Bill Aitken is Scottish by birth,
comparative religion at Leeds U
1959. He has lived in Himala
Maharani, freelanced under his middle name (Liam McKay) and
miscellaneous excursions—from Nanda Devi to Sabarimala—on an old
motor-bike and by vintage steam railway.

Aitken has written on travel and tourism for newspapers and
magazines in India and abroad for several years. His earlier books include
Seven Sacred Rivers and *Travels by a Lesser Line*.

BILL AITKEN

The Nanda Devi Affair

PENGUIN BOOKS

Penguin Books India (P) Ltd., 210, Chiranjiv Tower, 43 Nehru Place, New Delhi 110 019, India.
Penguin Books Ltd., 27 Wrights Lane, London W8 5TZ, UK
Penguin Books Australia Ltd., Ringwood, Victoria, Australia
Penguin Books Canada Ltd., 10 Alcorn Avenue, Suite 300, Toronto, Ontario M4V 3B2, Canada
Penguin Books (NZ) Ltd., 182-190 Wairau Road, Auckland 10, New Zealand

First published by Penguin Books India (P) Ltd. 1994

10 9 8 7 6 5 4 3 2 1

Typeset in Garamond by Fortune Publishers, Delhi

*To
Bharat*

Contents

Contents

Foreword

Till you can sing exultantly and delight in (the) God(dess) as misers do in gold, you never enjoy life

—Traherne

This is neither a book about Himalayan climbing nor a treatise on hill theology but a diary of mountain relish. If its emphasis on the warm updraughts of devotion is occasionally disturbed by the cold blasts of New Delhi's bane—bumptious bureaucrats—the lesson for these self-styled sporting administrators bears repeating, that in spite of narcissistic illusions of indispensability they remain the servants of those of us who pay the nation's taxes. Most of the action is far from the pliant corridors of power and centred around the feet of Nanda Devi at whose insistence this book was written. (I can therefore cheerfully avail of what most authors nobly deny themselves and disclaim all responsibility for the product: errors and omissions can safely be attributed to my patroness) Her commission was that I write down her captivating mood on high and render in print a whiff of her sensual fragrance that maddens and elevates our sea-level consciousness. Butterflies, apple-blossom, blue jays and fiery sunsets no doubt do the same but my marching orders were to report on the ravishing impact of the granite Goddess of Garhwal.

In my first attempt to capture the mood while the Devi's aura was still fresh I overshot the mark and ended up with a manuscript of Russian Ph.D. thesis proportions. Appropriately enough a Ukrainian well-wisher urged me to cut it down to size. Seven years later rather than reduce the original I rewrote the book, acutely aware of the loss that accrues from passion that has peaked. But as my orders had not been countermanded I can only hope that—as with any affair of the heart—the residual smoulder is enough to indicate the intensity of the fire.

Mussoorie   *Bill Aitken*
November 1993

Sketch Map of Uttarakhand
Nanda Devi Kshetra

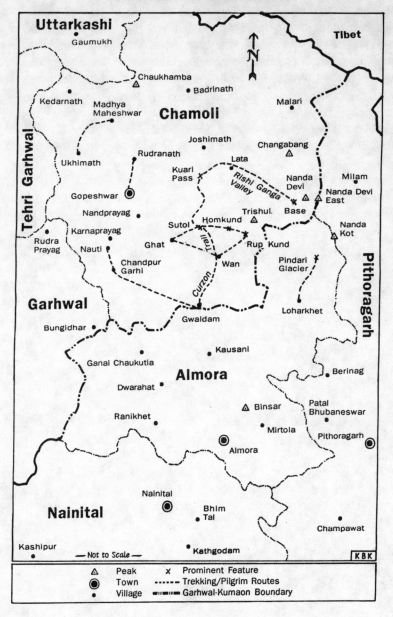

Uttarkashi

Gaumukh

Tibet

Chaukhamba △

Badrinath

Kedarnath

Madhya
Maheshwar

Chamoli

Malari

Joshimath

Changabang △

Rudranath

Lata

Milam

Ukhimath

Kuari
Pass

Rishi Ganga
Valley

Nanda
Devi

Nanda Devi
East △

Gopeshwar ◎

Nandprayag

Sutol

Homkund

Trishul △

Base

Nanda
Kot △

Karnaprayag

Ghat

Rup Kund

Rudra
Prayag

Nauti

Chandpur
Garhi

Wan

Pindari
Glacier

Pithoragarh

Garhwal

Bungidhar

Gwaldam

Loharkhet

Ganai Chaukutia

Kausani

Dwarahat

Almora

Binsar △

Patal
Bhubaneswar

Ranikhet

Mirtola

Pithoragarh ◎

Almora ◎

Berinag

Nainital ◎

Nainital

Bhim
Tal

Champawat

Kashipur

— Not to Scale —

Kathgodam

KBK

Tehri Garhwal

Trail

Curzon

△	Peak	x	Prominent Feature
◎	Town	- - - -	Trekking/Pilgrim Routes
•	Village	▪▬▪▬	Garhwal-Kumaon Boundary

ONE

The Moving Mountain

If it seems strange that the mere sight of mountains can arouse the most maddening of human passions it probably means the doubter has lived far from their lofty beckoning or lacks that inner 'lodestone, cherished as an implant of great price by those who possess it. According to the out-turned conventions of the Western mind I 'happened' to be born at the foot of the Ochil Hills in Scotland and further chance took me later to the Western Himalayas where I spent the larger part of my life. Looked at from the more adventurous angle of Eastern intuition it could be that one had chosen the Vale of the Forth to be brought up in just as one's needy soul had alighted upon the parents it deemed suitable for its growth. Certainly I am grateful to the sequence of events that provided an ego to be worked upon. Without that Western head-start others would have decided my destiny and rendered the priceless pearl of selfhood the empty spiritual cliche it has become in India.

The high ground of the Ochils appealed as a constant factor in a Scots childhood spent in reconciling a reflective nature with a conventional family dedicated to the dreary discipline of not offending God or neighbour. The negativity of our humble aspiration to respectability was epitomized by the lace curtains used in the village, behind whose veil the community timidly sacrificed any sensual yearning for the wine of eternity and settled for the water of passing genteel fashions. But my lonely quest had the crucial advantage of existing in the warm matrix of clan affection. My parents though not well-off were remarkably well-adjusted and for a soul striving to distinguish the certain from the unreal their example of fighting character and healthy self-respect provided a perfect springboard for later expeditions on the mountain path.

From an early age I discovered that the local peak Dumyat spoke more to me of God than the fusty kirk in Tullibody. Somehow the peak exuded belief whereas the local church and all its works invited ridicule for the way it stifled any passion for enduring things. It seemed a divine joke that Dumyat overlooked the greatest store of bonded whisky on our planet and an appropriate gesture that I should have been named after a grandfather who apparently dedicated his life to the prevention of its undue evaporation. The youngest of four siblings brought up in the bracing air at the head of Cambus brae, I shared Wordsworth's feeling of bondship with the woods and ditches, the bluebells and the heather. Carse and firth were friends and I would breathe gratefully atop Dumyat at the beauty and rightness of their spread. To experience those schoolboy moments of rich fulfilment when the poetry of existence coursed through one's being in a hallowing of flesh was to glimpse an essence soon lost in the filter of a doubting mind.

All of life's finer sensibilities are rendered impotent by the inadequacy of predication. Language castrates the buoyancy of mood experienced on a grassy hilltop where the heady mix of immediate beauties with the overarching drone of heaven's music is rendered stillborn under the label of nature-mysticism. What actually are life's treasured moments—the utmost wonder of the softness of Ochil turf with its immaculate spring, becomes on paper a pretty postcard scene. The halo of fresh scent that comes from the windblown wool of sheep and the dank odour and intriguing originality of their ordure never ceases to amaze this watcher of the craftsmanship of nature. The point being that language can only echo the truth of nature's breathing. It is in the miracle of unvoiced aspiration that we truly are ourselves, never in the literary sloughing off of intimacies. Why then strive to put on paper that which cannot be represented in words? Many reasons altruistic and otherwise can be advanced but for the peak in my life the answer was simple. The Goddess of the mountain commanded.

Dumyat at 1,375 ft is no great shakes in the list of mountain objectives yet by sheer strength of character its peak outshines many greater rivals. Crouched like a sentinel to the east of Stirling's outcrop, the verdurous run of its face sweeps up gently but formidably from the flats of the Forth. The impression of its startling rise to a brooding summit is oddly satisfying. This is everything a mountain should be despite the fact that its altitude credentials fall far short of the title of Ben—accorded to those summits in the 3,000 ft league. I did make the effort to climb Ben Cleuch, the chief of the Ochil vantage points which looked out on an extraordinary sweep of Scotland, but not even its dawn unrobing of the day could affect my fierce loyalty to Dumyat's craggy cockpit. All around the latter lay heartsease and even when in surly mood the mountain never bullied its locale. It loomed large in our lives, presiding over village destiny but never threatened to send down another boulder as huge as the monstrous ball of rock on which had been erected our Tullibody war memorial. That is not to say Dumyat lacked any numinous overtones. The villages around her base were steeped in the lore of fairies and a very real childhood terror was to run past the war memorial at night where some of those listed on the lych-gate, mainly of the Highland Light Infantry, may have found their way back from the bloody battle of the Somme.

My father's birthplace in Menstrie exemplified the usage peculiar to the Ochils, 'hillfoots'. The garden at No. 5 Long Row actually backed on to the sudden uprise of the hill face. The climbing turf swept one's feet as if by magic up to a tinkling glen under Craig Omas, a subsidiary peak. All the grim gagging of the kirk could not subdue that magic nor would it be silenced by the austere imported theology of Calvin. My brother and I had once stumbled back with a fisherman uncle over the crest of the Ochils from Sherrifmuir at midnight and seen the great spread of Midlothian lit up by iron foundries coughing their contempt for the pastoral heavenwards. The tantalizing paradox of opposites seemed forever to leap out and cry for reconciliation. The mountains would become in my life the symbol—and solution—of this conflict between the spirit and the senses, making straight the way to an understanding of purpose in life's stumblings. They would act as therapeutic agents to bridge the gap between earthly strivings and immortal goals. Like us they bore the fruits of deep contradiction within themselves. Unmoving was their nature yet they moved those who were drawn to their flanks. Did they possess a power of their own or was the affection the mountaineer showered on them the real occasion of their personality? These were the riddles that besieged my questing and as one grew in the study of religion the concern to appraise my spontaneous affection and desire for these outcrops of the divine manifestation (as they seemed to me) became an overriding passion.

My father moved from Menstrie to work in the English Midlands and I found myself at school in Birmingham. The deprivation of Dumyat spurred me to seek the lost constant in my life. Further education in Yorkshire helped assuage the loss but somehow neither the Lakes nor Wales, nor indeed the Grampians, held the thrall of the Ochils.

My course in comparative religion led to field work in India and one sight of the Himalayas was enough for me to jettison future plans for the respectable acquisition of academic qualifications. It was an ecstatic moment of confrontation where a symphony of the senses was conducted by the panorama of the snows and I succumbed to the lure of private research into the passionate calling of peak theology.

If it seems a sudden and spectacular leap from the puny but ancient outcrops guarding the gateway to the Highlands to the massive but exquisite ramparts of the Himalayan Abode of Snow the fact is that few other things on earth apart from mountains could have withstood that rainbow transition. I had arrived in the plains of India chastened by the rigours of an overland passage on a shoestring and the battering from strange custom and hostile thought processes had amplified one's sense of misfit. Fortunately the sense of selfhood learned intuitively from the loom of Dumyat had encouraged one to look positively on the solitary state. Equipped with an enquiring mind interested in the working of things (plus a general arts degree that widened one's appreciation of the cultures of the world), the process of adaptation to the challenges of India passed without undue trauma though it took five years.

I was too ill to appreciate the impact of the cousin range, the Hindu Kush, but had responded with electric regard to the sight of Mount Ararat. The religious hilltops of the Holy Land had failed to live up to their reputation and the lurid display of commercialised religion served not only to make me shake the dust of that hate-filled land from my feet but enabled me to extricate my beliefs from the infallibility of the Bible—an occupational hazard of all reformed Scotsmen. Undoubtedly one's emotional attachment to the mountains had been encouraged by the Psalmist for were not his hymns of praise referred to as 'songs of Ascent' for the pilgrim?

As an undergraduate I had accompanied some English Franciscans on a pilgrimage to Lindisfarne and the border abbeys. For my money the Lowlands are every bit as appetising as the greater ranges just as in many ways the Lesser Himalaya can compete with the Greater. Mere verticality is no measure of a mountain's beauty anymore than a tall woman should be accounted desirable before a shorter but more attractive companion. This might be a criterion for distinguishing the true mountain lover from the mechanical; the one drawn by the lure of aesthetic satisfaction, the other driven by the mass demand for statistics with their sheep-like acclaim for physical priority.

Whether the compulsiveness of the call to mountaineering is laudable or not, it is terribly real, an addiction almost frightening in its pull since the approach is always dangerous and the outcome on occasion less than satisfactory. Not at all interested in the physical aspects of mountain climbing—I shied away from the hearty masculine exudations that seemed essential to the Leeds University climbing club—it was the psychic and sacerdotal angle that fascinated me about upraised rocks. If God spoke from on high and delivered the tablets of His law unto the prophets, could not physical high points claim extra potential as the seat of holiness? Atop Dumyat the humblest shepherd could momentarily indulge in an omniscient view of the nagging problems left behind at base. These now fell easily into perspective and, more important, hardly seemed to matter.

Clearly there is a kind of brotherhood between man and mountains. The untamed nature of the rolling hillscapes injects a needed transfusion of blood into the urbanite's watery diet of artificial response. The urge to smell real things and pit one's atrophied animal cunning against the forces of the wild rises up and screams for early remedy. And yet those gifted with the bonus of residing close to the peaks rarely penetrate into their fastnesses. Himalayan pilgrims tend to congregate towards smooth passage while another touch to the definition of the true mountain-lover must be his willingness to wander in uncharted places and assume the responsibility of risk.

For those with the lodestone of an adventurous outlook implanted in their destiny there is no looking back. The inescapable logic of desire leaves the mountain traveller no choice but to plan his next expedition to the very peak that may have just rejected vociferously the most single-minded of advances.

*

What Birmingham had done to stimulate my love for Dumyat, a year in Calcutta did to cartwheel me nearer the beloved. In May 1960 I set out with a Bengali teacher friend on the Doon Express to Haridwar. Owing to the season the dust had settled over the face of the peaks and though I got as far as the threshold of the Great Himalaya (before being turned back by the police at Rudraprayag for lacking an inner line permit) I did not set eyes on the main range. Repairing to Mussoorie to learn the local language (as an aid to the next expedition) I did cast up my eyes and early in the morning glimpsed the floating wonder of Bunder Poonch, the monkey-tailed peak. It may have been the least of the snow giants that spread their glory across Garhwal but its thrilling lines spoke of an ecstasy that defied definition.

The following October I had occasion to visit Kumaon and still awaited initiation into the full effulgence of the Himalayas. As the mail bus toiled up the newly blasted gorge route to Almora one got blinding snatches of the snows, as dazzling as they were shortlived. From the town set under the lee of a high ridge one had fine views of the tailspread from Trisul west to Chaukhamba but the most immediate cluster from Nanda Devi to Panch Chuli were hidden by the march of conifer.

The next day must be accounted the happiest in my life since I glimpsed both Nanda Devi and my guru. I caught the early morning bus to Panuanaula along an excruciating unmade road and then climbed steeply through the sweeping forest of pine to the temple at Mirtola. It was situated with its back to Nanda Devi as it were, and nestled in a saucer to protect it from the blasts curling over the bald ridge at 7,200 ft. This aspect availed of a rare but rich spring whose water was pumped up by a hydraulic ram. The occasion was rather formal with my initial impression of the guru cool to hostile. After lunch on the floor, village style, my hosts walked me towards the ancient temples of Jageshwar and suggested I visit Kausani via Binsar since I had expressed an interest in the best snow view.

That evening I spent the night on the veranda of a tea shop in Dhaul Cheena half way to Binsar. By next morning I had struggled up the magnificent mountainside of Binsar to be confronted by the most mind-boggling vista of peaks imaginable. It was the grass-cutting season and the empty bungalow where I was to spend the night superbly sited to drink in this ultimate vision of mountain grandeur. In the orchard a tangle of cosmos—pink, white and maroon—were in bloom and their vibrant colours were enhanced by the sweet smell of freshly scythed grass. That night I slept on bare floor-boards in an empty room after a supper of water and a lump of sticky molasses provided by the chowkidar. I had never been happier in my life.

The peaks and particularly Nanda Devi spoke so directly and emphatically that there and then I made the decision to leave Calcutta and come and live among them. There was something commanding in the Devi's beauty as she lay before my eyes, essentially royal and feminine. All the cliches about Nanda as a queen surrounded by courtiers were appropriate for she towered above the rest with a regal detachment, the centrepiece of a priceless necklace. The gaping spread of the great range viewed from Binsar takes the breath away as 300 km of jagged grandeur pierces the vision. Only in Kumaon do the peaks wear such individual character. From the Kathmandu valley the summits may be higher and their statistics more impressive but for sheer breathless beauty the mountains stretching from Gangotri in Garhwal (above the source of the Ganga) to the western Nepal sentinels of Api and Nampa (guarding the outflow of the Karnali) exceed all others in their striking array of personality. The central spread of Trisul leading up to the Goddess Nanda is balanced to the west by the curious conning tower shape of Nanda Ghunti, in turn offset by the massive frontage of the fortress-like Chaukhamba, this Badri kshetra being spiked by the impressive spires of Nilkanth and Kamet. To the east of Nanda the peerless drape of the tooth-like Nanda Kot is followed by Panch Chuli the 'five cooking stalls of the gods'—those startlingly matched peaks that extend from Traill's Pass to the trading inlet with Tibet at the Lipu Lekh.

The blinding loveliness of the upraised ice curtain ahead is offset by the booming foreground abyss where Binsar's face falls sheer for 6,000 ft to spring up in the wonder of the Great Himalaya, a dramatic 20,000 ft increase. Nanda Devi tops the scene at 25,645 ft (7,817 metres) serenely aloof and set back apparently from the company of her courtiers. It took me twenty years to prise out the secret of her innermost lair and those who see only the outer majesty of the mountain would find it hard to apprehend the magic of her hidden fastness. Binsar sits almost due south of the twin peaks and gives the best frontal introduction to the mountain. From above the district town of Pithoragarh an angled view of the twin peaks yields a fabulous untramelled outline of the mountain. North of Binsar and closer to the face of Nanda Devi is the vantage point of Chaukori set near the tea gardens of Beринag. While this gives a stunning close up of the magnificent snow drape of Nanda Kot it fails to do full justice to the Goddess Nanda owing to the problem of foreshortening.

That thrilling contact with the core of Himalayan bliss was followed by a trek to Kausani further west along the watershed ridge. From here the tourist view of the great range is gained but Trisul in the foreground is the major attraction. Nanda tucked away in her sanctuary appears to be shy of revealing herself. The morning I left Binsar another delight was to wake to the extraordinary spectacle of the peaks rising out of an ocean of low layered cloud. All the intervening ranges had been blotted out by this carpet of oblivion and one gasped at the dramatic potential of the elemental interplay. As the sun rose the mist began to loosen its hold and most strange of all as I descended through its layers was to find it disperse around my head like the soul summoned to its source. The uncanny beauty of the morning gave that infinite feeling of being at home in the universe. The strange elation brought on by plunging through the sea of cloud confirmed me in my determination to move unto the place whence came my help. Kausani was an idyllic resolution of my short-term needs. The Gandhian ashram where I worked as part-time man enabled me to get into the slow rhythm so necessary for a foreigner who hopes to become part of India. It was no doubt an imposition on Sarala Devi, the English disciple of Mahatma Gandhi who ran the school for village girls, even more so for Radha Behn her local assistant and the girls who had to suffer my share of adjustment pains. Fortunately for the four years I lived in view of the Goddess at Lakshmi ashram my Gandhian commitment was sincere enough to withstand the temptations that inevitably arose from the proximity of a lone gardener to a bevy of flowering blooms. The scales of protective puritanism dropped after a serious illness and my eyes were opened to the essential Eros of the great wheel of life. With the revelation went my attachment to the cause of self-denial. It was time to seek the source of that juice which had flooded the being during my bodily flirtation with death.

Oddly it was the grace of the Goddess that had given me the disease. Down in the village the very thing the Gandhians scorned was to give me the key to enlightenment. Lakshman Singh a daily labourer at the ashram had invited me to attend a devta natch in honour of the Goddess Nanda. Though the Kumaon villagers made little show of affection to the visible peak (most of them would have been hard put to distinguish it from its neighbours) they worshipped the Goddess ardently in their village rituals. The annual Nanda Devi fair held in Almora during the month of August was the highlight of the Kumaoni social calendar. The influence of Gandhian reform was yearly reducing the superstitious content of the festival especially in substituting for gruesome buffalo sacrifice the symbolic vegetarian offering of a coconut. Back in the village such squeamish compromise was viewed with more than derision. The high-caste hillman forever squirming under the accusation of unorthodoxy by his plains brotherhood took this opportunity to defend the traditional mode of sacrifice since it included the bonus of a sanctified source of meat. Nanda Devi's popularity partly turned on her non-vegetarian tastes.

In the old days the missionaries had referred to devta natch—the summoning from the deep of local spirits—as 'devil dancing' confirming the widely held view that many of their impressions of Hinduism had been formed on distant assumptions rather than by immediate contact. It was a full moon night in the village and a charged atmosphere prevailed in the tense gathering above the river. The Brahmins dressed for the occasion were reciting the appropriate scriptures vociferously while around a hefty bonfire of blazing pine trunks the village bloods paced out a desultory dance. To one side the low-caste drummer heated the stretched skin of his copper drum, a tiny affair made more primitive in its musical potential by the crudely fashioned sticks. The old man with a turban wound round his dark head seemed to exercise a quiet authority over the company and it was he who decided when the Devi had truly entered into the proceedings.

Possession by the local spirit is still the way many interior Himalayan villages commune with divinity. The custom is fading as villagers become more exposed to sophisticated norms and it is now embarrassing to attend a devta natch where the outer motions are gone through by self-conscious participants who pretend possession by their guardian deity as a sop to tradition. The real thing is something else and no one can be in any doubt of the authenticity of the seizure. Obviously the candidate will be someone of loose integration or even feeble mind. However in Garhwal and Ladakh where women enjoy a higher status than in Kumaon, the vehicle of the Goddess can be a strong-willed woman whose performance can seem terrifyingly akin to the menace threatened by the Goddess Kali. The male oracle pronounces the ruling of the Goddess on the questions affecting the village which are put to him. He arrives on the shoulders of a strong companion and is summoned by a flourish of drums. The Shilpkar drummer emerges from the shadows of the bonfire and suddenly assumes a presiding presence. His small drum emits the most electrifying coda and one feels the hair bristle as 'forces from the other side' are challenged to appear in answer to these compulsive sorcerer's drum beats. Hissing, slavering and ranting the possessed shaman is borne into the ring of fire. Pop-eyed with the vacancy of a soul dislodged he shivers violently and has to be restrained from leaping off the shoulders of his bearers. Between his teeth is clenched the Devi's dagger to symbolize that the mouthpiece of the Goddess will brook no obstacle. As the drumming reaches its searing crescendo the demented entourage staggers round the leaping fire where semi-possessed attendants tread on live coals or grasp flaming pine branches to impress on the audience the genuineness of their inspired credentials. Grotesque shadows are thrown by the bonfire and weird shapes hover enlarged by the flare of raw resin. Mothers hold up their babes to be blessed by the passing of the Goddess Nanda. I expect to find apprehension on the face of both parent and child but am astonished to see instead serene grace and gurgling contentment.

It takes two weeks for the typhoid germ to manifest itself. Fifteen days after the bonfire night I found myself for the first time in my life experiencing the novel sensation of not wanting to eat; to be followed by the less appetising realization that death stalked my breathing.

TWO

Vital Statistics

*N*anda Devi may not get into the top twenty peaks on the score of height above sea level but curiously she did once enjoy the singular status of being the highest mountain in the world's greatest empire. The reason for this was that Mount Everest lay in the kingdom of Nepal and K2 in the princely state of Kashmir. The British who took their heights seriously, understood the symbolic value of being on top and though they could not disturb Nepal's neutrality in order to fly the Union Jack over the world's highest peak they did by a clever stratagem assume protective custody through the imposition of their nomenclature.

Everest's importance above that of Nanda Devi is revealing of the confused attitudes that surround modern mountaineering. After the British success on Everest in 1953 the Indian authorities continued where the imperial sahibs had left off. Colonel John Hunt's expedition that put Sir Edmund Hillary and Tenzing on top was described by the London *Times* correspondent, Jan Morris as 'military manoeuvres'. Inspired by the khaki assault mentality, the defence bureaucrats in New Delhi turned Indian expeditions to the Himalayas into similar extravaganzas, following the Hunt recipe for success by leaving tons of junk on the mountain.

Unlike Everest which is a very plain peak (except when viewed from the north) Nanda Devi is scintillatingly beautiful from any angle. It shares with Everest the blandness of an easy route to the top, by which is meant a testing plod as opposed to a challenging display of technique. It is often said that the first ascent of Nanda Devi by an Anglo-American team in 1935 was accomplished without the use of crampons. What is not told is that the saddle-bags bearing this crucial equipment accompanied the pack goat into the growling gorge of the Rishi Ganga rendering the use of crampons higher up the mountain academic. It could be argued that this unwitting sacrifice of an animal caused the Devi to smile on the expedition since a goat is considered a proper offering to the Goddess. On the other hand village custom was outraged when it heard that mortals had stood atop the sacred summit, defiling the gold pavilion of Vishnu with their boots. On the day of the first ascent—August 30—Garhwal experienced a cloud-burst and the hill station of Mussoorie reeled under eighteen inches of rain. In the village of Tharali the Pindar river, rising on the eastern flank of the mountain, drowned twenty men and it was widely believed that this reflected the anger of Nanda Bhagawati (as hillmen call their protective deity).

One of the two successful summiters, Bill Tilman mocked the connexion between flood and sporting success. He took an unglamorous view of the religious associations supposed to reside on the summit and declared that all it amounted to was a slab of snow admeasuring 200 yards by twenty. Curiously when it came to the final reckoning and the most outstanding climber of his generation turned his back on the Himalayas for the adventure of sailing the seas in a small boat, the Goddess appeared to have settled scores. Tilman, his crew and his boat disappeared without a trace, the ultimate squelch for one who attempted to make invincibility his calling.

Like Everest, Nanda posed serious problems of access. Attempts to crack a route to her base coincide with the beginnings of Alpine climbing in the Himalayas and the first man to take on the challenge was W.W. Graham whose startling success was announced in the *Times of India* in 1883. Along with two Swiss guides he had entered the outer sanctuary of Nanda Devi and claimed to have climbed two of its most impressive peaks, Dunagiri (amongst its toughest challenges) and Changabang, perhaps the most raved about beauty in the gallery of aesthetic contenders for the title 'most ravishing mountain.' Significantly Graham fails to mention the extraordinary impact of Changabang with its incomparable sweep of grey gleaming granite fingering the threshold of eternity. This is suspicious when the rest of his diary is absolutely authentic in recreating their hair-raising passage above the plummeting gorge of the Rishi. Clinging to tufts of grass he had dragged himself miserably in the monsoon downpour towards the goal of the inner sanctuary only to be brought up by an impassible canyon on its doorstep. Bad weather had prevented Graham from setting eyes on Changabang and the peak they most probably climbed was Hanuman, a modest but commendable neighbour. But Graham's venture was not in vain if only because it highlighted the perils of inaccuracy in the reports of those desperate to add cubits to the stature of their expeditions. Thanks to Graham's optimistic overreaching of the bounds of possibility the science of forensic examination of mountain claims was born alongside the sport of Himalayan climbing.

The sanctuary of Nanda Devi is remarkable for its unique wild grandeur. Even more remarkable is that this uplifting terrain sacred to the folklore of popular Hinduism has been written about by some of the finest pens in mountaineering literature. Starting with A.L. Mumm's *Five Months in the Himalayas* (1907), the impressive difficulties of the way have been chronicled vividly. Mumm was a well-heeled publisher and with the restless explorer Dr Tom Longstaff and the ebullient alpinist General Bruce in his party this strong expedition had originated as an attempt on Everest, diverted to Garhwal by the spoilsport expediency of politics. Whereas Graham had beaten a way along the gorge during the trying monsoon Mumm's party had flailed an exhausting passage through the snow over the dangerous Dharansi Pass in May. Brought up before the dead end of the canyon walls at Rhamani the party retreated for a daring outflanking manoeuvre. They would withdraw from the confines of the booming Rishi and move north to the village of Dunagiri, to attempt to breach the 19,000 ft curtain above the Bagini glacier. It seemed the Goddess had smiled on their temerity for surely after that cliff-hanging entry into her sanctuary no further obstacle would be encountered. As they descended the steep glacier to Rhamani their hearts must have sunk. Confronted by the same fawn canyon walls they were back to square one.

Vexation at the forbidding nature of the Goddess brought out the best in Longstaff and as consolation before a second retreat he zoomed up with the Swiss and Gurkhas to score the maiden ascent of Trisul, an achievement that was to stand in the record books as the highest mountain climbed until 1928. (A Gurkha swore he could see Buckingham palace from the top)

Longstaff had probed the east sanctuary curtain and fought his way to 19,000 ft up the Lawan Gad from Milan with the Brocherel brothers in 1905. His was the satisfaction of being the first to peer into the southern inner sanctuary but he realised he could never hope to get loads up and over the divide. His name has been given to the col on which he stood but like Traill's Pass it was an honorary landmark at least until Tilman, exiting from the sanctuary after the first ascent of Nanda Devi, beat a remarkable pioneering retreat over this feature to add to his reputation for misogyny a working knowledge of masochism. He was accompanied by the American Dr Charles Houston and the Sherpa Pasang Kikuli of K2 fame.

Following Longstaff's track was the unlikely figure of Hugh Ruttledge whose slight physique was offset by the enormous advantage of his status. He was the deputy commissioner for Kumaon and his dedication to ferreting out approaches to the curtain-bound sanctuary earns him a place beside the other great hill district administrators, Traill and Atkinson. Ruttledge joined Longstaff on two more probing expeditions of the sanctuary curtain. In 1927 they visited the Ronti Saddle and in 1932 (with Emile Rey) attempted the even more formidable Sunderdhunga Khal which originally was named Ruttledge Col. (Two failures on Everest guaranteed his name would be dumped) Atkinson's famous *Gazetteer* of Kumaon derived largely from the findings of Mr Traill, the first trade commissioner. Traill's perseverance in crossing the dangerous ice-fall linking Milam with the source of the Pindar was rewarded with the naming of an unfixed pass after him. On top of this his eager explorations have been accorded sporting status. It seems more likely his search for a shortcut had been occasioned by the East India Company's desperation to get a share of the 'shawl wool' filtering over the passes from Tibet. (Shatoosh happens still to be the most expensive fabric in the world)

If Traill is to be termed the discoverer of the pass what does that make Malak Singh, the villager who guided him up and over the ice-fall? The descendants of Malak Singh continue to remind all visitors on the Pindari glacier trek of their ancestor's prowess but unlike the Chomolungma lobby that deplores the imposition of 'Mount Everest' there is as yet no insistence on dislodging 'Traill Pass' for 'Malak La'.

Atkinson in his *Gazetteer* (1888) gave the sum of knowledge regarding

Nanda's inaccessibility to nineteenth century eyes. 'It appears like a spire of greying rock sprinkled with snow and lying to the north-east of Trisul and north-west of Nanda Kot and rising far above the similarly snow-clad summits which surround it. The summit is altogether inaccessible. The natives maintain that smoke is sometimes seen to issue from its summit which they regard as the kitchen of the local deity.'

Ruttledge indicated the problems surrounding entry into the sanctuary in a letter to the London *Times* in 1932: 'A seventy-mile barrier ring on which stand twelve measured peaks of over 21,000 ft which has no depression lower than 17,000 ft except in the west where the Rishi Ganga rising at the foot of Nanda Devi and draining the area of some 250 square miles (799 square kilometres) of snow and ice has earned for itself what must be one of the most terrific gorges in the world'. If Ruttledge made no mention of the extraordinary beauty and symmetry of the inner sanctuaries—magnificent rolling meadows to the south being matched by the marvellous cathedral-like ramparts to the north—it was because no one had yet cast eyes on these extravagantly improbable assets. Only the traditional seven rishis who gave Hinduism its scriptures would have been privy to the gloriously wild and idyllic landscape that lay locked in Nanda's embrace. The mountaineer who helped discover (and best described) the ravishing realm of the Goddess was Eric Shipton, perhaps the perfect choice since his romantic inclinations were miles away from the military manoeuvres school.

The meaning of Nanda Devi is 'bliss-giving Goddess' and in his book *Nanda Devi* on the first successful penetration (after eight attempts) to her base, Shipton's lyricism provided a classic of mountain literature. He had come to India with Tilman on a shoestring expedition in 1934 and mounted what must be reckoned as Garhwal's most cheekily successful expedition ever. (Their six-month voyage cost Rs 3000) With the help of three Himalayan Club sherpas—Ang Tharkay, Pasang and Kusang—the two tough coffee-planters from Africa forced a passage up the canyon walls into the south sanctuary. Shipton's description of the mountain paradise they discovered after the gruelling challenges of the way does full justice to the dramatic scale of the sanctuary. I had stumbled upon his book in the library of the Asiatic Society in Calcutta and made up my mind in 1960 that come what may one day I would visit the booming gorge and win a way through to this Hindu garden of Eden.

With the onset of the monsoon the small party withdrew from the sanctuary and transferred its attention to solving another Hindu mystery, whether it was possible to find a shortcut between the two shrines of Badrinath and Kedarnath. When they recovered from the ordeal of their abortive temple shortcut they re-entered the sanctuary to explore the north inner sanctuary as the monsoon weakened. Marching and measuring they managed to map the basic outlines as well as climb those peaks that did not demand any reserve of energy. Shipton managed to struggle up a glacier leading to Changabang to give his name to a col on the divide overlooking the Rhamani glacier down which Mumm and company had passed in their belief that they had broken into the real sanctuary.

To climax their extraordinary season of firsts the whole party exited from the south inner sanctuary by the Sunderdhunga Col over a spectacular wall down to the Pindar valley. This cornucopia of exploration has never been exceeded nor has the enthralling versatility of its five expedition members been equalled, a rare example of sahib-sherpa harmony. Certainly Shipton's book has never been bettered for conjuring up the mood and majesty of the inner sanctuary. The following year Shipton declined (and Tilman accepted) the American invitation to climb Nanda Devi, preferring instead to return with the great-hearted Ang Tharkay to do some more plane-tabling in the area. Tilman's book *The Ascent of Nanda Devi* is a model of expedition reportage; terse, telling and modest though the vital ingredients of poetry and passion seem missing. The narrative is characterized by the freeze of British emotions kept firmly on a leash. Victory allowed a formal thaw to the extent of a stiff Masonic hand-shake on the summit with Noel Odell who in 1924 had become famous as the last climber on Everest to see Mallory and Irvine before their disappearance. Tilman's ode to the Devi is nearer to a national anthem than a border ballad.

Shipton's oneness with the Goddess made him an odd man out and it was inevitable that his philosophy of an 'overriding passion' as the motive force for mountaineering would be ruthlessly ignored by the English climbing establishment when they came to choose a winning leader for the 1953 Everest expedition. When peaks have to be conquered for prestige and funds poured in to guarantee the flutter of a flag from the summit it is only proper that corporals who aspire to be sergeants and brigadiers smitten with the passion for full command should be recruited before poets and mountain mystics. It is a coincidence that Nanda Devi has never hosted the conquerors of Everest—Hunt, Hillary and Tenzing—but in beckoning back Shipton and Ang Tharkey the Goddess proved that she could recognize her own.

Sadly the post-war expeditions to the mountain organized by the Indian Mountaineering Foundation (IMF) all followed the military mode. The first president of the IMF enjoyed the status of Cabinet Secretary, a position that for protocol purposes exceeds the rank of Field Marshall. S.S. Khera was an advocate of the Shipton and Tilman 'gur and sattu' school of lightweight enterprise undertaken with a minimum of official interference and done for fun rather than self-promotion. In 1941 he crossed Traill's Pass from the more difficult southern side. Unfortunately his successor H.C. Sarin was more interested in administering the sport of mountaineering than in climbing.

It was inevitable in a Third World scenario that possession of a prestige range of mountains would be capitalized on for political and personal advantage. The compromise can be dated from Khera's order to the first Indian Everest expedition that he wanted the mountain climbed 'at all costs'. From that moment the infant sport of Indian mountaineering became a bureaucratic tool for narcissistic administrators to play their favourites and curry the favours of politicians. Sadly the thinly veiled racism that had marked the pre-independence Survey of India was carried over into the Himalayan Club when it was founded in 1928 and the exit of its leading lights after 1947 cost the new nation an objective and expert sponsor of the sport. The IMF stepped in to manage mountaineering as it would a government department which meant that all decisions were based on political expediency rather than sporting sense. A typical example was the expedition organized to put a woman on top of Nanda Devi as a prelude to a female ascent of Everest. What this compulsion derived from was the political need for a spectacular Indian presence in the international year of women. So weird were the compulsions for female success that when a male climber decided to go solo for Everest in a heroic oxygenless bid he was roundly accused of sabotaging the best laid plans of the expedition's bureaucratic sponsors.

Nanda Devi experienced from 1964 onwards the indignity of several hush-hush expeditions to place a nuclear spying device on her summit. Ten years later when the sanctuary was thrown open to mountaineers the stampede of young Western climbers eager to make their mark in the record books led to an environmental disaster. Owing to the short season, pressure tactics were applied to get pack goats in and the forests were hacked to build bridges and provide fodder.

Fragile juniper slopes above the tree-line were deliberately fired to provide charcoal for the porters whom the foreign expeditions had neglected to supply with warm clothes. The IMF snarled in its red tape (demanding to know Chris Bonington's father's first name and whether Joe Tasker was competent to lead in view of his failure to attend any outdoor course vouched for by the Duke of Edinburgh) was so busy collecting peak fees from the foreigner that it neglected the area it had been created to protect. Instead of closing the sanctuary to save its unique status the IMF simply jacked up the fees for the peaks in its cirque.

Three expeditions to the realm of the Goddess deserve some mention. In 1976 an innovative and well-provided Japanese team managed to pull off a spectacular traverse of the three-kilometre knife-edge ridge that links the east and main peaks of Nanda Devi. In 1981 the Czechs, tough and regular entrants to the sanctuary managed to force a route up the north face of the main peak to arrive at the summit only a few hours away from the successful imprints of Rekha Sharma, the first woman to reach the top and an Indian to boot.

For the lore of the mountain Goddess the arrival of an American commemorative expedition in 1976 promised to yield good copy. It followed hard on the spectacular traverse of the twin peaks by Hashegawa and Teramoto and was led by the irrepressible Willi Unsoeld of Everest east ridge fame and pucca American alpinist Adams Carter. Star of this nostalgic re-run of the first successful climb was Willi's twenty-two-year-old daughter whom he had named after the mountain. All that now remained was for Nanda Devi Unsoeld who was young, blonde and beautiful (and had been with the Peace Corps in Nepal) to surface at the summit and make this American dream come true. Tragedy struck just below the summit and the girl died suddenly at Camp IV succumbing to complications from a hernia she had contracted in Delhi.

To the grief-stricken expedition members was naturally extended the consolation of the girl's absorption into the mythology surrounding the mountain. But the hill man's well-known distaste for the flouting of tradition had been stimulated by the young lady's scanty dress and much more unforgiveably by her lax instinct to share a tent with her fiance: '*Sara Kailash chut hagi*'—the entire mountain had been polluted. Any female daring to flaunt her sexuality would be dealt with summarily for Nanda was known to be an angry and jealous Goddess.

Ten years after the tragedy John Roskelley, the young successful lead climber of the expedition, vented American disenchantment with the sentimental motivation of its planners. In his book *Nanda Devi—the Tragic Expedition* he argues that the girl was neither competent nor well enough to scale the mountain. Unfortunately Roskelley's jarring and loveless view of events reduces his argument to a clinical justification of his own drives. (The Americans refer to this recurring high altitude phenomenon as 'R and R'—rest and recrimination!) Preferring the romantic version Kiran Kumar, the Indian paratrooper, (who later died on Everest) erected in the south sanctuary meadows an iron plaque to the memory of the mountain's namesake. It quotes from Nanda Devi Unsoeld's diary some lines more profound than melancholy that should set at rest all controversy: 'I stand upon a wind-swept ridge at night with the stars bright above and I am no longer alone but I waver and merge with all the shadows that surround me. I am part of the whole and am content.'

THREE

'Beru Pakho'

*N*anda Devi is the patron Goddess of both Kumaon and Garhwal. These rival cultural provinces with their distinctive dialects and customs have feuded belligerently over the centuries redeemed solely by their belief in the visible grace of their common mountain. Known since ancient times as Uttarakhand, the combined terrain between the western border of Nepal and the course of the Tons (that demarcates the eastern frontier of Himachal Pradesh) has featured prominently in the Puranas as the playground of the gods. Almost all hill provinces claim to be dev bhumi, the land sacred to the deities of Hinduism but the only true claimant to the title is Garhwal which possesses all four of the char dham, the quartet of sacred Himalayan shrines. Kumaon is the poor relation in terms of pilgrim goals and only provided a convenient route to Kailas-Mansarover in Tibet, the ultimate pilgrimage to Shiva's abode.

To confuse the primacy of Garhwal, instead of referring to the geophysical combine of Kumaon and Garhwal as 'Uttarakhand Himalaya' British surveyors wilfully and unscientifically introduced the misnomer 'Kumaon Himalaya', on the flimsy pretext that British 'Kumaon' included in it a part of Garhwal. After ridding Uttarakhand of the Gurkha regime the East

India Company allowed the Maharaja of Garhwal to rule over Tehri Garhwal while Pauri Garhwal remained British.

To Hindu hillmen 'Kumaon Himalaya' instead of Uttarakhand was a gratuitous insult and to students of geography it became a baffling riddle that gave rise to hilarious assumptions totally at variance with ground realities. The worst victims were mountaineers in transit who, ignorant of the Wars of Roses situation that holds between Kumaonis and Garhwalis, failed to understand that this usage to a Garhwali is like describing Lancashire as part of Greater Yorkshire or Harvard as an outpost of Yale.

The reason why Garhwal enjoys sole possession of the title dev bhumi is due to the exclusive flow of the Ganga and her affluents in this province. Kumaon for the most part is innocent of glacial torrents off the great range and its heartland is watered by the kinder flows from the Lesser Himalaya. Nanda Devi occupies a position that overlooks Kumaon but is not a part of it. Her sanctuary curtain forms a right-angled boundary between the two warring provinces, but her peaks lie east of Almora, the capital of Kumaon. This is explained by the slant of the Himalayas that has caused the Ganga to flow not in a north-south direction as supposed but south-westerly. The profile of the Devi varies according to the province. From Almora and the heartland of Kumaon it is the twin peaks that identify the Goddess and inspire the local lore—as in Naini Tal—of worshipping the mountain in the form of two sisters. The obvious suggestion of feminine uplift is nowhere better seen than from the east in the Bhotia valley of Milam where the twin peaks rise in majestic symmetry. From Almora the main peak overshines the eastern summit not just by altitude but from its sturdier formation. Some Almora pundits hold that the hump of the main peak proves that Nanda is a corruption of Nandi the bull, sacred vehicle of Shiva. They argue that rather than a Goddess the mountain is the footstool of Shiva who dwells on Kailash. The male chauvinist ingenuity of Kumaon's Brahmins has to be kept in mind when reading Atkinson's *Gazetteer* since it was compiled largely from lore related by one of its imaginative number.

The devious employment of the intellect to make physical facts fit spiritual theory can be listed as one of the differentiating characteristics of the two provinces. Garhwalis are invariably found to be simpler in their mindset while Kumaonis are acknowledged as masters of mental agility. It is true that the very first reference to the mountain in English gave us 'Nundi

Deva' (in 1840) and it is likely that some pilgrims to Kailash did easily relate to the main peak as the preliminary bull of Shiva. But this was a regional perception that would cut no ice either in Milam (where the bosom of the Goddess is so well-defined) or in Garhwal where the end-on view of the main peak seen from the west could just as easily be said to resemble a thrusting lingam. Then there is the problem that if Nanda Devi were the outer guardian of Shiva's holy Mount Kailash, how to explain that the vehicle is higher than the deity ? (Nanda Devi exceeds Kailash by nearly 3000 ft)

When I arrived in Kumaon in the autumn of 1960 everything appealed after the humid scrum of Calcutta. The station master at Kathgodam had made one feel immediately welcome and the first thing that cheered my eyes outside the station was a sepoy of the Kumaon Regiment feeding a dog called Tommy. The diamond air of October tingled as the sun enlarged the day. On the hillsides women sang as they scythed the tall grass with their sickles, one girl leading from high on the slope to be followed by a chorus from below.

On Calcutta's street stalls I had picked up Swami Pranavananda's guide to the holy mountain and in his list of essential equipment for the pilgrimage was a revolver to be sounded off each night to advise any would-be robber that the party's non-violent approach did not extend to renouncing the use of a deterrent. The secret of how to arrive on the shores of the pilgrim lake unscathed was told to me by a Kumaoni villager from Garur. He had gone as a visibly poor man and remained not only unaccosted by the robbers but was helped along the way by their Robin Hood instincts.

One noted immediately how Kumaon's southern slopes (to Bhowali) ambled up with pine covering and then fell more precipitously on the cooler northern face to the shade of oak. It was also obvious from the start that the women did all the work. Those not athletically cutting grass on steep hillsides staggered under the weight of wide baskets of manure on their heads, awaited by lines of more toiling women wielding hoes. Cheerful and tough, the lot of the Kumaon village woman was as captively confined as the regime of the menfolk was effete and exploitative. Closer acquaintance with this monstrous regiment showed women to be child-bearing chattels and the joke about whether a buffalo or a village woman had right of way was easily settled in an economy where livestock cost more than a wife. The men loafed their lives away in the tea shop huddled around the caste hookah, the Brahmins disdaining even to plough. *'Sir dukko devi'* was their constant advice to women: Cover your head, divine female—but the contradiction lay in their open disgust at the physical manifestation of female mysteries. On the one hand the Devi principle was worshipped as inherently sacred, on the other women were revoltingly untouchable for the duration of their menstruation.

This basic hangup is crucial to an understanding of the Nanda Devi cult and can be considered the best evidence of how hill religion exactly shadows the pattern of a high-caste male dominated society. The most popular folk song in Kumaon whose lilting tune has become a popular military march begins *'Beru pakho bara masah, kafo pakho Chaita meri chela'*. In these lines are contained a lexicon of social habit. Translated,it is the observation of a village woman on the seasonal fruits of the jungle. The wild fig (beru) ripens all the year round while the tree-raspberry (kaphal) fruits in the summer month of Chaitra. The milky fig grows to a modest size and if the latex is patiently boiled out, does make a kind of poor man's substitute for a vegetable. What is important for Uttarakhand is the symbolism of this ubiquitous tree. The most sought-after shrine in Hinduism derives its name from this humble fig. Badri, the seniormost temple of the sacred char dham apparently gets its name from the 'beru' of the folksong. (Lord Vishnu while performing penance in the bleak Mana valley was forced to live off this unappetising fruit) So limited is the range of diet in the Himalayas that hillmen will wax lyrical over the stringiest of Bageshwar mangoes or sound paeons to ordinary sliced hill khakri (cucumber). In a Kumaoni equivalent of Guy Fawkes night bonfires are lit in the autumn when cucumbers abound and a resounding victory over Garhwal is celebrated by resort to this bland delicacy.

*

I once walked from Almora to Srinagar in a cross-grained recapitulation of the forager's route in 1962. That was the year I was made aware of the Chinese aggression in the Himalayas by the slogans floating across the valley from the Kausani college students. 'Chairman Mao hai! hai!' went the refrain and if the usage of the Chinese leader's designation seems improbable this would be to underestimate the educational impact of English on Kumaon. Up till quite recently Almora boasted of being the most literate district in the whole of Uttar Pradesh. While Garhwal languished as a native state secure in its Maharajah's custodianship of the Badri-Kedar high places, Kumaon availed of the opportunity modern education gave to blossom along influential avenues. One of independent India's most successful Home Ministers was the Kumaoni Govind Vallabh Pant, to indicate the potential of an area the rest of India assumed to be both backward and unprepossessing. To the plainsman, 'Garhwali' signified a menial domestic servant who religiously sent home his earnings by money order. Those who measured up to the required size of chest for recruitment to the infantry would sign on for their manhood years and swell the chorus of sadness in the hillside songs. Ideally the Kumaoni strove for the minor but respectable post of government· chaprassi at the State Bank of India. The job provided quarters, a uniform and a bicycle—and made no undue demands on the body. Best of all it yielded a pension and the unstated glow that in the peasant world view attaches to sarkari naukri.

It followed that my journey through the villages of Kumaon and Garhwal was viewed with extreme suspicion. The very first students I fell in with on the descent from Dwarahat to Ganai Chaukutiya concluded I must be a spy. 'Kofiyas' (police informers) abound in the hills and are more testimony to the effectiveness of British skill in raising to an art the Brahmanical pastime of embroidering rumour. As an inmate of a Gandhian Ashram I carried with me a small spinning wheel which when compacted resembled a book and indeed was called 'Ramayan Charkha.' At the border confluence of Deghat I ran into the first arrogant statement of caste. Kumaon is famous for its orthodoxy but it is a tribute to the native ingenuity of its high-caste trend-setters that in an age when twice-born privilege is under scrutiny they manage most effectively to disguise its unchanging pattern. The shopkeeper where I enquired for a meal sold me rice and lentils, provided a pot for cooking them and called upon a Christian convert to cook them for me. As a kitchen religion, Hinduism has survived on the loyalty of compliant cooks who perform the ceremony of preparing dishes for the household deity according to the most rigorous rules of psychic hygiene. The top Brahmin families in Kumaon are known as 'lumbi dhotis' to indicate the scrupulous custom of disrobing before meals—sewing-machines having post-dated the shastras, the cling of any stitched garment is considered impure. One's place in Kumaon's pundit hierarchy is arrived at according to the length of one's cotton wrap. Unfortunately the urge to apportion spiritual clout does not extend to the sanitary sphere and next to the length of the dhoti its unsoaped Brahmanical equivalent of clerical grey is usually another unfailing indicator of holy ratings.

My walk took place before the panic of Chinese attentions unleashed a fury of so-called hill development. No motor road traversed the tangled terrain where the Ramganga river announced the end of one culture and my introduction to another. In Kumaon the men wear forage caps often of the white Congress pattern while the women work in the fields to the hitched whirl of the crinolined ghagra. Formerly only Brahmin women wore the sari but with the coming of the motor roads—deemed strategically necessary by the Chinese threat—the custom has spread to put the ghagra almost out of fashion. Similarly the wearing of slippers that once would have signified a prostitute has thirty years later been accepted as a token of polite advancement. The women of Garhwal by contrast do not wear the tough black drill but favour a brown woollen blanket traditionally folded back and pinned. The men of the interior likewise affect the warm simplicity of the Highlander's wrap whereas in more sophisticated Kumaon it would have seemed unmannerly for a male not to have boasted of either a coat or 'pant' in imitation of their erstwhile British overlords. Very few hillmen took to the Gandhian ideal of homespun as a political gesture but many wore it as a natural extension of their propensity to spin wool as they tended their flocks.

In Garhwal the absence of fertile valley floors compelled the menfolk to add their labours to those of the women. Their houses were also that little less prosperous than in Kumaon where the whitewashed upper stories with the family quarters above the stable still dazzle from afar. The carved woodwork of the veranda likewise delights with the work of local Shilpkars, Kumaon's untouchable craftsmen. It is an irony of caste that these despised 'Doms'—the original inhabitants of the lower Himalayas—earn more money than their manually shy social masters. You can often tell a Brahmin in a hill village by his poor dress and pinched looks. The price of his fair skin is not achieved without worldly reparation to the darker Dom.

In Garhwal the mud-washed houses give a less salubrious appearance to the village. Caste flourishes though not quite as vibrantly as in Kumaon where General Bruce once claimed the natives were so particular about ritual hygiene that they even washed their firewood before cooking! Garhwali food differs in some respects from Kumaoni but both regions are wedded to the morning meal of dal-bhat. Without the daily ballast of rice— and a hillman can shift a kilogram without blinking—a man will complain he has not eaten no matter how many chapattis he may have consumed.

The crucial place of rice in daily life has been transferred to the realm of religion and some grains applied to the auspicious forehead paste are the hillman's confirmation of the blessings of the gods. At devta natch ceremonies the questions put to the oracle are answered with hurled rice grains to symbolise the Goddess throwing out her grains of wisdom. According to the number of grains the supplicant manages to catch so the strength of the answer is to be interpreted. The rice cooking pot can be viewed symbolically as the caste womb. None but the authorised cook dare stir the seed therein. Rice however does not ripen much above 6,000 ft and the higher valleys must make do with wheat which in turn does not flourish above 8,000 ft. Thereafter millet is the poor man's grain and at the top of the habitation chain buck wheat and barley must do for the Bhotia and other tribals who hover between Hindu censure and Buddhist acceptance. The absence of rice in their diet indicates a deficiency in holiness.

The higher up the hill one travels the more difficult it is to subdue the hillman's taste for meat. Amongst the nomads mutton inevitably forms their staple and to illustrate the elasticity of Hinduism's embrace, both those who sacrifice a coconut in Naini Tal to the Goddess and those who slice up raw goat's meat at her temples in the interior of Garhwal, are accommodated as devotees of the same Mother principle.

Most of the teashops I halted at in Garhwal were more concerned with establishing the caste of the stranger than in serving him tea. I spent the night in forest bungalows, those convenient rest houses devised by the British at regular halts no matter how far they may be from the amenities of daily life. With apple wood logs sizzling fragrantly in the grate and the chowkidar's brave attempt at currying eggs one lapsed after the vegetarian regime of Kausani into the local convenience of dedicating the meal first to Nanda Devi. There was snow still on the high ground above Tulliasen and the brilliant splash of rhododendron cheered up the silent tread of the bridle path with its British milestones. From Almora to Pauri was eighty-eight miles and it was fascinating to watch the wide snow face of Trisul grow daily nearer to its trident nomenclature. Clearly the peak had been named from the perceptions of Garhwal. From Pauri a fine and intimate snow view awaits the visitor and this small hill town on a secondary artery from the plains maintains the charm lost by so many other stations that have been overwhelmed by the pilgrim bus.

My destination lay further down the winding trail in Srinagar where Sunderlal Bahuguna, the Chipko leader, had called a meeting to protest against the side-stepping of prohibition. The hill districts along the pilgrim route to Badrinath are officially dry but to get around the ban self-styled doctors would acquire a homeopathic degree by correspondence and open up a shack selling 'tincture', an Ayurvedic alcohol-based tonic. As Srinagar was an important staging place for the converging pilgrim buses it was feared the effect of too much tonic on the driver would endanger his passengers, hence the meeting to try and control the sale of substitute hooch. I confess I had been put off by Sunderlalji's commandeering of the town's primary school children whom he harnessed into shouting slogans as they walked through the town's streets (of which there were but two). It seemed to me a greater evil to attempt to manipulate children than to dispute adult rights to abuse their own bodies with drink. One also noted that hill politicians used the Gandhian sense of outrage selectively. If shouting support for prohibition would discredit an enemy leader in Lucknow the local neta was ready to go to jail for his belief in the harmfulness of alcohol. But when his own party leaders took a soft view of the subject on account of the revenue-earning properties of alcohol, all thoughts of martyrdom evaporated.

It is only in recent years that Kumaon and Garhwal have been linked by an all-weather road. Because of the slicing nature of the rivers off the Great Himalayas it has always been quicker to proceed to the plains and catch a train paralleling the foothills, then return into the hills. The creation of hill universities has helped stimulate the demand for a separate hill state carved out of Uttar Pradesh and the idea gained weight when the Bharatiya Janata Party adopted the notion under the contrived name of Uttranchal. The whole point of a hill state is to offset the resentment felt by the locals at the successful presence of outside businessmen. Owing to their negative work ethic and stultifying caste pride it is not surprising the hills of Uttarakhand have been developed by enterprising neighbours, especially the Punjabis. In Naini Tal the traditional pahari end of town, Talli Tal, reflects exactly the apathy of the work-shy village male while at the other end of the lake, Malli Tal exhibits a vibrant modern image. It is peopled by Sikhs and other go-ahead communities from the plains. The contrast in energy flows was brought home when in an interior village where the menfolk sat huddled around a game of chance, I asked a Punjabi driver what stakes they were playing for. 'The world ludo championship' was his witty reply.

The odds against an easy destiny for the united tracts of the U.P. Hills seem high but there is one indisputable uniting factor—the Goddess Nanda Devi. Visible daily on my week-long trek from the Kosi to the Ganga the beauty of the peak is great enough to overcome all obstacles. From the furthest corners of Uttarakhand the Devi is visible, even from Chakrata far to the west. Throughout the panorama of peaks most villagers own some localised knowledge about the status of Nanda as queen of all she surveys. To much of inner Garhwal the peak is not visible though she can crop up in the most unlikely of view points, such as from outside the Scottish cemetery in Landaur (above Mussoorie) and in more magnificent detail from the temple of Rudranath, one of the five Kedar shrines.

While the peak is elusive in Garhwal this is made up for by the level of local devotion. As with other modern trends the conscious urge to Sanskritize has meant that the Devi cult in the accessible parts of Kumaon has become indistinguishable from the plains worship of the mainstream Goddess Durga, a deity of comparable dignity, strength and beauty. Nanda however includes elements of Saraswati, wife of the creator Lord Brahma. But primarily she is the shakti of Rudra the fiery form of Shiva, echoing the *Song of Solomon:* 'Thou art beautiful my love, and terrible as an army with banners.'

It was hardly surprising that in my own choice of physical partner I should have chosen a woman who combined the fiery power of Durga with the devotional instincts of Saraswati. Prithwi was a close devotee of Sathya Sai Baba, himself an extraordinary blending of the Shiva-Parvati avatar. As a Sikh her contact with Kumaon had been confined to a childhood in the palace at Bhim Tal where she was brought up, grand-daughter of Maharaja Ranbir Singh of Jind. Ranbir Singh was remarkable for his outdoor sporting gifts that enabled him (in the opinion of his neighbour Jim Corbett) to overcome the handicap of total deafness and qualify both as a crack shot and as the best trainer of gun dogs in India. Our interest in religion brought Prithwi and I together and was strong enough to withstand the strains that arise when East meets West. In 1972 I moved from Kumaon to Garhwal. Prithwi had a house in the hill-station of Mussoorie and this was to prove an excellent base for our explorations of the pilgrim sites in dev bhumi.

FOUR

'Barah Masah'

*T*welve fruitful years had been spent in Kumaon, a period known in Hinduism as a yuga, the completion of a satisfactory cycle. Adjustment to the simpler, slower and sometimes bafflingly strange lifestyle of the hill villager was not easy but the physical pleasure of living in sight of the great peaks made up for the traumatic inadequacies of a learner whose behaviour was equally slow and strange in the eyes of his hosts. Yuga also ties in with the Nanda Devi cycle. According to the lore of her priests 'After twelve years the land is polluted from an unmarried girl's menses'. Hence the twelve-yearly yatra to appease the anger of the Goddess.)

In the Kausani ashram my enthusiasm for taking the weekly day off in the surrounding hills spread to the girls and probably for the only time in their careers they experienced the unusual exercise of climbing mountains just for the joy of it. Needless to say the women of the villages we passed through looked on in bewilderment when we returned empty-handed. It was unheard of in Kausani for a woman to climb the steep face of Pinat that stretched to 9,000 ft and not stagger home under a load of oak leaves for the family buffalo or a shaggy bundle of pine needles for bedding down the cattle. On one remarkable outing to Pinat in the heat of summer when the going was difficult and the gloss on the carpet of needles (phirule) made one skid and rendered any upward ambition to a scramble on hands and knees, the problem I feared most was the lack of drinking water. The hysterical chiming of the cicada did not help and their tone was so deafening that physical waves of sound added to the discomfort of one's sweat. To my astonishment the girls and a couple of women wardens were observing a fast and climbed that whole day in the blazing heat without letting water touch their lips. Their normal voluble cheerfulness was not in any way subdued nor was their rate of progress. It seemed funny that in Delhi self-important mountaineering bureaucrats should spend vast amounts to try and get a woman on Everest. By easy recourse to these Kumaoni village ladies, fully trained in the arts of tough survival and uncomplaining in the face of the extremes of nature, the desire to fly flags over summits could have been fulfilled at a fraction of the cost and by an innumerable bevy of belles. When the Chinese scare galvanised the government into creating a home guard for the hills it was found during rifle practice in the villages that women proved to be the crack shots. This did not surprise me in the least for their daily round was so harsh and muscle-building that most of them for all practical purposes were fully trained Olympic athletes.

My admiration for the women of Kumaon was based on a close study of their routine and the perpetual grind of their existence. They always got up long before dawn, then trudged in the cold morning greyness to lug water on their heads from the spring. From early morning to last light their swaying muscular grace was invoked as the copper ghara was hoisted effortlessly on to the head and the struggle to gain the lost altitude back to the village embarked upon. Next the family had to be given tea and a snack of last night's leftovers, if any. Then the livestock demanded attention. The buffalo had to be milked and mucked out, wood for the day's cooking chopped and the rice and dal for the morning meal cleaned. Before preparing the fire they would honour the family gods and offer flowers to the local deity.

After the main meal of the day they would gird their loins and embark on the agricultural demands of the season. During sowing or harvests they would be in the back-breaking mode of the labourer but even in the midst of their animal lot the fluidity of their bodily motions maintained all the grace of their feminine birthright. It would be an unusual day if they did not exchange words with a neighbour over the habitual transgression of coveting other people's crops. The instinct of the peasant is to apply the shrewd and

31

amoral policy of cutting one's neighbour's grass before one's own. Daily heated arguments sound off the slopes and like barking dogs whose glands have been enlarged the slanging of shrewish tongues continues until the stores of expletives are exhausted or night intervenes.

When the fields were not in need of attention the daily load was transferred from the back to the head. The women would set off single file with a rope around their waists and a sickle tucked in to their cummerbunds. Their objective could be a hill five miles away to collect grass or cut wood on, or even to prise out lichen for medicinal purposes. Free of male disapproval they would sing and sport lasciviously and some would resort to the hidden pleasure of smoking. Then it was back to work with their flashing sickles to hack the oak leaves for fodder or rake the slippery *phirule* into heaps. As they worked they chattered loudly to keep in contact with their group. On a steep hill it is easy to slip. Other real dangers are lurking snakes underfoot and the even nastier prospect of a bear rearing up out of the undergrowth to maim and hideously disfigure any object that comes in its way. The hillman has evolved a safety code for these threats. You must run up hill when chased by a snake, downhill when an enraged bear is after you. The problem is to remember which way to run when surprised and the brain automatically surrenders to panic. Downhill a snake can go like greased lightning while a bear's paws, so useless on a steep descent can be used to propel him smartly upward, his four limbs enabling him to outrun your two.

One of the Kausani wardens claimed to have had a close encounter with a bear while cutting grass. The animal had got her in a close embrace but instead of screaming the woman had faced her molester and bravely tapped her sickle on the bear's chest to indicate a counter threat. The bear, unaccustomed to a non-wriggling victim and puzzled by the insistent tapping, let go of her. It might be added that the woman was a hardy Bhotia who though not technically beautiful enough for a bear to lust after, was such an extraordinary character that her story seemed perfectly credible.

My own experience with bears was confined to crop protection. In Lakshmi Ashram they would come in summer for the apricots and peaches, climbing the trees to stuff themselves, then falling off with a thump when they were gorged. In Mirtola they came later in the season for the ripening maize. One night I sat on duty as midnight crept past and was very edgy as the tall plants rattled in the cool breeze. The inky surroundings were relieved afar by Almora's lights that glowed like a necklace some ten miles distant. To add to my nervousness was the slender pike with which I had been armed. What would one do with a six-foot pole if the bear appeared at close quarters? In fact these shuffling animals are highly sensitive to human presence and avoid contact when they can. They are also extremely athletic and when on another occasion I was armed with a shotgun, a bear I caught raiding the maize terrace raced for the boundary wall and before I had time to train the gun on him had leapt with one fluid motion up and over a six-foot stone dyke leaving me blinking at the speed of his exit.

That night in Mirtola the bear did not turn up but I experienced a very scientific puzzle. In the still blackness of the cool silence I could make out the steady throb of a diesel generator. Its distinctive drone gave off an audible beat and I knitted my brows trying to work out how sound waves (which do travel considerable distances in the silence of night) could manage to ripple out from Almora, the only place that could conceivably boast of a motor.

Next morning when I described the mystery at breakfast my guru laughed and said 'That was no distant engine. That was your own heart beating'.

It was these simple but stunning discoveries about the blindness to our own make-up that the great spaces of the Himalayas could stimulate. Uncanny details abounded for the superstition-ridden villages were eagerly accustomed to all the horrors attendant upon the spilling of blood in a deliberate sacrificial frame of mind. My best ghost story related to the most popular devta of Almora district called Golu (Goril). The most famous temple of this impish nature spirit (who was suspected to be of princely lineage) is at Chitai overlooking the Himalayan peaks on the outskirts of Almora. The temple is festooned with bells perhaps as a cover-up in a modern disapproving age for the actual offering which traditionally is a fattened goat. The other curious feature of Chitai that reflects on how well the local Brahmins have assimilated the advantages of British administrative procedure is that petitions to the resident demon have to be formally made on government-stamped court paper. That way a record is kept of the petitioners while the U.P. government avails of an unexpected steady source of revenue.

Golu, after the custom of hill Rajputs, is accompanied by the sound of drums and an account of his powers was told to me by the Gandhian worker Sarala Devi, who incidentally disbelieved most strongly in such local superstitions. She had been in the neighbouring valley of Salem staying at the house of a Gandhian worker who was visibly upset at the condition of his daughter. The girl was possessed and prophesied that Golu would come and claim the sacrifice owed to him. Sarala retired early to the closed confinement of her upstairs room, tired after a long march. Late at night she was awakened by the characteristic sound of a wedding procession which in Kumaon is preceded by a band of furious drummers. A mighty racket was raised before the door of her host and Sarala thought it strange that she had not been informed of the auspicious ceremony to be held in the village. Next morning when she opened the window she was surprised to find the paved courtyard bare with no signs of the aftermath of any celebration. She asked her host over the morning glass of water (since to Gandhians the intake of tea is considered anti-poor) who had got married at his house last night. The man looked blank. Then, when he learned that Sarala had also been privy to the sound of drums, he confessed that Golu had come to fulfil the prophecy.

In my researches on the lore of Nanda Devi many similarly spooky situations had to be skirted for one was concerned primarily with the brighter side of the Goddess. There was nothing sinister in Nanda's mountain form though there too some cruelty could be detected if one were to accept the hillman's notion of jealous revenge wreaked on Willi Unsoeld's daughter. Almost all my associations with Kumaon's ranges were sunny though as one reached the very top of Pinat to pass through a strangely brooding canopy of cypress that crowned the mountain there seemed undoubtedly a sighing presence. It seemed to finger the passing tread with a silent restraint almost as if these trees belonged to Tolkien's race of Ents. Clear of them on the summit one's rejoicing knew no limit.

The bell of the tiny temple was clanged with the sheer exhilaration caused by the spread of such bounteous beauty all around. One was level with the snows, sailing above the lesser peaks of Kumaon. The heart swelled to its fullness and for the duration of the stay one breathed as a conscious human being, allowing the instinct to worship to well up spontaneously. With each step back down the mood weakened and one was finally shocked back into the pain of ordinary reality by stumbling in the failing light into a bank of stinging nettles at the base of the mountain.

Another similar mood descended in late February while collecting firewood in the pine forest around Mirtola. I sat resting in a clearing when the sun suddenly smote the winter foliage of dried-up saplings. One sensed the precise moment of the first stirrings of spring in the initial creak of expanding wood as the sap began again to pulse and signal a flutter to the still wings of insect life. To be privy to the great secrets of nature's limitless storehouse was one of the rare blessings the Himalayas provided. Whatever her poverty the singing cheerfulness of the oppressed village woman of Kumaon confirmed the essential unquenchable joy of life. Hill society in its brutal compulsions seemed to be a doomed exercise in human relationships where male arrogance in punishing its women had led to its own emasculation of purpose. In the silent jungle often strange coincidences could be reflected on and it was not unusual to think of a friend out of the blue and return to the ashram and find a letter of his awaiting.

One curious coincidence stands out as a sort of link between my departure from Kumaon to reside the next yuga in Garhwal. Above Lakshmi Ashram had stood an empty bungalow maintained by an irascible chowkidar and I always puzzled why its owner chose to remain far from such a sensational view. Moving to Mussoorie I found myself now facing south across the lush kindly aspect of the Doon Valley. Immediately below our residence was a large empty property set in a magnificent sheltered estate possessed of every variety of mature conifer. Again I puzzled why the owner should disregard such a privileged viewpoint and deny to the soul what most aspire in life to attain. One day in Landaur I entered the South Indian restaurant for a dosa and found myself sitting next to an attractive woman who (most improbably, in view of her curvaceousness) admitted to being a fairly senior bureaucrat. It turned out that her family not only owned the house below my Mussoorie look-out but incredibly also owned the bungalow above where I had stayed in Kausani.

The mountaineering ladies of the village would return with headloads weighing fifty kilograms, swinging powerfully in their wrapped up skirts, then return ten kilometres at a fast gait, fortified only with a handful of gram. Their evening round would involve milking and bedding down the buffalo, then cooking the evening meal of chapattis and vegetables, if available. Hard work on a harsh diet had not made these exploited women any less maternal. On the contrary their willingness to go the extra mile showed their infinite inner strength, the distinguishing mark of the feminine. No physical labour could break these tough ladies. However on emotional grounds they could come to grief and it was not uncommon for those unhappy under their mother-in-law's jurisdiction to be sullen and shrill. A few miserably matched with a wife-beating husband might end up taking their lives and be found hanging from an oak tree.

Only at festival time did they find relief from the unending grind of duty. On the morning of the big day they could be found chirping eagerly on the river bank washing their ghagras after a month's hard wear, spreading out the folds to dry on the rocks. The mela might amount only to the buying of a few trinkets at a stall or enjoying the prospect of replacing broken glass bangles but it gave the body rest and allowed if but for a day the womanly delight in her own seductive mysteries to flicker into flame. The menfolk hogged the dancing but in the upper Bhotia regions the women also form a circle and do their own sedate pacing. At the time of marriage the joyous feast which meant a break from the monotony of a grim diet was followed by the real sadness of leaving forever one's mother's hearth.

A common sight in the hills is the distraught condition of girls torn away from their home valley to work in the strange rigours of an unknown terrain. At childbirth they may return and sometimes when work is slack the married woman may visit her mother's house on family matters. Happy indeed the girl who is married into an understanding home where both husband and mother-in-law support her bewilderment at the sudden change of scene. The husband quite often can only find employment in the plains and the bride has to adjust to this added loneliness. Sometimes she will accompany him to the plains and face the daunting heat to experience the alternative cruelty of a purdah existence, mother to her husband's children, cook and servant to her lord, captive inmate of a cultural impasse.

These seasonal miseries of the female lot have great bearing on the Nanda Devi lore for though she is viewed as a royal princess in both Kumaon and Garhwal, the Goddess remains an ordinary hill woman who must work the treadmill of dismal custom honoured by the theory of traditional respect but abused in the everyday expression of it. The main harvest season in the hills follows the ripening of the rice in September. This leads to the busiest time of year in the hay cutting for winter where the women work long hours on the hillsides flashing their faithful sickle. Winter is slack only marginally for when the wheat is sown in November they prepare dried vegetables for the lean months ahead and perhaps make pickle. Pumpkins line the veranda of the houses and maize cobs dry golden on the roof. In the higher villages it is the time for weaving when the yarn spun by the menfolk on their spindles as they walk is fashioned into warm clothes or blankets.

Winter in the hills is a visibly quiet time when much of the male population descends to the lower regions. The days though cold are magnificently serene and viewing the snows now is to experience the distinct sensation of nature aslumber. A somnolent azure lies about the winter snow-line where the cold air traps the wood smoke of village fires. The flattened cling of this heavenly shade lazily gives way to the deeper blue of the winter sky caused by the sun's southernmost journeying. Unlike the plains where the cosmic junction at the turning back of the sun makes little impact, in the Himalayas one is aware of the solstitial reversal process. Southwestwards the sunset becomes more hauntingly beautiful than in the monsoon when the bruised texture of the clouds had caught scarlet inspiration. The January twilight horizon is the most moving of natural spectacles when the sky changes dramatically from the fury of red to the promise of gold then briefly yields to the poignancy of green that brings tears to the eternal witness in man.

Winter reveals the limitation of orthodox Hinduism's ability to encompass the physical reality of Hindustan. The Vaishnav temple where I spent seven years proved hard to service and attain the required level of ritual purity. At 7,200 ft it effectively marked the ceiling of any attempt. Higher than that and only temples to Shiva could survive, less concerned as they are with the niceties of a hygiene evolved for the humid needs of the Gangetic plain. Shivering in cotton garments one's feet were apt to freeze to the marble floor of the sanctum sanctorum and to remedy this threat of circulation failure one had to keep a bucket of hot water outside the garbha for constant plungings of one's numb extremities. Hot water itself is not rated much as a spiritual substance and in Kausani where such luxuries were not available one could manage to bathe in the icy spring by the expedient of first applying mustard oil to the body. Certainly these tingling encounters with the raw edge of divine elements whose five manifestations were worshipped daily in the arati ceremony stimulated self-consciousness, if only for the sheer thrill of having survived them. Never has one been more physically alive than after the extreme resort of bathing at these icy sources of the Ganga.

In the hills there is the usual friendly rivalry between the majority who follow the religion of Shiva (and his consort Nanda Devi) and the minority of better-off devotees of Lord Vishnu. The latter are more likely to be found in the towns and to show their subtle superiority would hold their celebration of the same festival a day later. Just as she unites both Kumaoni and Garhwali so Nanda Devi transcends the sectarian loyalties of the orthodox to include the tantrics as well as gather in the vote of the aboriginal outcaste. Alone in Uttarakhand the Goddess soars above the differences of dress and language, custom and diet. This ability to ennoble the primitive strivings of hill society make the peak an object of reverence as well as a fascinating study in the power of religion to integrate warring parts. Devotion for the Devi flowers 'barah masah'—all the year round.

FIVE

Well-Earned Bliss

*T*he chance to follow in the footsteps of Shipton arose in 1980. One had read the expedition reports of the flood of foreign entrants to Nanda Devi sanctuary when inner line restrictions were lifted in 1974. This eagerness to get into the record books by knocking off virgin routes to little-climbed mountains helped my solo effort greatly by stimulating the infrastructure of approach. Willing and knowledgeable porters now existed to transport parties successfully through the gorge and the only factors that lay between the candidate for darshan of Big Nanda, and the fulfilment of his dreams were the resolve not to end up in a watery grave and the ability to come up with the requisite finance. The previous monsoon I had been to the Valley of Flowers and the utter plenitude of the outcome had won me over to putting to the test Shipton's proposition that the rainy season was no time to be in the sanctuary. Besides I had no choice. It was only in the month of July that I could get away for the space of three weeks. At this time Prithwi went to Sai Baba's ashram in the south for Guru Purnima, and life in Mussoorie—thanks to the non-stop rain—came to a halt anyway. If I did not seize the moment it would mean another year lost and, having reached the age when spectacles had become necessary to read the newspaper, one knew that soon the problem of finance would be overtaken by the even more depressing condition for which there was no remedy, the drop in energy consistent with middle age.

Like most maiden assaults on the serious ground of the Himalayas my aspirations were ludicrously unrealistic. My earlier expeditions from political necessity had been confined to the lesser range and amounted to no more than treks with a light rucksack containing a sleeping bag, a handful of peanuts and a lump of jaggery. What other mountaineers consider basic to their welfare I have always scorned. My years in Kumaon were spent entirely in the barefoot mode and the soles of my feet had grown impervious to cold or puncture. However eight years had elapsed since I had turned my back on that level of fitness. Another oddity extended to rations and the taste of chocolate has never excited me to any furtive munch. I was for all practical purposes a hillman in my habits, never so happy as when shifting a healthy spadeful of home-pounded rice.

For my imagined triumphal exit from the sanctuary over to Milam I optimistically packed a pair of crampons. Funds did not rise to arctic tents but I had fashioned my own from khadi along with a pair of tent poles whittled by hand. I had an Indian-made feather jacket that emitted clouds of (possibly) DDT and a motley of other bodily coverings nearer to the age of Shipton than Bonington.

My 'approach march' boots had also been acquired from Old Delhi and seemed to weigh a ton which was at least preferable to a friend's experience from the same source. Having chosen the lightweight alternative he found that the weight had been offset by absorbability: the soles of his boots were apparently made of cardboard. So strapped are humble Indian expeditions for funds that often snow fields are traversed in canvas boots and the number of frost-bite casualties from this economy alone is frightening. My rucksack was second-hand from a French expedition which had wished to lighten its return flight. For those in Delhi keen to land the latest gear the arriving East European parties were the best bet. Their government-sponsored expeditions did not rise to providing pocket money to the members and immediately on arrival they would sell their unused equipment to raise cash for private pleasures—and claim the luggage had been lost on the mountain.

Fifty feet of nylon rappelling rope and an ancient wood-shafted ice axe completed my kit. The axe was innocent of any contact with ice though its spike was well-worn from doubling up as a tent pole.

Earlier that year Sathya Sai Baba had visited Prithwi's Delhi house and the hostess invited the holy man to bless my proposed trip to the sanctuary. This Sai Baba readily agreed to do. He smiled as he took the proferred ice axe and then proceeded carefully to rub vibhuti (sacred ash)—which he had created for the purpose from thin air—on the pick of the axe but not on the spoon. Then he handed it back with the words: 'You will be successful.'

As a regular overnight commuter between Delhi and the hills I travelled to the Kashmiri Gate terminal to book a seat on the bus to Rishikesh. To my pleasant surprise I found the roof of the bus crowded with the luggage of a Bombay mixed expedition. It was a joy to travel with these genuine mountain lovers doing their pilgrimage on a shoestring with none of them suffering from the handicap of official sponsorship nor encumbered by the patronising handouts of the Indian Mountaineering Foundation (IMF). The IMF had replaced after independence the Himalayan Club as arbiter in mountaineering matters. While the latter had been formed of a band of enthusiastic sahibs with a genuine love of India's great range, there was little doubt that their prime allegiance lay with George and Elizabeth rather than Shiva and Parvati. With the heavy exodus of expatriates in 1947 the Himalayan Club stumbled along thanks to the efforts of a few remaining Britishers in Calcutta but its style was foreign to the Bengali milieu whose grand passion for the Himalayas equals if not exceeds that of any other nation. Finally the Himalayan Club regained its footing in Bombay where a sound working mixture of sport and finance enabled it to bounce back as a badly-needed objective force in the increasingly politicised mountaineering circles of India.

This mountaineering conscience was sorely required in view of the distortion the sport suffered at the hands of non-participant bureaucrats who tillered its furtherance in a blaze of pompous self-importance. Tenzing's ascent of Everest did for Indian self-respect what the sinking of the Russian fleet in 1904 had done for the Japanese. Obviously the need of the hour was to produce more Tenzings so the plains babus set about creating a string of institutes for training young climbers. They overlooked the fact that Tenzing had never been to any institute (nor was strictly an Indian for that matter). They could have saved much time and money by simply improving the native skills of the hillman with his strengthened lungs rather than start from scratch with unenthusiastic candidates from sea-level who too often joined the courses to use the certificate awarded at the end as a crude means to promotion. (These novices could hardly be blamed for their blatant self-advancement when the same principle was employed by those at the helm of the mountaineering scene) Just as the arrogant outpourings of the *Alpine Journal* against plebian climbing skills on the Eiger had set back British mountaineering attitudes by ten years, so the strangulation of Indian climbing prospects was accomplished by the armchair bureaucrats. They guaranteed that India would never break out of the big expedition syndrome of Everest by the South Col route.

The U.P. Roadways bus slewed its way through the night with the driver's foot flat down on the accelerator and the palm of his hand flattened over the horn button. We arrived in Rishikesh at four in the morning and managed to hire an empty fruit-stall on wheels to get the luggage from the bus stand to the office of the hill bus company. As we comprised a large group and the chances of everyone getting on the same bus were slight we were advised to accept the offer of an empty bus run by a smaller company which promised to get us to Joshimath by the evening. What with hold-ups from the damaged road and the need to constantly stop and check the run-down condition of the bus tyres we did not get to Chamoli (three-quarters of the way) until 5 p.m. The driver then declared he was too tired and would complete the remaining part of the journey in the morning. It dawned on us that his bus company belonged to Chamoli and that he had got us there deliberately so he could spend the night at home. As all of us were on budgeted time we informed the local police of how we had been tricked and the driver against his will was forced to honour his commitment. However we only got as far as the next village of Pipalkoti before we learned that the loops up to Joshimath were blocked by landslides. So we stopped over at the sparse Baba Kala Kambliwala dharamsala and ate in one of the halting-place's famous dhabas before sleeping on the wooden floor in our sleeping bags.

We were in Joshimath by ten the next morning and parted ways. The Bombay party headed towards the Valley of Flowers while I made enquiries about porters in the rickety town. When it became apparent I would have to hang about indefinitely on the off-chance of a climbing porter turning up, I decided to continue to the sanctuary roadhead at Lata. But three miles before Lata I alighted at Renni since someone on the bus had told me there were one or two HAPs (high altitude porters) who lived thereabouts. Once again I was invited by the relaxed teashop assembly to sit and see what would turn up. I decided instead to hump my load (now approaching thirty kilograms from the rations bought in Joshimath) and stagger along the road to Lata.

On the way I passed one of the HAPs I was looking for but neither of us concluded we were in need of each other's services. The path up to the summer village was exceedingly steep and by now the sun was scorching down. By great good luck the next person I met was Bal Singh Butola, one of the village worthies who was due to become headman. He immediately responded to my request for a porter and retracing his steps with my luggage hefted on his back, invited me to spend the night on his veranda. The businesslike command of Bal Singh sorted out my ambitions in a matter of minutes. There was no question of finding any porter to take me beyond the sanctuary. The question was whether there would be any willing to lead me in for the price of Rs 750, which is all that was left of my thousand after buying rations. These were deemed inadequate by Bal Singh who argued that because of the dangerously slippery terrain in the monsoon two men would have to go in support. I could hardly insist that I knew better. My sole aim was to get into the sanctuary and if Bal Singh's economies could help get me there he was welcome to everything I had. By adding the value of my equipment to the cash balance and accepting items (like the academic crampons) in lieu of later payments, it was found the expedition could be arranged. But since the normal rates for the ten-day trek to Nanda Devi base camp were still not met by my circumstances it was agreed that we would do double stages and accomplish in five days what normally involved ten.

That night, fed from Bal Singh's kitchen, I slept happily on his veranda high above the growling Dhauli Ganga. Hill rivers in the rains take on a more masculine voice and the Dhauli declared its violent intentions loudly as it bore down between Lata and Chamoli to perform the spectacular task of cleaving a passage through the Great Himalaya. The river's grumble accompanied us next morning when after tea and parathas Bal Singh in the company of Pratap Singh Rana led the way up the muddy lane to clear the messy environs of the village. There had been no time to visit the old temple of Nanda Devi and the new one I had seen had been built hideously in cement presumably to cash in on the sudden mountaineering interest stimulated by the opening of the sanctuary. I was introduced to the headman Jagat Singh, a person about whom it was difficult to be neutral. With the influx of foreign expeditions he had been instrumental in fixing up porters and pack goats for them. According to the bulk of expedition opinion, the Lata headman required close watching as unaccounted equipment loads were apt to be cheerfully written off as 'missing'—presumed fallen (with goat) into gorge.

My own essay was too humble to require the filling of saddle bags but Pratap Singh by profession was a shepherd and out of habit he kept whistling for his goats. The plan was for Bal Singh, a man of means who had no need to labour as a lowly porter, to deliver my rucksack to Lata Kharak at 12,000 ft where it would be transferred to his younger brother Nathu Singh. From his supply of old expedition leftovers Bal Singh had dug out a day-sack for me to carry and this had come with the confident assurance: 'The porters will do everything. All you have to do is get yourself to the sanctuary.'

I soon learned that the shepherd rule of approach was forever *diretissima*. Where steep shortcuts were available they effortlessly entered upon them leaving me gasping and floundering in the rear. It was a hands and knees scramble to pull ourselves up beyond the cool shade of the cedar forest to gain the tree-line at Lata Kharak. Ahead the ridge ran up knife-like to part the waters of the jade green Dhauli from the raging white of the confined Rishi.

We camped under the last great deodar and a cache of salt confirmed that Nathu Singh had passed by yesterday delivering this essential part of a goat's diet. Within minutes of arrival Pratap disappeared to locate the spring and returned after ten minutes with a large bulging plastic bag tied at the neck to announce the expedition water bottle. Bal Singh proceeded to set up the kitchen and put my pressure cooker on to make khichdi. To serve it he whittled away at a piece of driftwood to produce the expedition spoon. This cheerful improvisation extended to the setting up of my khadi tent over a piece of plastic stretched out as a ground sheet. Protected by the great tree the drizzling mist hardly permeated the woollen blankets of the two men as they lay down in the open. The smoke from the wood fire made me weep copiously but to counteract this the porters were content to puff away at their bidis. They had fulfilled their promise of doing everything that needed to be done.

The altitude had got to me and not being able to eat from lack of appetite I now found I could not sleep from lack of oxygen. On Bal Singh's advice I decided to jettison the tent since he assured me that all the camps ahead could provide cave accommodation. The tent only added to my sense of claustrophobia and without a cold stream of air playing directly upon the nostrils I felt I might suffocate.

The morning saw no let-up in the mist and everything including the lichen dangled shaggily from the trees, drooping in a sag of sodden misery. Voices from the mist announced the arrival of Nathu Singh but they came from downhill while his had been expected from the next camp across Dharansi. It turned out he had gone down to the village the previous night by a shortcut and only learned there that he was needed 6,000 ft higher. It took him two hours to accomplish what it had taken me the best part of a day to attain. Bal Singh left and we set out over a terrible stumble of slewed slabs, some of them rocking to add to the weird sense of walking through a cemetery.

Along and up the ridge we toiled in the unyielding fog until a cairn announced the long winding passage of the pass that led over to Dharansi. Here the wind tore away shreds of cloud to reveal brilliant surrealistic emerald alps. A long wind down from the exposed rocky edge brought us to the ease of springy turf that away from the path gave rise to plashy clumps of potentilla soggy from the weight of moisture that burdened our passage. We continued down to a stone pen at Malathuni passing under a goat's *arc de triomphe* at Ranakhola. These were but names on the map, the camping sites of itinerant shepherds but lacking in water and shelter except for the stone walls flung up to keep out the worst of the wind. At each of the camp sites the porters would ferret about prodding the ground with my ice axe or sliding their fingers into crevices. They were looking for items stashed away from earlier expeditions—one of the basic precautions of men carrying loads into the sanctuary was to deposit promptly in hiding any commodity that would not be needed until the return voyage. But all the Malathuni foraging yielded was a dug-up blue plastic pyramid of salt and a sealed packet of injection ampules, both jettisoned in disgust.

After milkless tea the porters quickly packed and trotted off into the mist. The loads had been reapportioned and Nathu was now lugging the bulk of our supplies. I was carrying my rucksack with warm clothes in it and as the path shot down steeply I found the weight of the sack top-heavy. By the time I had adjusted the straps the porters were nowhere to be seen. I stood on the brink of the misty abyss puzzling which way to go until yells and whistles from below indicated a plunge was needed.

Then followed a near-vertical descent over more upended slates that as we neared the alp of Dibrugheta turned into a muddy slide from the steepness of the slope. As we entered the spruce forest fringing the Dibrugehta nala the verticality increased even more improbably and one had to scrabble desperately to grab passing tree roots to arrest the skid of unclinging boots.

Instead of halting after this dramatic quickfire descent the porters leapt nimbly on to a tree trunk conveniently jammed across the furious stream and nonchalantly ambled over with their loads. I was petrified by the roar of the angry water and scared that the wet log would cause my boots to slip on it. I had to call back one of the porters to take my load, then crawled across barefoot on all fours before the danger was overcome.

The camp site was an overhang higher up towards the level alp. The river had sculpted out the rock and it was difficult to find a hold up the smooth bank. Eventually I dragged myself up by a muddy detour and peered over a shelf to find Nathu busy blowing up a fire with enormous spurts of wind from his seasoned lungs. That night we sheltered under the cold overhanging rock whose dankness was considerable. The porters taught me how to divert drips from the cave roof. The tiring slog had guaranteed my appetite again refused to switch on and I had to force myself to eat a few mouthfuls of rice and dal against a rising urge to throw up.

In the morning the rain slanted down and the misery of packing wet clothes to add to the weight on our backs did not slacken until we had crested Penikhola Dhar to look down in clearing conditions upon the Rishi. Since we had started the mist had not revealed a single snow summit and the doomsday advisors who had warned against entering the sanctuary in the rains seemed to have a point if you had come to identify the peaks.

We jogged down to the racing river lightened by the stashing of the tent and some supplies against our return in the rocky recesses of the cave. Another steep slide through fir to the river bank was made trickier by the formation of several streams underfoot. As we charged towards the rickety temporary bridge over the Rishi Ganga the porters put up their hands cautiously. It seemed from the tilt of the fragile structure that it might collapse from the first footstep on its tindery planks. For a moment I thought the expedition was off. There was no way I could have forded the Rishi against its extravagantly hostile display of naked muscle. But I had not reckoned on the initiative of the porters. Pratap tied on my rope and eased himself over lightly to test the structure. He managed to get half way across before the rope ran out. Nathu scorning such safety devices picked up his load and clomped confidently over. I tip-toed after him trying to forget the awkward question of having to cross this teetering lifeline on our return.

Now we were in the midst of the lush and paradisiacal jungle Mumm and Shipton had written about, with a good trail skirting the river. We worked our way past the camp site at Deodhi and headed for another at the junction of the routes for Rhamani and Trisul base camps. The birch forest with its undergrowth of bent rhododendron was bearded with the elegant drape of lichen and lower on the approach to Trisul nala head-high stands of soaring rhubarb kept us company. By now the morning had begun to steam as the sun worked to dislodge the hold of the mist. Sunflowers and a whistling thrush helped cheer our mood as we slashed a way to the stumbling block of the Rhamani cliffs. The confluence of the Rishi and the waters off the Trisul-Bethartoli combine is not mentioned as an obstacle to expeditions outside the monsoon. The danger can usually be overcome by a bridge of sagging birch logs that need span only a few feet when the river was not in full spate. The bridge the porters now expected me to negotiate was both slim and terrifying and the more I enquired about its fastening (there wasn't any) the less eager I was to commit myself upon it. The bridge had in fact been laid by Pratap and consisted of two logs placed in a 'V' over more than ten feet of howling torrent. It was the mesmerising hurl of the water more than the flimsiness of the bridge that one feared. The attendant clash and fury seemed to wish destruction on any who risked themselves to its crossing.

As it was growing late we decided to camp under what the porters described as an overhang but which seemed to be more of a token gesture in the way of rocky projections. We would reconsider the option of crossing in the morning when the night's freeze-up would reduce the water level.

The porters soon had a huge kindle of fallen birch toasting the night. The first patches of snow proved we were getting near the heights but the driving sleet that plastered our alcove could get nowhere near to soaking us thanks to the abundance of stoked flame that reared out into the gloom to cheer our sinking prospects.

Next morning without ado we hid what luggage we did not need and climbed down to test the spring of the bridge. The water seemed to be no lower in its fury but I had made the conscious effort to exclude all thoughts of a river from my mind as I performed the gymnastic feat of crawling face down over the dashing torrent without disturbing the unanchored logs.

It was a yogic task to be performed detachedly. The porters marched across confidently while I tied on the rope and began my crawl. It was agonizing as the 'V' opened to exchange the security of both poles for the transfer of one's destiny to either fir or birch. For a moment my clothes snagged. Then, panting with fear from the desperation of holding off a killer stream, I was free and leapt with a whoop to a rock midstream. A further leap involved no great jump and one almost cavorted across the second instalment of the nala to gain the shore. 'Nanda Devi *basekin chalo*' shouted Pratap and we hared up through the tangled undergrowth of the gloomy Rhamani cliffs to emerge alongside the slick, ferocious mainstream. The Rishi rode unstoppable between the great black rock curtains and on one wall I saw in silver paint the sign of a visit from the Naini Tal mountaineering club of which I was a member. Normally one would have disapproved of such inappropriate advertisement but somehow in the threatening inclose of mountain and river it seemed a hopeful sign.

We did not linger to make tea but emerged at the foot of a towering brown canyon which had defeated so many stronger parties. The porters swarmed up, smoothly pulling on birch saplings to aid their grasp. It was fun to leave the sulking river so easily and my maiden encounter with unavoidable rock climbing seemed so enjoyable that I was lulled into a false sense of cragsmanship. A narrow chute had to be straddled and the porters in their bare feet soon got purchase from the sides and kicked a way upwards. Had it been on a less exposed part of the gorge one would have concentrated on overcoming the paucity of holds. But looking between my feet, I was suddenly aware that the river lay booming straight below. I panicked and proceeded to make a silly move. Unable to reach up with my fingers I used the pick of the ice axe to drive into the earth wall of the gully, hoping to get enough purchase to allow myself to find a toe-hold. But the pick sank in only two or three inches before it hit solid rock. The weight on the axe caused me to slip, boots frantically scrabbling to find a brake. Luckily Pratap who was ahead backed down in a lightning crab movement and managed to grab me by the scruff of the neck. With the holds carefully worked out in advance I managed to get up and out of the chute and nearly broke into tears when I saw at the exit a piton hammered in precisely to avoid my predicament.

But the porters felt we were too light a party to bother with ropes and besides we would need them higher up. I was now miserable with fright and as the brown walls reared all around and the mist again settled to encourage despair I wondered if I would ever be able to get out alive. How the hell was I going to get down that chute?

Fortunately at the parav (halting-place) called Bhujgara where the last of the birch surrendered to the dominion of the cliff there was some turf to get a foothold on and though sheer and scary the climb was now bearable. Clutching a way upwards on tufts of grass one came out to the 'quarry' site of Patalkhan. We sank down breathlessly for tea while my palpitation wore off. We were nearly there and if I could just hold on for the last lap up and over the tumble of huge boulders the sanctuary portals lay at hand.

As usual the porters rummaged around the back of the cave, pushing in their arms to try and locate some hidden souvenir. Incredibly they came up with a large brown plastic bag in which, wrapped in reams of toilet paper was another paper bag, in which again was wrapped a thick book. Pratap solemnly presented it to me saying he had rescued it from an accident that had befallen an Australian expedition. A member's rucksack had tumbled into the gorge and shrugging off their loss the team had continued homewards. The porters hanging back had managed to find a route down to the river and indulged in some beachcombing. The paperback turned out to be Sir James Frazer's anthropological classic *The Golden Bough* and its arrival at my lowest ebb served to give me the lift to perform the last struggle into the sanctuary. This book in many particulars echoed the lore of Nanda Devi albeit in Greek dress. The fact that it had been recommended reading for my religious studies and that I had never got round to perusing it seemed to point to the Goddess mocking me gently with a personal interest. How else to explain this prize awaiting at the head of the gorge, except in terms of the bliss-giving Nanda?

Fortified by her grace I took in my stride another nasty slip off the slabs beyond the Patalkhan cave. Then we leaped and balanced wildly like the Bolshoi ballet to cross the bouldered shoulder of the last obstacle. There ahead lay the splendid rolling promise of the south sanctuary meadows. With the wind in our hair we passed the cairns raised to announce the portals of the sacred mist-bound mountain.

Six

Escape from the Sanctuary

*I*t felt good to be alive as we sloped down to the sanctuary camp. The all-encompassing mist prevented the fixing of landmarks but the green expansiveness of the rolling moors announced this could be nowhere but the sanctuary of the Goddess. We headed towards the roots of the mountain where across the sunken bed of the South Rishi the black ragged rocks supporting Nanda Devi reared up to reveal ramparts eroded by the undermining, scouring elements.

Expedition litter announced the main camping site where a small stream ran past white encrusted rocks to make more vivid this emerald dell. Alongside was a rock shelter built with stones to make a reasonable if constricted cave. Against our better instincts the porters pulled up roots of the brush undergrowth to make a fire. Normally we did not abuse the hospitality of the environment but now were too tired to bother about the ethics involved. The porters went off rummaging but their beachcombing did not yield anything useful. Next morning they declared they would continue the march to Nanda Devi base camp (another eight-kilometre scramble up the South Nanda glacier) to rescue some tinned supplies they had hidden from a previous visit. I was undecided about my programme, feeling quite happy to have got this far and unambitious to cross the river and set foot upon the mountain. The cave was cold and any comfort totally lacking from its claustrophobic dankness. We spent a wretched night unable to sleep, my exhaustion from failure to eat now catching up to add to the misery of altitude.

In the morning I decided I wasn't up to the extra march. Prithwi had given me a tiny image of Nandi the bull to offer at the feet of Nanda Devi and I decided I would begin the day by building a small shrine on the roof of our rock shelter for this offering to the Goddess. This meant searching around for slates to pile up around the metal image. To keep warm I fell to the job with a will. After fifteen minutes I was pulled up with a pain in my chest and realized how careful one has to be at altitude. By now the morning was distinctly warmer and wisps of cloud streamed away to announce a weak sun trying to break through. The five days I had been on the trail had not yet yielded a single snow peak but in spite of the aesthetic short-changing I remained happy at having broken through to my goal. It was a joy just to be there in the riffling winds off the meadows, where snow pigeons went screaming by and black choughs with yellow bills performed their leisurely stalls. Bird life had not been abundant but the need to keep one's eyes glued to the dangerous trail had not allowed for much straying interest. I was also disappointed at not sighting any herds of bharal. The porters advised me to accompany them to *'base-kin'* (base camp) where I could be sure of a sighting but I was content and had no wish to leave the meadows.

They then decided their round trip of sixteen kilometres to collect a tin of mince was not worth the effort. They also preferred to laze and recoup their lost energy. The cave was forever full of billowing smoke that wrung out our tears. Brushwood was the only fuel as the juniper bushes had all fallen victim to earlier expeditions. This denudation was not the only trace these earlier visitors had left behind. The unacceptable face of the sanctuary was the sprawl of expedition junk rusting along the stream. One could actually deduce from the junk the nationality of the parties. Yugoslavian biscuit wrappers lay alongside British sardine tins and Coca Cola cans from America shared space with jettisoned medical supplies from Indian military sources. The mess was an affront to the Goddess and the illusion that the people who could do this to the most beautiful of Himalayan wildernesses qualified as sportsmen never stood more exposed. Shipton and his sherpas had honoured their surroundings by the limited size of their party and genuine exploratory motives for being there; since then the sanctuary had been violated by the greed for fame and the mindless urge to keep up with the record books.

As I sat on the cave roof facing the black ramparts across the echoing river, the shredded mist higher up the mountain suddenly revealed a patch of blue. It was the first hopeful sign in five days of wet marching that the weather might clear. Contented, I sat back to breathe in the pleasure of the moment and as I idly stretched in the warming air the great moment happened. The top layer of cloud began to thin and tantalisingly the outlines of the main peak began to flicker into recognition. I couldn't believe my eyes. Unknown to me I had built the temple to Nandi exactly facing the Goddess. It seemed a minor miracle that the sun should choose this moment to reward my labours. As the reluctant beauty of the mountain strove to outwit the parting cloud cover I was aware almost painfully of the strong erotic pull this peak of passion had on me. It was almost as if a spiritual striptease was being performed. I could only gape as the revelation neared its climax. The sun climbed to disperse the upper band of mist and lo! the full breathtaking face of the mountain coyly floated into focus. Only her peak was revealed, as lovely a portrait in ermine as any queen could wish for. She sailed majestically against the brief blue of eternity and I could not take my eyes off this stunning apparition. Everything I desired had come to fruition. There was a feeling of utter fulfilment and a song of thankfulness welled up from that core of contentment that follows the union of heaven and earth; the perfect end to all our striving.

The Goddess remained clear for the hour it took the porters to pack our reduced baggage. Having experienced darshan of Nanda Devi nothing remained but to return and share it with those I loved. It was early afternoon when at last we tore ourselves away from her loveliness and turned our backs on the Goddess' enchanted realm. Still the mist clung to the base of the mountain and obliterated the extent of the swelling moors. Unlike the other parts we had traversed, here the grass of the sanctuary overcame all attempts by the flowers to hold sway. There were brilliant clumps of searing yellow along the small sanctuary camp stream but these served only to highlight the immense expanse of turfed delight that sprawled to the horizon.

Intoxicated by the glow of our surroundings we slowly made our way to the portals and sat down under the cairns to bid a final farewell to the peak. The porters dozed off in the warm sun and left me to breathe in the full wonder of this extraordinary manifestation of sanctified nature. It was now clear enough to look down the branching course of the North Rishi and spot the great white rock that marked the junction of the Changabang glacier. The Goddess carefully kept her snow treasures under lock and key as if to suggest I must come back if I wished to see more of her jewels.

We climbed slowly over the boulders and made camp for the night at Patalkhan. The small cave seemed perfectly adequate and I found all my fears of the descent had evaporated. To aid our retreat I had picked up a pilgrim staff with a ferrule from the sanctuary camp that would ease the next day's passage. The porters produced a tin of mutton from their renewed searchings but my stomach was totally turned off at the suggestion of any non-vegetarian article of diet. I lived on packets of soup powder since the effort to swallow anything more substantial made the act of swallowing a gamble against the urge to vomit. Despite the battering the body had undergone my mood was buoyant. That night the moon shone as the river growled in the echoing canyon. Now to my rejuvenated ears its music was no longer menacing. The Devi had muzzled her watchdog and the gorge no longer held any threat.

The challenge of the Rhamani slabs was put behind us early next morning. Aided by my stick and the helping hand of the porters we cleared the face with only one stretch of protective rope required to be threaded through the conveniently placed pitons. Vaikunth Siri was successfully negotiated (the so-called Stairway to Heaven) and as we eased our way along the catwalk discovered by Shipton and Ang Tharkay one had to marvel at how this impassive gorge could yield such subtle links that guaranteed access only to the most ardent of probers. In the cold morning the panic that had accompanied my scary ascent was missing. Similarly the return crossing of the Trisul nala was done with business-like despatch. My earlier petrified crawls were now turning into more confident assessments of the challenge. It was thoughts of failure that sapped one's ability to take victory in its stride. Not skill but conscious poise was the lesson of that descent.

Once across the first danger the porters accelerated towards the second, the creaking bridge over the Rishi at Deodhi. Now there was no stopping us.

We simply took the obstacles at a run, one at a time, but with never a thought of the consequences. We were free of the menacing river and, happily tired, seemed to have won our way home. The day's retreat had covered three paravs and our speeding feet had put thirty kilometres of the gorge behind us. We settled under the dank Dibrugheta overhang to eat a dish of celebratory sweet porridge confident that we would be back in Lata the next day to make offerings at the Devi's temple. At three in the morning I was woken in cold drifting rain and told it was time to start. The nala was noisily swollen and the log by which we had entered was now under six inches of crashing white water. I stared glumly at this development while the porters examined other reaches of the spoiling stream and concluded we had to try from where we were. Another log reared out of the river at a desperate angle but did not span the entire width. It fell short by some six feet and any progress by its slippery offer was doomed to end with a plunge into the icy swirl. To add to the pall of defeat the moon that had struggled against the drizzle now chose to go behind the mountain. The porters leapt up on the upreared log and began to prise out boulders along its lie hoping to ease the surging flow by their removal.

Nathu's strength was so uncontained that he managed to break off the ferrule of the ice axe. I was reminded how Sathya Sai Baba had blessed the pick and wondered why his protection seemed now to have deserted us. The porters were shouting for me to get started but I bawled back that there was no way I could cross the log—I couldn't even see it under the white pressure of furious spilling water.

Then Pratap shouted words that gave hope—*'Peet per jayega.'* Nathu would carry me across on his back. I had never been in any doubt about the porters' strength and initiative but to risk their lives to bail out a comparative stranger seemed a remarkable display of loyalty. Each season sanctuary streams washed away mountaineers and porters and so fierce was their bore that the bodies were never found. I was all for waiting till morning but Pratap argued that the earlier we tried the lower would be the level of water to be contended with. With an enormous hoist Nathu took me on to his shoulders. I found myself clinging like a monkey as he kicked a way across the full force of the water. He was wearing an old pair of discarded expedition boots which he saved for special occasions. Most of the time he went barefoot but wore boots out of caution at camp sites to guard against the danger of broken glass (another sad comment on modern mountaineering culture). It seemed to take an age for his one foot to risk another step. I had closed my eyes to the clamour of the hysterical drumming water that seemed to bay for blood. Though I dread getting my feet wet—let alone relish the prospect of drowning—I had never felt safer than on Nathu's back. There was a reassuring smell of goats about him and as he slowly worked his way across the rising log his full strength revealed itself. Without dunking me in the white swirling cascade he managed to lower himself from the log into the full sweep of the raging torrent. Then with the river bed under his feet he crashed a way through to deposit me on to the sandy edge.

It was a heroic moment and I thumped him on the back in appreciation. It was not just the achievement of fulfilling a voluntary responsibility that impressed but the inherent fighting qualities of a simple village thakur on display. Lesser men would have waited till morning or left me to find my own way across. But the code of the Lata men demanded that contracts entered into for darshan of the Devi were to be honoured fully. It was this tremendous demonstration of loyalty that touched me most and I presented my watch to Nathu as a token of affection for his big-heartedness. It had been given to me by my guru and so would pass from one compassionate hand to another.

Nathu now would leave us to divert to a shepherd's camp at Malathuni. He had to collect a goat for a village ceremony and would meet us later at Lata Kharak. I climbed very slowly up the steep bank of conifers lining the nala then leaned to the incline of the tiresome pull up to Malathuni in the pre-dawn stillness. The grass was sloshy underfoot and gave off the swish of monsoon saturation. The fullness of sap seemed appropriate to our condition. Here we were staggering up a killing slope more dead than alive, half-starved from the rigours of altitude and worn out by the punishing nature of the trail, yet we felt absolutely fulfilled and tingled with aliveness even unto the uttermost pore. A sort of mystical veil of wellbeing seemed to descend over our vertical slog and as we crested the ridge an air of hushed holiness overtook the sanctuary and all that was part of it. Nanda Devi reared up grandly in a royal sweep of purple power as fire flashed upon her summit in the first arrows of an eager dawn. Against this kiss of life the rest of the sanctuary peaks rose in solemn array, a stunning spread of spires, towers, crags and pinnacles awaiting in the grey stillness the promised touch of regal warmth. No cathedral had ever stood out grander than the awesome architecture of that noble cirque of Garhwal nor the breathless atmosphere of natural sanctity struck one as so real. Beyond my state of heightened inebriation the soul had momentarily glimpsed itself.

My diary was full and to sketch the thrilling lines of Nanda's soaring peak, emerging from the depths of the gorge, I had to resort to the medium of birch bark, a soft and permanent record easily torn off from the trees along the way. We turned our steps plashily through the sopping meadows that led up to the Dharansi crossing. Soon the sun climbed over the barrier of Nanda Devi's huge configuration and played upon the colours of the flowers underfoot. With the wind in one's hair and the simple pleasure of walking homewards through the emerald expanse around Raj Kharak I found myself possessed by a conviction every bit as commanding as the vow that had led me to savour the sanctuary. Just when I had achieved in full measure the culmination of a twenty-year-old desire I discovered another spontaneously settling upon my brow. There was the distinct impression of the Goddess prompting me to write about the wonderment of her sanctuary, to get down in print before it faded the maddening fragrance of her spangled monsoon largesse, and seek to convey—no matter how feebly—the benison of her grace, even through this crude medium of a mountain lover's notings. I can never forget that walk to Dharansi for it happens to be the only time in my life when I was aware that I was *fully* conscious.

The mood did not last beyond Lata Kharak but the certainty it generated did. It was as if instead of falling in love one had become one with the beloved. It never pays to analyse the affairs of the heart since love refers to the mysteries of eternity rather than derive from the products of time. My feelings in the sanctuary echoed uncannily the words of the alchemist Thomas Vaughan, brother of the poet. In his *Golden Treatise* of 1650 he wrote : 'All things when they first proceed from God are white... of a celestial transcendent brightness... there is nothing on earth like it... she yields to nothing but love... This is she and these are her favours. Catch her if you can.'

Vaughan summed up my mesmerising darshan of Nanda Devi when the peak so languorously had shaken herself free of the clouds, for all the world like a beautiful woman aware of an admirer, watching and arranging to show herself off to maximum effect. Vaughan's description of the felicity that follows the seeker of nature's secrets closely resembled my feelings on that walk, a hallowed experience of passing through a minster without walls:

'Look on the green youthful and flowery bosom of the earth. The stars and planets overlook her and they shed down their golden locks like so many tokens of love. Do but look on the daily sports of nature, her clouds and mist, the scene and pageantry of the air. What glorious colours and tinctures doth she discover. A pure eternal green overspreads her and this attended with innumerable other beauties, roses red and white, golden lilies, azure violets, the bleeding hyacinths with their several celestial odours and spices... Know for certain thou hast discovered the sanctuary of nature. There is nothing between thee and her treasures but the door. Thou hast resolved with thyself to be a co-operator with God. Have a care thou dost not hinder His work. Take heed therefore lest thou set nature at variance with herself.'

The remarkable merging of ecology and theology in these alchemical formulae catches exactly what Dr Jung was later to describe as the fierce animality of nature. It was extraordinary to find in Vaughan the very thoughts that had coursed through my mind in the negotiation of the sanctuary. The crossing of the Trisul log had been a vivid exemplar of the alchemical art—the union of fire and water. One of the mantras of the medieval enquirers into the art of transforming gross nature into gold was vitriol, a codeword whose first three letters invited the seeker to 'enter into the earth'. The brute impact of the sanctuary had caused a profound shaking up of my consciousness. Its naked threat had served to bring back the raw edge of fear and the sense of blessed relief that follows survival. Crossing the rivers one was acutely aware of both the destructive potential of water and its limitless energy. Nature taught that any force one-pointed in its drive was unstoppable. Clinging face-down on the birch and fir poles above the maelstrom one was entirely at the mercy of the elements but at the same time wholly in charge of one's fate. It was the resolve to work with nature that would extricate the body from its predicament. Any negative reaction might result in the wrong move and quicken dissolution: 'For this fire and this water are like two lovers; they no sooner meet but presently they play,' noted Vaughan. Here he catches the paradox of the Devi, both gentle and ferocious and states the incongruity of her mountaineering devotees who approach with love yet leave behind their litter. The conflicts in nature and oneself were brought home by the dangerous quest to touch the hem of Nanda Devi. The experience, had I undertaken it just for altitude gained or a place in the record books might have missed out on the real trophy—the rare opportunity to learn more about the mystery of selfhood.

The feeling of plenitude that peaked after escape from the frank facing of difficult challenges was the result of what the modern alchemist George Gurdjieff would have called a super-effort. One was distinctly aware of Gurdjieff's definition of choices: 'Better to die seeking to wake than live in sleep.' The truth learned in overcoming the physical odds was that Nanda Devi's beauty and religious appeal were both real, the physical upthrust of granite as well as the subtle presiding presence of the Goddess of Uttarakhand.

The next challenge was to recognize the benevolence of the Devi in the animality of village worship and stomach the crude sacrificial behaviour of her more primitive devotees. The courage and loyalty of the Lata porters had introduced me to this lower element in the mystique of the Devi and one would have to face the reality of squalid reactions in religious practice as unflinchingly as the noble. The wholeness of nature had been the chief lesson of the sanctuary. The grim facing of one's goal left no time for the conventions of caste and hierarchy. One learned eagerly from everyone and everything. Shipton's description of a paradise where the wild blue sheep grazed unafraid of man had been outlived by the pressure of mountaineering ambition. The Bhotia mastiffs who from habit trailed after their Lata masters had caused the bharal to withdraw from their traditional grazing meadows, now no longer safe from man. Crop protection guns were brought in to take advantage of the innocence of nature's original arrangement. By the mid-Sixties Indian mountaineers were boasting in the *Himalayan Journal* of how many bharal they had shot for the pot. The smuggling in of a nuclear spying device had apparently been the occasion for the building of our flimsy bridge across the Rishi. Thus we were in no position to blame the plutonium back-packers for without their efforts we would not have been able to enter the inner sanctuary.

*

Nanda Devi had come into the news in 1978 but for political not religious reasons. The story broke in America when a former CIA agent gave the San Francisco fringe magazine *Outside* a story entitled "The Nanda Devi Caper". It supplied details of the placing of a nuclear spying device in Nanda Devi sanctuary to monitor the deployment of Chinese missiles along the Tibetan border. The cloak and dagger rumours that went around international climbing circles (even the staid *Alpine Journal* referred to the subject) gave off too much smoke for official denials to be taken seriously and the involvement of top class climbers in CIA operations was widely assumed.

In his *Himalayan Handbook* (a remarkable work of reference that lists the ascents of the main peaks) the mountaineering historian Joydeep Sircar notes under the entry 'Nanda Devi' that a secret Indo-US expedition in the mid-Sixties sought to install a nuclear-fuelled device. Presumably the main peak with its flat top described by Tilman was the logical goal, and the most likely route to it up the Coxcomb ridge from the south sanctuary. Since no official details have been published from the Indian side beyond confirming that the device was planted—then lost—to be substituted by another device on a neighbouring peak which was retrieved—we only have newspaper reports and mountain hut gossip to go on. The well-known American climber Galen Rowell in his book on the 1975 US attempt on K2 feels obliged to end with vigorous denials that the team was in any way part of a CIA operation. The vehemence unintentionally indicates that American spying involvement was suspected to go beyond the Indian Himalayas.

The folly of placing a nuclear device above the last discovered source of the Ganga as well as illustrating the panic-stricken nature of modern political decisions serves to distinguish the mountain lover from the modern breed of mountaineering mercenary. It appears that a whole generation of India's climbers were seduced to work against nature and were forced by their official calling to conspire to pollute the sanctuary. There is a poignancy in such folly and the saving grace of duty unquestioningly performed when our insecurity leads to panic and snowballs into collective hysteria. Instead of viewing the presence of a nuclear device ticking away at the heart of the world's most ravishing mountain wilderness as the outward sign that idiocy and not freedom is our human birthright, we can see this curious paradox of beauty and the beast as proof that Shiva's wife also swallows the world's poison. In accepting both the crude villager and the complex mountaineer as her devotees the Goddess Nanda shows herself even-handed in her bliss-giving.

While re-writing this book in the English Midlands twenty-six years after the air crash in the Alps, the wreckage of Dr Homi Bhabha's aircraft was stumbled upon by some British climbers. Amongst the litter of frozen cargo were the gruesome carcasses of Indian monkeys destined for the loathsome laboratories of vivisection. What irony that Hanuman, the healing agent of the gods who flew to Nanda's neighbouring peak to pluck the life-saving herb, should in our more enlightened age be caged for commerce, reduced from the status of divine messenger to that of dollar earner. It confirms the planetary insensitivity of the extraordinary decision to risk pollution of the headwaters of the Ganga and marks modern blindness to the long term environmental fall-out of hasty reactions. Perhaps it is an honest indicator of the human situation that at the heart of one of the world's last pristine Himalayan wildernesses, now declared a Heritage site for the delectation of future generations, we deliberately introduced the deadliest substance known to our species.

SEVEN

Shining Failure

Mountaineering bangs can be followed by a whimper, as the first ascent of the Matterhorn shows. The 1980 visit to the south sanctuary did end with a bang for the same day that started with my peak experience around Dharansi, ended most dramatically in Joshimath. Nathu had turned up with his sacrificial ram at Lata Kharak and we eased ourselves down to the village by lunchtime. I took my farewells after darshan at the Nanda Devi temple and was impressed by its ancient artistry. Also intriguing was the character of the officiating priest, known locally as a charasiya (marijuana addict), a fine crop of his addiction standing in his garden next to the temple.

I caught the evening bus to Joshimath and checked into the tourist bungalow. At 9 p.m. I went to a rickety eating place next door and ordered a plate of rice and dal. My departure from the village had included drinking a toast to the Devi from Pratap's home-made supply of daru, the excellent distilled spirits the highlander's wife had produced from barley. As I ate in the dingy Joshimath restaurant my plate suddenly began to wobble and then the table began to shake. Was I victim to the after-effects of too much grog or was this the beginning of eschatology?

Then the lights went out and screams confirmed that an earthquake had struck the town. The damage was minimal but one felt shaken to remember the nights spent in rock shelters where the claustrophobic fear of their confinement had been enlarged by the knowledge that the Himalayas were still growing and their instability a notorious fact of life that people who build large dams pretend to ignore. Nonetheless, it seemed only proper after an adventure on a Hemingway scale that the world should have moved.

It would have been remarkable if my second attempt to enter the sanctuary almost a year later had come off, considering the speed at which it was arranged. On hearing at tea-time in Mussoorie of a three-week free period I dashed around throwing gear into a rucksack and staggered out to catch the last bus to Dehra Dun. The following morning when I woke up in a friend's house I could hardly get out of bed. I had strained my back running with the heavy load.

In Rishikesh I decided to try and hire a porter from the Garhwal Tourist Development Board, hoping that this would save the bother of lugging the load further. But the only porter available waited at the tourist bungalow in Joshimath. Having missed the early bus there was little one could do except catch one that went as far as Srinagar, half way. I had come a little later in the season than last year and the monsoon had set in fully, sweeping the valleys with a heavy downpour that triggered off crops in a wild sprout of abandoned green. In the rice paddies the last of the communal transplanting was being effected to the sound of the village drum, the women seeming double-jointed as they bent over to swiftly thrust the seedlings into the churned up mud.

As the driver revved up the cold engine for an early start the following morning he remarked on the lack of down traffic, which signified a road block higher up. As we manoeuvred the muddy ascent we were overtaken by a foreign mountaineer loaded down with luggage and a pillion rider on his motorbike. A while later we stopped to help him when he took a toss in the mud. Finally when we came to Helang at the bottom of the loops up to Joshimath he was there again arranging to have his bike manhandled across the break in the road. The Helang nala had washed away the culvert.

The foreigner turned out to be a research student attached to the forest department on his way with a forest guard to the Nanda Devi sanctuary. Michael Green was forthcoming about his enthusiasm to study the reclusive habits of the musk deer and had settled at a breeding farm near Tunganath (Garhwal's highest shrine) to further his Ph.D. project. However he was very chary of discussing his plans once inside the sanctuary and it was not until

I met him again in Delhi a year later that I learned why. The musk was a protected species and a well-known character of Joshimath had offered temporarily to snare one to enable a film of this elusive animal to be made. Yashu was an enterprising Bhotiya from Bampa who displayed all the initiative of the border trader free of caste or indeed of any other hangup. Most expeditions found it worthwhile to cultivate Yashu if only because of his reputation as Mr Fix-it. Charming, cheerful and possessing the untroubled conscience of an ardent capitalist Yashu's ingenuity could provide a way round most problems. His reputation for turning water into wine guaranteed him a loyal following in a strictly dry pilgrim area. But his popularity with foreigners (he is mentioned in Sir Edmund Hillary's book *Sea to Sky* on river running up the Ganga by jet boat) made him many enemies amongst the more orthodox, less corner-cutting porters of Lata.

The porter awaiting me in Joshimath was S.S., a tough young HAP from Lata. Unfortunately for my tastes he represented the modern trend in hill society to reject outright all the traditions of his elders. I found myself saddled unhappily with a young man who didn't know where he belonged. His dress and bearing aped the film fashions of Bombay and his language maintained a ridiculously high content of macho expletives. It was not until we arrived in his home village that I understood the problem. He was bitter and resentful of the fact that despite his qualification as a trained mountaineer his youth and economic status made him low in the village pecking order. I had unwittingly upset the other porters by employing an upstart. I found it difficult to get Nathu Singh to go with me because in terms of social seniority his family stood much higher than S.S.'s. Either I would have to pay Nathu the equivalent of a high altitude porter or scale down S.S.'s rates. Bal Singh, now the village headman (he had superceded Jagat Singh) jeered at me for employing a sarkari nauker. Eventually, the miserable S.S. agreed to share lower rates with Nathu.

Nathu was a strong and willing porter but so accustomed to being overshadowed by his brother that he always let others impose their decisions on him. I learned this to my cost next morning when travelling lightly up to Lata Kharak to arrive by midday, I expected to spend a lazy afternoon sorting out the supplies S.S. had bought in Joshimath. But he had other plans. He talked Nathu into convincing me that we could easily reach the next camp beyond Dharansi where Nathu's goats were camping. Instead of hanging around on the windy ridge at Lata Kharak we would have a tent and the comforts of a kitchen awaiting us. I was horrified at the thought of doing another slog when my back was just beginning to feel less painful. But as I had wasted two days in getting to Joshimath I was tempted to make up for lost time. Nothing on this trip seemed to be working out. On the second night out of Rishikesh I had assisted Michael Green's motorbike across the flood. He magnanimously offered to come back from Joshimath to give me a ride but in the fading light I felt it was unwise. Also I could get a lift in a contractor's lorry ready to take the road repair gang back to Joshimath. I recrossed the roaring river to collect my luggage from the bus. But by the time I had painfully got my luggage down from the bus roof and staggered back across the river the truck had gone. That left the option of employing a Nepali porter to lug my load up the steep twelve-kilometre bridle path to the town. To thwart that plan two young trekkers from Rajasthan beat me to the draw. They were in a hurry to reach the Valley of Flowers and had booked the last available porter. That night was spent with no advantage to my strained back on the only flea-proof surface in the area—the roof of my bus which meant crossing the torrent yet again.

Spurred on by S.S.'s youthful chivvying we started up the ridge to Dharansi. Gusts of icy rain hit us as the afternoon weather closed in and tormented our progress all the way to the pass. It was like being flailed by steel knives, the impress of the howling elements stinging us to tears. I gasped for breath in the discomfiture of this hunched battle to make headway and every step gained drove home the folly of our haste. Tired beyond expression and battered to a pulp by the relentless sluicing freeze I fought my way over the pass and through the arch at Ranakhola to stagger down brokenly towards the distant shepherds' camp.

The grass came up to our knees plastering more cold into our beaten frames. Nathu yelled across the valley for the kettle to be put on but there was no one in the camp. In a patch of bright golden evening light that suddenly squeezed through the billowing murk we could see a long line of black and white sheep brilliantly framed returning down the emerald shoulder of an alp perched above the Rishi gorge. A shepherd in attendance whistled them home while a sheepdog recognizing Nathu's voice raced ahead to meet us.

The tent had been raised around a stone pen and we stumbled in without any introduction to collapse on a pile of thick woollen tulmas (blankets), too far gone for any manners to apply. I felt I would die of pneumonia if I did not get warm immediately. The shepherd recognizing my scrabble for survival put me to bed and piled on the blankets. Later, he offered me some gruel but had added so much chilli powder that it seared my lips. I was totally exhausted whereas S.S. and Nathu were only mildly exercised. My dislike of S.S.'s brash behaviour took a further turn when I heard him boast to the gathered shepherds that he had to be back in Joshimath soon to lead an Australian expedition to a peak above the Valley of Flowers. He had put us through the day's agonies for his own advantage.

Kalyan Singh our gentle shepherd host made up for the modern generation's confused priorities. He preserved the best of the warm nomadic instinct to extend hospitality graciously. Whatever he had he shared and that extended to information on the aloof schedule of the sanctuary shepherds. He was an authority on the wildlife that roamed the skirts of Nanda Devi and like any good herder could distinguish between each and every one of his flock of 300 sheep and goats and knew exactly which one of them had gone astray. My own familiarity with goats was enhanced when, worn out by the exertions of our double march I lay snugly amidst the pile of sweet-smelling blankets and wondered if their warmth would be sufficient to pull me through the cold night.

I need not have worried. The goaty cling of the outdoors mingling with the smoke of wood fires gave off the same reassuring smell I had experienced riding across the Dibrugheta nala on Nathu's back a year earlier. Weighed down by the warmth of Kalyan Singh's thick hand-woven rugs I slept soundly. When I awoke next morning I knew immediately that my body had won the battle with yesterday's exposure. The back may still be painful but the expected weariness from the chill factor had gone. I felt deliciously cocooned in the layers of rugs and turned in contentment. To my surprise, I found my body was pinned down by the weight of the bedding and even more bizarre, I heard a gentle burp in my ear. I opened my eyes to find half a dozen goats parked sleepily on top of me. The one near my head was the source of the ruminant belch of contentment. It was then that I recalled the various alarums and excursions during the night as the heat-seeking goats edged nearer to the warmth of our sleeping bodies, only to leap up and thunder out of the tent whenever a dog barked.

We left lazily after an ample breakfast of thick chapattis and sloshed up in the rain to catch the path for Malathuni. As a memento of my stay Kalyan Singh presented me with a lead-goat collar deftly woven from goat's hair that tied on with a wooden toggle. In return I earmarked a warm jersey I was wearing to be presented to him on our homeward journey. As it happened, our paths did not cross again for another year but I left the present with Bal Singh to be given to the closest dwelling of the Devi's devotees.

The slide down to Dibrugheta was followed by the prescribed steep pull up to the cave. As we optimistically spread out our clothes to dry in the choking wood-smoke we were joined by two young shepherds from Lata. It was raining again next morning and we set off miserably to find that within five minutes our nominally smoke-dried clothes were again sopping from the downpour. As we crested Penikhola Dhar and eased our way down over rocky outcrops to come within reach of the roar of the Rishi, Nathu held up his hand for silence. We were crossing an icy stream that cut a way for itself noisily through a black litter of slate. Nathu held up some fresh droppings in his hand, sniffed and whispered that we had just disturbed some blue sheep while they were drinking. We crept slowly out of the riven bowl and there, a hundred yards away, peering cautiously from a rock above us were three bharal ewes, identifiable by their short horns. At this season the long-horned males usually turned solitary and took themselves off to higher ground. Unlike that other sanctuary resident, the cliff-hanging thar of distinctly shaggy aspect, the sleeker bharal prefers to range on open ground withdrawing to the crags only for safety when disturbed. What the two species do have in common is the fatal habit of curiosity and had we been armed our three ewes would have made easy targets as they sought to squint down at us.

Instead of crossing the river to Deodhi we kept to the north bank and began a long haul to regain height on a steep turfed slope that led to Changabang base camp. We passed a badly littered camp site that betrayed evidence of an East European expedition having sheltered there recently. Nathu instinctively went on a rummaging excursion but found nothing we could use. Once more, our exposed scramble up the face of the mountain was subject to the steel knives of driving rain. Mist had settled over the entire outer sanctuary and it was difficult to remember a more depressing day in the mountains. Eventually with aching back and anguished mind we topped a rise to find the way barred by a cascading torrent of water that dashed down violently to sweep the line of our proposed crossing. It resembled a fireman's hose in intensity. There was no way I was going to cross that and I lacked the energy to explore for alternative routes. We retreated to the shelter of a rock cave through which the wind howled and rain drove in while Nathu went ahead to reconnoitre.

If I haven't spoken much of what we ate in the sanctuary camps it was simply because I didn't eat much. The thought of food made one ill and the higher one got the more hostile one's stomach grew to the mention of a meal. The porters ate well and regularly but for me it was an achievement to swallow a spoonful of rice above the height of 10,000 ft. This is the altitude at which the body is safe from the deadly onset of mountain sickness. Those who suffer from the sudden affliction of pulmonary oedema can survive by the simple remedy of retreating below this crucial barrier.

Another grave mistake on this expedition was for Prithwi to have provided me with the luxury of a large tin of ghee. This meant that whatever was cooked was now soaked in butter fat and to add to my strained back was a stomach reeling from rich and spicy food. Nathu was a bad cook at the best of times but brash S.S. only pretended to be better. I was visited with a violent attack of diarrhoea after nibbling S.S.'s ghee-drowned food and all pleasure at being in the sanctuary evaporated in worry for one's health.

No doubt if the rain had slackened and the sun smiled sympathetically one would have put up more of a fight to reach Changabang base and behold the immortal lines of the loveliest of mountain profiles. And no doubt if Nathu the born follower had not been seduced into retreat by S.S.'s double-dealing (he was eager to get back to Joshimath for bigger pickings) we would have found a way over the blocking torrent. That night was easily the most coldly miserable I have ever spent. Quite apart from mental depression (worsened by having to decide whether the weather was more disgusting than S.S.'s disloyalty) and the physical distress of a bad back and weakened bowels, were the utterly gloomy surroundings in which we were forced to spend the night. The sodden mountainside was once clothed in juniper but this had all been blackened by shivering expedition porters who had set the hillside ablaze in the expectation of ready charcoal awaiting their next visit. The torn out roots of wet juniper now added to our misery as Nathu strove manfully to blow them into flame. We had buried my stove at Dibrugheta and Nathu recalled he had hidden his stove ahead at Changabang base. Caught now between stoves we had to depend on the sodden fuel in a freezing charnel-house of rock. It was too cold to sit up with the wind howling through the shelter and too painful to lie down. The night crawled along as Nathu performed more heroics in stirring up a lid-full of charcoal embers for me to huddle over to try and still my shivers. Lying comfortably after his rich evening meal S.S. announced that he had got his dates wrong and must now positively leave for Joshimath in the morning. To Nathu's surprise there was no bitterness in my prompt acceptance. Maybe things would get better with the absence of this ornamental government guide I had inflicted myself with.

At last morning light reluctantly eased its grey glimmerings to confirm that our sufferings were real and not dream-like. As always when the faintest possibility of hope arises with the new day the body slumps into a coma of relief. I woke to find S.S. packed and ready to leave. Nathu and I planned to make a dash for the Rhamani glacier and spend the night under a plastic sheet to enable me to get an early morning photo of Changabang. But this would depend entirely on the weather clearing. There was no point in camping out on the freezing glacier if the following morning lacked blue skies. Rid of S.S. we hunkered down to see if the day would clear. In a way I hoped it wouldn't for in my weakened condition it would need a lot of heroics to get the photograph of Changabang.

Nine o' clock came and passed as we sat huddled under our plastic capes. We made gloomy surveys of once-familiar landmarks that had been turned by the greyness of the cloud cover into unfriendly objects. Looking down at the Rishi we could make out where we had crossed the perilous bridge of birch and pine to outwit Trisul nala. Two crows swirled up and settled cawing on the roof of the cave as if to confirm the bad omens. The expedition was over. Everything had conspired to hasten the drawing of a line under this poorly cobbled enterprise.

More ghee-flooded parathas for breakfast sparked the final break with ambition. Changabang would have to wait. My insides were more important. Somehow the presence of the crows eased the pain of turning back. Their symbolism was clear. Do not attempt to enter the sanctuary unless you are fit, acclimatised and as impervious as a crow to the monsoon.

Other lessons emerged more slowly. I was disappointed in Nathu's level of support but had to accept that he was even more dismayed by me in having appointed S.S. before reaching Lata. Also Nathu's urge to initiative had been blunted. Recently Bal Singh had invested 20,000 rupees in his marriage. I was forced to view S.S.'s behaviour more leniently for the whole cycle of disloyalty had been sparked off by my ingratitude. What need was there in view of Nathu Singh's magnificent performance last year to bypass his expertise? Only then did I understand the teaching of the Goddess. Like most mountaineers I was jealous of a little success and had sought a high altitude porter in the hope of maybe reaching Shipton's Col to enter — who knows — the northern inner sanctuary in a blaze of victory. Nathu was too canny to be drawn into such climbing histrionics. He assessed the physical dangers rationally while I cultivated the fantasy of being a latter-day Shipton. It can be argued that the extraordinary run of success both in and outside the sanctuary that followed Shipton, Tilman and the three sherpas, could not be due simply to their toughness and skill. The fact that no other expedition has ever come near to what they achieved ought to be proof of the uniqueness of their team. Convention might call it a good run of luck but devotees of Nanda Devi would prefer to attribute their extraordinary safety record to the protective hand of the Goddess.

I concluded that my washed-out attempt on Changabang might have been to save me from the misfortune of unrealistic ambition. Had the weather cleared it would have been difficult to resist the urge to press on and court serious illness on the glacier. As an even-handed Devi it was acceptable that my southern success the year before should be balanced by the disappointment meted out now in the north of her sanctuary. And possibly I had learned the valuable lesson that while success may derive from the grace of Nanda, failure assuredly originates from one's own bad decisions.

These balms of rationalised wisdom were not instantly available as we glumly picked our way back down the tricky slope to the Rishi. Another night in the cold wet cave at Dibrugheta at least treated us to an unscheduled display of shepherding skills. The two shepherds we had met on the way in were now poised to lead their flocks across the roaring nala and next morning they spent an hour trying to goad the lead-goat across the famous log that was now clear of the rushing water. Every ruse was tried to get the ranks moving but the goats just refused to trust themselves to the slippery pole. Salt was liberally scattered along its length but this also failed to move them. Then Nathu stepped in to repeat his rescue act. This time he lugged over the lead-goat on his back and positioned it at the other end of the log. This spurred the others to follow but now the crush to get across caused a few animals to be knocked off and fall in the water. Panic-stricken they began to swim to try and get across under their own power. Only the stronger ones succeeded. The sodden fleece of the smaller animals guaranteed they would be washed away and suddenly the river bank resembled a rugby scrum as the shepherds and Nathu rushed up and down dragging out drowning animals. One bedraggled sheep was washed away but even quicker was a young shepherd who sprinted downstream where another log slowed the flow. With a spectacular dive he managed to divert the beleaguered animal to shore.

After these heroics the climb up to Malathuni and the walk back to Lata seemed tame. And with my bodily aches there was no chance of any mystical mood settling over our retreat across Dharansi. Loose bowels I discovered are incompatible with mysticism. Perhaps emphatic rejection and the fruits of failure are the enemies we ought to love for their teachings. I was beginning to learn that the great mountain views do not lie only in the physical meeting of coordinates. By depriving me of the wonder of Changabang's upthrust glory the Goddess had forced me to question whether I could live without capturing the peak on camera. Or would I die forever unfulfilled, with 'Changabang' engraved on my heart?

The answer that has come slowly, painfully and platonically is that Changabang is but a reflection of the true mountain within. Of course the external beauty is real and its outer form sacred but all reality arises from the same source as our sense of wonder. Here is the paradox of our condition. How to unite inner and outer perceptions? Nanda Devi speaks to both states for she is the source of wonder springing in the heart of those who love her; enlarging our individual perceptions until they include all opposites.

EIGHT

Stampede and Hit List

*T*he removal of restrictions on entry to the sanctuary led to a stampede of mountaineering expeditions that ranged from elaborate Indian military ventures (who hired a hundred porters to ensure a blaze of regimental glory) to the alpine ascents of a compact party of 'hard men' who achieved their goal with almost clinical detachment. Serious doubts about some of the military claims have troubled civilian opinion but since defence personnel maintain a monopoly on access to the Himalayan interior it is difficult to prove malafide intent. But debunking has increased to the level of a companion sport when expedition reports are too short on route details.

Sometimes these reports were not forthcoming at all and in one of the most remarkable instances of bureaucratic ritual I remember meeting Mr Khera in his office at the IMF as he sought to elicit the report from the leader of the first expedition to reach the top of Shivling. This was some half dozen years after the event and since the mountain was of great interest to the international climbing fraternity everyone was puzzled why the Indian authorities had not trumpeted their achievement. Was it that having badly burned their fingers over the disputed claim to Nilkanth they were themselves doubtful of their success on Shivling? Obviously Shivling did not bristle with the difficulties that surround Nilkanth and it was well within the professional competence of the Indo-Tibetan Border Police team to scale the technically challenging but comparatively modest height of Shivling.

To settle the matter once and for all Mr Khera banged the table and told the leader that he should go that very night to Mussoorie and collect the expedition diaries. More than twelve years have passed since I witnessed that impressive display of table-thumping and as far as I know the report has still not been made public. According to some it was because the para-military personnel had used vast amounts of rope to reach the summit in an age when alpine fashions dictated that the less complicated the equipment the purer the achievement. Rather than risk being laughed at the authorities took refuge under the cloak of security and implied that Shivling had been climbed as part of defence drill. Hence the report remained privileged material.

On another occasion the bumbling bureaucrats celebrated the first female ascent of Nanda Devi by printing the wrong route in their official publication. The map of the route that found its way into print was entirely different from the actual line of ascent. It seemed inevitable when the sport of mountaineering was being run by a demi-official organization (most of whose staff had never set foot on a mountain) that the scope for bungling knew no bounds. Applications in triplicate, father's name, leader's climbing credentials, peak fees according to the height of the objective, imposition of a non-climbing liaison officer to whom new climbing gear must be gifted, were the kind of rules that made India the genial butt of jokes in every mountaineering hut around the world.

Unfortunately for a generation of young Indian climbers the absurd and pompous incompetence of the sport's supposed experts at the IMF could blight their careers. Instead of being as in the West a discipline self-acquired, the Indian novice was expected to join a basic course and receive an official stamp of approval before he dared venture upon the mountains. Obviously the social mores differ between the Alps and the Himalayas and the injunction upon Hindu sons not to risk their necks in order to dutifully light the parental pyre, thus guaranteeing release to the souls of their progenitors, were factors that hardly troubled Don Whillans or Joe Brown when they sneaked out on to the crags with their mother's borrowed washing line.

The hierarchy in the Indian setting assumed monstrous shapes and unfamiliarity with modern trends exposed the IMF as an administrative white elephant. Young climbers from Delhi eager to arrange transport at the weekend to take them to the rocks at Dauj or Dam Dama found their pleas fell on deaf ears. Those at the top seemed genuinely ignorant of the connexion between keeping in shape on a local wall and its crucial bearing on the ultimate success of the prestige expeditions to a big peak. Worst of all was the sinister threat held out about the inviolate nature of IMF rules. One young Indian climber deputed to assist a foreign expedition on a well-known peak in Kashmir found his base camp duties too enervating and decided to scale the summit solo. In the ensuing enquiry into this insubordination, the authorities from the depth of their armchairs came to the conclusion that the climber's well-attested achievement deserved to be dismissed as doubtful in view of this failure to toe the line.

Yet the babus' regard for the Himalayas was real if secondary to a career and if their haste to establish a chain of training institutions to produce more Tenzings was crude and missed the whole point of encouraging mountain delight, it was a genuine mistake probably based on high-caste unfamiliarity with physical realities. The babus responded to the nobility of the sport and felt as moist-eyed about Mallory as any Englishman. But they were primarily government servants and if the politicians wanted to introduce a dangerous nuclear device into the Nanda Devi sanctuary the bureaucrats manning the defence ministry had no qualms in putting policy before principles.

The mountain experience that was supposed to make men free in mind and limb was thus turned by the exigencies of life in a Third World situation to make them voiceless instruments of state doomed to veer by unkind circumstance and indecision between self-importance and self-disgust. To protect the honour of the Goddess was too much to expect from these eminent creatures of circumstance. Everywhere reports were coming in of the defiling of the Himalayas and of the need to take stern measures to stem the threat to the fragile environment.

The scars left behind by expeditions to the sanctuary could never hope to be healed by the fees paid to climb the mountain. It was becoming a national scandal that India's most unique wilderness area was being destroyed by rich foreign parties while ordinary Indians unable to raise the finance were deprived of entry. In an extraordinary decision to address the problem the IMF simply raised the peak fees for Nanda Devi. This meant that now only very rich foreigners—those most likely to lack any commitment to the environment—could afford to go there, a classic case of bureaucrats taking careful aim and shooting themselves in the foot.

On each of my entries to the sanctuary it was distressing to note the callous disregard of the climbers for their surroundings. Undoubtedly their attitude had been hardened by the demand for peak fees. They felt they had already paid a tax to protect the environment and if their porters in lieu of not being provided warm clothes set fire to the juniper slopes, that was not the expedition leader's worry. If the rules had been more realistic it should have been made obligatory for expeditions to carry sufficient kerosene for porter's fuel and provision made to remove rubbish after a climb.

But the romantic notions of idealistic bureaucrats did not allow them to believe that heroic climbers could turn anti-social immediately their objective had been achieved. They were ignorant of the fact that the harsh terrain meant for the climber a choice between getting out alive or dying from exhaustion in digging a pit to bury his refuse. Both administrators and mountaineers were fooling themselves about their true motives. The administrators really wanted to bask in the rubbed-off glory of successful ascents while the climbers, whatever their protestations of respect for the mountain, were dedicated solely to making a name for themselves on the top. Neither side seemed serious in honouring Shipton's sense of wonder at just being there.

In 1977 Luvkumar Khacher, a member of the Bombay Natural History Society, entered the sanctuary with a mountaineering party and published an excellent survey of the area. His sober appraisal of the dangers to the flora and fauna by the unrestricted stampede of expedition and porter trains provided the basis for an action plan. He called for protection under the national park scheme which would provide wardens on duty to monitor the situation. To its credit the U.P. government promptly elevated the sanctuary to the status of a wildlife reserve but went overboard in flattering the then Prime Minister by naming the park after her son. The risible situation of Nanda Devi having been derecognized in favour of Sanjay Gandhi served to show how ludicrous overnight fancies could become fact in the capricious shifting sands of Indian politics. From Shipton's time the sanctuary had been under the protection of the forest department and it came as a jolt to learn that in all the thirty-five years since it was discovered not a single senior forest officer had penetrated to the inner sanctuary in his official capacity. It was well-known that the crop protection guns issued to the Dhauli Ganga valley villagers were misused to poach bharal, musk, ghooral and monal in the sanctuary. Military expeditions made no bones about shooting for the pot, since being a law unto themselves in border areas restricted to the public they were answerable to no one. The danger of 'inner lines' behind which the democratic process is suspended is nowhere better seen than in the interior of Uttarakhand where in the name of defence the forests of the region have been vandalously destroyed. One of the greatest ironies of modern Asian history is that in replying to a threat of foreign invasion on her borders India's own defence forces have caused much greater and irreversible damage to the Himalayan environment then any invader could.

What is true of Uttarakhand is applicable to other parts and the entire stretch of the Himalayas from Kashmir to Arunachal Pradesh has fallen victim to a more insidious enemy than the Chinese.

So, for every climbing success on Nanda Devi there was an ecological price. When I got back to Delhi in 1981 after my abortive trek to Changabang I read of a successful Czech expedition whose achievements were splashed in the national dailies. It so happened that I had followed in their footsteps and had marked how all the birch trees around Dibrugheta had been slashed to provide fodder for their pack goats. They were in a hurry and there was no time to unload the saddle bags to let the goats graze naturally. The Japanese who scored the ultimate climbing feat by performing the traverse linking the two peaks of Nanda were notoriously beneficient in paying porters to hasten their supply trains by felling trees to make bridges over side-streams. This depletion of fine stands of timber eventually exceeded a limit enough to arouse the wrath of the easy-going forest department and the difficult alternative route into the sanctuary via the Rishi Ganga gorge was declared closed. This approach had necessitated a colossal waste of timber since most of the freshly felled logs were soon washed away and the next expedition was required to cut its own for replacement.

At this critical juncture when the IMF was more concerned with collecting climbing fees and the local villagers were likewise earning huge amounts from their portering activities it seemed like the grace of the Goddess that there should appear in Delhi the right man to take the bold decision. Nalini Jayal happened to be a Joint Secretary in the environment ministry and was rare among bureaucrats in actually having had personal contact with Nanda Devi. He had visited the sanctuary with an expedition to Trisul. Also his family had close ties with the former ruler of Garhwal. All his instincts were to save Nanda Devi from further violation by upgrading the area to a centrally protected reserve which would guarantee the funds that the earlier well-intentioned scheme of the state government could only promise.

The beauty and variety of life forms in the magic circle around Nanda Devi were so raved about by the more discerning mountaineer that the sanctuary soon became the subject of further protection. Dr Michael Green wrote from Cambridge with the good news that plans were afoot to include Nanda Devi sanctuary in the World Heritage list. This would require ratification by the Indian government and UNESCO and would provide full protection of the area as a biosphere reserve chosen for its unique character and preserved for future generations. The presence of one single-minded mountaineering bureaucrat thus arrested the decline of a ravishing corner of the Himalayas that seemed doomed to become another Everest slum trail.

Nanda's falling short of the magical 8,000 metre mark also helped save her from the eager boots of ambition. The fact that she is a much more beautiful objective than Everest says a lot for the concerns of modern mountaineers whatever they may claim for their motives. The articles legalising the protection of Nanda Devi seemed a long way away in 1981 when on the bus to Joshimath I had spotted a wayside addition to the characteristic high count of government notice boards. This sign advertised 'Nanda Devi National Park.' Often erecting boards seems the sole activity of the departments who raise them and in this instance it certainly seemed true for when I enquired at the forest office in Joshimath no one had any information on how matters stood. A similar board had been erected at Lata roadhead and Bal Singh (who had built a shop next to the bus stop to cash in on the flow of expeditions) informed me that a tent put up at Renni housed forest guards now renamed wildlife wardens to check on any entrant to the sanctuary. Since the authorities themselves did not seem to know or care about the rules and the notice board at Lata spoke about 'parking fees for heavy vehicles' (inside the sanctuary!) the creation of the national park was just another occasion for a public laugh at government expense.

But there was trouble brewing between the villagers who defended their hereditary access rights to the sanctuary grazing and the wildlife wardens who had orders to charge all entrants a fee. When I asked what fee I would have to pay the villagers laughed and said they would beat up anyone who dared collect it. As a guest of the headman I had effectively bestowed on myself the privilege of a free pass.

What the wildlife guards were being paid to watch out for were poachers of musk. The pod of the male fetched more than the price of gold. The Japanese seeker of its supposed aphrodisiac boost and the French fashion salon marketing the latest range of perfumes, alone threaten to wipe out the entire musk deer population because in trapping the male the females and adolescent deer are also slaughtered. The musk is an elusive but by no means untrappable animal. Its significance to science lies in the suspicion that it holds the key to a missing-link species between the deer and the antelope. Not a very gainly animal, the male musk deer sprouts a pair of down-curving tusks which seem singularly inadequate defence against its many enemies.

Snow leopards above the tree line and pine martens lower down are two of its known attackers though a worse fate lies in the snares of the indiscriminate poacher. During British rule musk was an honoured article of Himalayan trade and when the deer population shrunk from over-exploitation and its shooting was banned it was not surprising to find that after independence the same Indian families who had controlled the trade legally were now involved in the illegal hunting of musk. Michael Green had given me a lot of information on how the poaching ring operated and asked me to follow up any leads that could help protect the musk from the depredations of the Delhi businessmen who used the proceeds of smuggling musk to build a new five star hotel (which prided itself on the vegetarian attraction of the capital's best salad bar.)

It was late in October 1984 that I first crossed the trail of musk poachers. I had received the sad news of the disappearance of two young Bengali climbers who had tried to repeat Shipton and Tilman's route across the crest from Badrinath to Kedar. To commemorate the fiftieth anniversary of the occasion the two mountaineers from Calcutta had set themselves the harder task of reversing the route which meant tackling the tricky Kedarnath end first. Shipton and party's difficult days had been intensified by losing the way in the mist. By setting off after the monsoon the Calcutta attempt hoped to avoid that danger. They also took a better line to reach the crest and from Gaunder had climbed up a great connecting ridge that looms above Madhmaheshwar to join near the terrific drop of Chaukhamba's face. Most optimistically they only took one porter and their plans were further weakened by the loss of time in seeking inner line permission. With a lot of luck they might have squeaked through but a severe blizzard caught them as they struggled to gain the crest and only the porter survived, badly frost-bitten, to record their tragic disappearance.

As fate would have it the weather remained clear and calm for the next six weeks. In response to a telegram from the family to try and find out what had happened I set off to Guptakashi, the roadhead for Madhmaheshwar. There I engaged a Dhotial porter and on the first day of our thirty-five kilometre trek to the temple we managed to reach Raun Lekh and slept on the paved courtyard outside the village shop, which lay below the bridle path.

In the middle of the night we were wakened by the tread and pant of a party of running men. Normally in the hills no one would go abroad at night let alone travel without a flaring torch of pine to scare off any bear or leopard. Also to keep up their spirits along lonely stretches of jungle, hillmen will talk loudly to make their presence known. This party obviously wished to keep its movements unknown and one could only make out the flickerings of a torch amidst the heavy breathing of a fast-moving group.

Next morning we met two armed wildlife wardens who informed us that they were in pursuit of a party of musk poachers. Had we passed anyone suspicious on the way? Sadly for the deer the law favours the smugglers. Even when caught red-handed with the strongly scented pod they could not be convicted unless a witness testified to having seen them snare and shoot the quarry. The government even when supplied with details of the smuggling operation and in possession of the whereabouts of the poachers (ranging from a village in Pithoragarh district to the address of the kingpin in New Delhi) still shied away from applying the law. Later events suggested that the offenders enjoyed political protection for when I submitted a report to the government my information was not so much received gratefully as confiscated angrily and I never saw it again.

NINE

The Jeeves Factor

The third visit to the sanctuary finally allowed me into the sanctum sanctorum, the north inner enclosure. Although I only stayed there overnight the impact was powerful and I had a real sense of standing on holy ground.

For the third consecutive year I found myself in Bal Singh's house at Lata but fate had been kinder and I was able to make the trip in the post-monsoon season. With increasing porter rates I had had to raise Rs 1,500 to cover expedition costs and I was still smarting from the loss inflicted by the Changabang fiasco the year before. Mid-September found me on the bus out of Rishikesh bound for Joshimath. At Deoprayag where we stopped for tea I met a party of Bavarian climbers also bound for the sanctuary. Among their number was an Eiger soloist so it would not be difficult for them to overcome Kalanka, their target peak alongside Changabang.

For second porter I was given Kundan Singh, the village carpenter. Wiry and enterprising with a foxiness that comes easily to craftsmen's fingers he was the perfect foil to Nathu Singh and senior enough to bring out his strengths. The greatest asset was Kundan's skill in cooking and I came to realise that a lot of my suffering on earlier outings could have been mitigated by a more imaginative diet. Nathu was only as good as his fellow porter allowed him to be and with Kundan he blossomed for the last time.

(On later expeditions, unaware of the pattern, I employed men younger to Nathu and the overall results were never satisfactory)

When I arrived at Bal Singh's house I was told I would have to wait a day as expedition traffic had increased enormously and every able-bodied man in the village was away carrying supplies into the sanctuary. I decided to spend the day by crossing the cliff on the high path to Renni from Lata to meet Ummed Singh, the shepherd who had worked out the new route that would be disastrous for the future of the wild blue sheep. Wearing only a pair of thongs I slipped during my descent and scraped the skin off the ankle bone. In the humid atmosphere it soon turned septic and later necessitated some surgery to my right boot. The dense gloomy conifer slope that beetles over Renni to witness the dramatic exit of the Rishi from its gorge led to the wildlife warden's tent and before I knew it I was being asked to pay a fee to enter the Nanda Devi national park. When I questioned the guards about the recent entry of pack goats to the inner sanctuary they shrugged and said they had neither the equipment nor the instructions to set up a picket at Trisul base where the new route started. As a free-ranging seeker of greener pastures the nomadic shepherd by nature was hard to track. As grazing in the sanctuary was free the forest department had no tradition of sending its guards in to collect fees.

That evening Nathu arrived late from Lata Kharak. He had taken a double load for the Bavarian expedition in the morning and was happy at the boom in traffic. A large skiing party from France had required porters for Trisul base and after they had climbed and skied down the mountain they would be replaced by an Italian group expected soon in Lata. Two Indian expeditions from Calcutta were in the north inner sanctuary and the rumour was they had managed for the first time to get pack goats into the last preserve of the bharal.

I had not been able to meet Ummed Singh in Renni so followed the narrow path into the gorge to visit his village two kilometres inside. Paing is peopled by porters of great character but like Lata not a single able-bodied man was available that morning. All were inside the sanctuary delivering loads.

As I left I met a young HAP returning from a successful climb in Kashmir. Tough and modest, the villagers of Paing were reluctant to discuss their achievement in finding the pack-goat route to bypass the Rhamani slabs. It seems Ummed Singh had worked it out from his own sightings while on shepherd and porter duty. He calculated that sheep grazing above Trisul base on the flank of Devistan could by the simple expedient of going over the top just before the snowline find themselves high above the sanctuary meadows. If it seems odd that no mountaineer for a century preceeding Ummed Singh's finding had worked out this plain fact and that only a slope peaking at 18,300 ft required negotiation to outwit the Rhamani canyon, it is further proof of the exhausting nature of the sanctuary trail. Most early explorers were too tired to think by the time they reached Trisul nala. Ummed Singh's discovery of this straightforward climb into the sanctuary meadows served to dash the impregnability theory built up by the romance of Shipton's hairy passage along the gorge. To the ancient Hindu myth that only the seven meditating rishis could ever have hoped to get in to that mystical cirque, Ummed Singh's discovery added the distinct possibility that poachers could claim some professional acquaintance.

I could now piece together the elements that led to the discovery of Nanda Kharak pass (as the shepherds referred to the new crossing) on Devistan's curtain that divided the inner and outer sanctuaries. A year ago Pratap had mentioned that he had got his flocks into the south sanctuary by a route that went to 22,000 ft on Trisul. The absurdity of this height (which I had reported) was pointed out by Jagdish Nanavati, the eagle-eyed authority on claims.

Apparently Ummed Singh had made the maiden crossing a year earlier in 1980. His arrival in the meadows had been promptly criticised by some members of an army expedition who threatened to report the enterprising shepherd for causing environmental damage. This so scared the pioneering instincts of Ummed Singh that he never went back. When in the following year Pratap Singh had got his flocks over the same Devistan ridge, Ummed Singh, fearful of being fined by the forest department, was only too glad to accord to Pratap the status of discoverer thereby absolving the original trespasser from guilt.

As we climbed to Lata Kharak we sat and had tea with the descending flocks. By mid-September the sanctuary grass had turned brown and the livestock began their long passage to the winter grazing slopes in the foothills. In view of the tightening restrictions on entry to the sanctuary the shepherds were philosophic about transferring their grazing grounds. While they talked the shepherds sheared their sheep with the old-fashioned squeeze of metal tongs.

I was surprised to learn that some of the shepherds had come from as far away as the Kangra Valley. It seems that they all had this wanderlust to check on grazing possibilities outside their district, forever in search of the other side of the hill where the grass is greener.

For the first time I awoke at Lata Kharak to the thrill of snow peaks all around. Added to this was the appetising breakfast Kundan prepared and I was made fully aware of how limiting the monsoon season can be for the lover of the sanctuary's bounty. Instead of the dank grey jungle, green tits fluttered amongst the deodars and the pleasure of dry clothes and boots made for a march of pleasing prospects. The debit side of the bright blue post-monsoon skies was to miss the emerald brilliance of the meadows now no longer picked out with the bejewelled glow of potentilla. Underfoot the scene was as drab as the overarching sky was blissful. Nature evidently balanced her seasons carefully and what one gained in staying dry you lost in that missing elixir of wild flowers and their shout of infinity amidst the moody swirl of obscurity. There was little challenge now in the familiar lurch from stone to stone to the Bukfena cairn to gain access to Dharansi. With the element of struggle removed the day passed unremarkably and whereas the sting of spiteful rain had stimulated the will to overcome, now the warmth of benign recovery lulled one into the mechanical mode of dull forgetfulness.

The contrast with previous visits was so palpable that I recalled the misery of last year's experience with an affection the present voyage could never hope to arouse. At this juncture last year on my way out past Tolbaljinti I had sat depressed and defeated in the first faint gleam of sunlight amidst the tumble of rocks. Then at arm's distance first one and then another weasel had presented itself with expressive cat-like face upturned to sniff the stranger. They disappeared with the same lightning flick of motion as they had come when I returned their look of interest but were immediately back twittering and frozen by turns. Their mix of fearless proximity and whiplash retreat made me laugh out loud and all my bodily miseries dropped from the therapy these companion creatures provided. For more than fifteen minutes I sat as they writhed, cavorted and dazzled with their pirouettes. Prior to this the only acrobatics one had feasted on was the lazy stall of choughs as they unconcernedly neutralised the sanctuary winds and nonchalantly peeled off a sumptuous range of aerodynamically outrageous manoeuvres. The languor of the yellow-billed chough was now perfectly complemented by this flickering fluidity of the Himalayan weasel.

That night we camped beyond Dibrugheta but because of the balmy evening eschewed the cold confines of the rock shelter for the pleasures of a soft bed of needles amidst spreading spruce. It was a wonderful camp site chosen unerringly by Kundan. Again it was brought home to me how important it was to acquire a guide with imagination. Nathu was incapable of choosing any site but the most obvious. As the delicious aroma of the conifer surroundings was added to by the skills of Kundan's stove I realised that for the first time I could respond to the sanctuary's beauty with all my senses intact. The cold and wet had foreclosed the option of both smell and taste buds performing adequately and all one could associate with my earlier treks was the acrid smoke of wet wood that choked even as it leached moisture from one's system.

To our astonishment descending towards us as darkness fell came a Hindu holy man dressed only in a cotton wrap. He was a local figure who resided at the hot springs near Tapovan and the porters made it callously clear that while they would share a bidi with him they had no intention of inviting him to join us for supper. Eventually the holy man took the hint and went further down the Dibrugheta alp where the tonk of bells indicated a shepherd's camp. The kind of person who settles at a pilgrim spot like Tapovan is a fairly good indication of his sincerity to the calling of an ascetic life. It came as no surprise that this mendicant had attached himself to the French skiing party when some of its members had evinced an interest in his spiritual achievement of living at high altitudes in scanty cotton clothing. What the French admirers may also have been interested in was the holy man's means to beatitude, a plentiful supply of marijuana which grows bountifully in the raw state around Tapovan. Otherwise by their reckoning the nudist camps on cold British beaches should have yielded a bumper crop of mahatmas!

The religious paraphernalia of village worship did not exceed the confines of Lata. The temple was ancient and artistic and well-honoured in the district of Chamoli as possessing the shakti (primal power) of the Goddess. Before we had set out we went to have darshan of the Devi and a cup of tea with Rattan Singh the pujari. On the flagged courtyard the remains of a sacrificial goat were being sliced into slivers of consecrated flesh. They would go as prasad—the blessings of the Goddess—to the households of the village who had contributed to the sacrifice. A tiny tot sat on the compound wall watching the men run their knives expertly through the meat, chewing a raw ribbon of the red offering. As anyone who has hired Lata porters knows, mutton is their favourite article of diet and they will go to any length to sink their teeth into it. As it happened, the very next day at Deodhi while burying some of our supplies for the return journey, Nathu uncovered a hoard of meat belonging to Harak Singh, a fellow villager. Overjoyed my porters stuffed the cache in a pressure cooker and scoffed the lot, their pleasure heightened by the illicit nature of their windfall. As fate would have it we met Harak Singh descending the Rhamani slabs the following morning and Nathu and Kundan kept straight faces as the weary villager returned to what he thought was his waiting larder.

Caste determined the distribution of prasad and little of what I had watched being carved up in the Devi's courtyard would have reached the other Lata across the ravine where at a safe distance from the thakurs lived the low caste doms. As the headman, Bal Singh was obliged to make an appearance at their ceremonies if only to honour the illusion that untouchability had been outlawed by government decree. While waiting for Nathu I had accompanied Bal Singh to the dom village to view a jagran (the Garhwal equivalent of the Kumaon devta natch) and hear the lore of the Devi recited by the professional gitol (bard). The mood was very subdued and slightly theatrical, the typical outcome of a village perched above the motor road where easy access to town culture had made its residents self-conscious about their oracular traditions. The meeting did end on an unintentional fiery note when the thatched roof of a cow-shed caught fire. Even during the height of the flurry to put it out, the bard whirling like a dervish in a white robe continued his narrative to prove that in some respects at least the ancient concern to give primacy to the religious affairs of the Goddess had not been conceded in a doubting age.

If the low caste in Lata were kept at a physical distance at least they were not excluded from the role of porter. But Yashu being a Bhotiya and neglectful of the respect that was due to socially (but not financially) superior Hindu hillmen had a year earlier been banned from using the Lata route into the sanctuary. The Bukfena cairn marking Dharansi pass had as its climax an old iron blade sticking out. The display of upraised iron in most Himalayan areas is associated with demon control. The saint-sorcerer Milarepa would place an axe with the blade facing upwards in a ripening

Nanda Devi from the last birch at Tilchaunani

A small temple to the Devi at Bedni

Harak Singh has a laugh, unaware that his larder has been raided

The Garhwal pilgrim bus introduces most visitors to Uttarakhand

Kundan tests a bridge of birch thrown across
Trisul nala

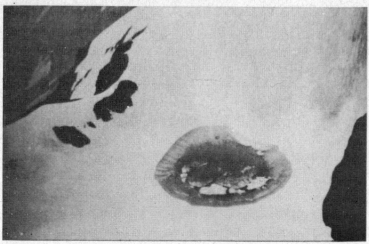

The mystery lake of Rup Kund, seen from the ridge above

Nathu Singh making rain at Malathuni

The author amidst grazing horses at Bedni Buggial

Snow leopard tracks on the South Nanda Devi
glacier

The tail-less Himalayan mouse-hare, sporting in Nanda Devi's Bedni shrine

The author's sketch of the Devi at Kot Kandhara

The author with the headman's son outside Lata's temple

Temple at Srinagar where the Shankaracharya traditionally upturned the Sriyantra

Garhwali devotee receives the lingam offerings as they fall into a yoni receptacle

The paratroopers' memorial to Nanda Devi Unsoeld under the main peak

Nanda Devi by moonlight from Auli Buggial

Photographs: Bill Aitken

barley field to ward off hail storms. It seems an Australian party in search of a souvenir of their climb in the sanctuary had offered to buy the Dharansi sword. At least that was the assumption since it was unthinkable that any guide would upset local demonology without adequate financial recompense. There were no witnesses to its removal but as Yashu's party had been spotted on the route he was held responsible for offending local sentiment.

No one familiar with the Nanda Devi trail could object to the proposition that the hand of Yashu was ubiquitous in the affairs of the Goddess. My only regret was that travelling on an Indian budget the skills of Yashu were beyond my means to employ. Undoubtedly he was the best guide to the area. He had a perpetually sunny personality that could only stem from a not-too-close acquaintance with the ethics of the conventionally law abiding. Typical of his unflappability was the fact that a year ago I had met him on the bus for the short stretch between Tapovan and Lata. I was surprised to find he was continuing to the next stop, Surai Tota, where a Czech party awaited him to blaze a new trail to Lata Kharak. The banishment from the Lata village approach (which was more likely to have been caused from jealousy of a rival's popularity with foreign expeditions rich in pickings than from any religious pique at the removal of an iron blade) instead of working to diminish Yashu's reputation only served to increase it. He now announced to his Czech clients that they were privileged to pioneer an exciting new route to the sanctuary. The more I saw of Yashu the more I suspected he was a role model for Latu, the impish herald of the Goddess, a spiritual artful dodger who always produced dramatic results.

Our next camp right on the Rishi near the Deodhi bridge was again delightfully chosen. Kundan's feminine touches had seduced my reluctant appetite into life and the climb next day up the Rhamani wall to another relaxed camp at Bhujgara went with the good feeling a full stomach exudes. It was the mental cloud that had worsened my bitter refusal to eat on earlier occasions though undoubtedly my condition had not been helped by Nathu's dispassionate mode of butlery. All this time I was limping with one boot cut down to avoid aggravating my ankle. The septic wound had caused the glands in my thigh to painfully enlarge. Each evening I would boil some hot water in a dirty billycan and add salt to try and subdue the inflammation, but nothing seemed to help.

The camp at Bhujgara enabled me to explore the enigma of Shipton's camp which he had referred to as 'Tilchaunani.' None of the porters knew what this meant nor where it was situated. My guess was that it was near Bhujgara which was named to indicate the very last of the birch trees in the ascending gorge of the Rishi. Rather than struggle up to the bleak Patalkhan (so named because it resembled a quarry from which slates had been extracted) the shelter of these gnarled trees looked towards the main peak of Nanda Devi narrowly framed in the fall of black rock. The picture would have appealed to Shipton's tastes. That night for the first time I found the drama of the brown canyon attractive. The moon shone over the seething river but the mood was no longer hostile. A serene note was now sounded, the anger of the monsoon spate having been but the opening movement of a varied symphony.

In the morning we woke to a wonderful image of Nanda Devi beckoning and this soon brought us up over the creaking field of boulders to her Elysian meadows. But now they wore the russet tones of a spent autumn. The brilliance had all gone and the flowers wilting on dry stalks rattled in the breeze, a solemn reminder of the fleeting nature of physical beauty. One of the most extraordinary floral effects of this unique community of plants is how within the space of six weeks they have to perform the whole cycle of growth, flowering and seeding while those at lower elevations can do the same thing in the relaxed spread of months.

Perhaps this inbuilt intensity of life at high altitude conditions rubs off on to the viewer. Looking up to the main peak in this sunnier season I found the peak bathed in a brilliant coppery dazzle with the bands of compacted granite appearing to glow with a green fire. The sober grey peak with its white striations had been the Devi's monsoon dress. Now in the translucent air of September her glossy greyness was overshone with a spectrum of soft colours that gave off that marvellous feel of the archetypal treasure at the end of a rainbow. Whereas in the rains the beauty had lain all around in the emerald flow of grass enlivened by the carpet of flowers, now that faded garland at the feet of the Goddess had been replaced with a gorgeous tiara worn around her golden brows. The same sheer physical pleasure coursed through the observer at both seasons. It was an enormous privilege to have won through again to this sensuous theatre.

We camped near the cave and the first thing I did was to check on the mini-shrine built two years before. I had been told by Bal Singh that the small image of Nandi had been removed by porters to a village temple in the Dhauli valley. This had been done to ensure proper respect was paid to the vehicle of Shiva. The propensity of many mountaineers to rip off whatever took their fancy as a souvenir had taught the more sober of porters to guard their cultural artefacts against the temptation of a quick sale. I had also left a hand-printed visiting card depicting Radha and Krishna and was intrigued to see whether this relic (wrapped in a cellophane envelope and slid under a slab of stone) had survived the intervening winters. It had, and wore the separation without any noticeable change.

Wandering around the litter of the south sanctuary base camp was a sad duty where amidst the dull rust of autumn the only object to shine was a junked tin can. Further afield the grass had turned in patches to a vivid blood red and these violent exceptions to the sloping fade of colour that ran uninterrupted down to the brink of the South Rishi helped heal the scars of insensitive human intervention. Near the site set aside for the helipad was a cairn to mark the passing of Nanda Devi Unsoeld. Her body lay near the summit but this memorial notice had been erected—where all could mourn her—by an expedition of Indian paratroopers. Because of the beauty of its wording the metal plaque did not offend the skyline and as another reminder of the fragility of all life in the sanctuary fixed on it was the skull of a slaughtered bharal, its bleached horns sweeping back as ugly evidence of the price of climbing ambition.

TEN

'Base-kin' Chalo

The later season meant the sanctuary was cold at night and all the streams froze up. Nathu who had gone on a rummaging mission the evening before had spotted a herd of bharal near the snout of the South Nanda Devi glacier. It was almost certain they would be in the vicinity next morning so we drew up plans to enable me to get nearer for a photo. It was agreed that Kundan who had not been in the inner sanctuary for three years would accompany me while Nathu, who visited Nanda Devi base camp at least once a year, would stay back to guard our supplies.

My ankle which had seemed to be on the mend suffered a set-back when I skidded on the icy surface of the first stream we had to cross and gave the tender spot a hefty knock. The excitement of actually setting foot on the mountain, however, overcame the inconvenience of a dragging boot. We crossed from the meadows to the skirts of the mountain using a snowbridge that straddled the curving South Rishi. The river drove its course in a deep grey cleft away from the massive ramparts of Nanda Devi and swinging round, aimed for the easier slopes that drained Devistan on the southern rim of the cirque. The glacier rose evenly before us to present a fairly easy approach but first Kundan offered presents to the Goddess. He broke off the corner of a throat lozenge I had offered him. One did not start ventures before getting the Goddess on one's side.

For me to set foot on the mountain was an erotic moment of fulfilment, the passionate climax to a serious affair. The physical thrill of having at last made brute contact with the flanks of the mountain is an experience I will always relish, a simple act but how hardly attained. As we climbed up picking a way through the rubble and skirting the pools of mud we could see the imprint of dozens of fresh bharal hooves. Then, perfectly imposed on a stretch of mud that ended in a pool, was a clear set of snow leopard pug marks. The animal had suddenly halted, crouched and then backed off from the water's edge leaving an immaculate visiting card.

As we got higher the peaks on the sanctuary curtain began to declare themselves. Devistan ran to a soft summit from this angle and Nanda Khat was obscured by the great sweep of Cream Puff, a whorl of snow that loomed in front of base camp. We knew we had arrived when an empty tin clanked down from above. With a bit of luck we could expect beans for lunch!

The reason we were so sure of a favourable reception was that an Australian expedition on a lightweight attempt of the main peak was known to be well advanced in their assault and the cook left at base was a young recruit known to Kundan from Lata.

We were now fairly high on the middle stroke of the reversed letter 'E' that is used to depict the layout of Nanda Devi in relation to the encircling sanctuary. I could see the steep wall that culminated in Longstaff Col and marvelled at the glorious improbability of Nanda Devi's black convex base competing with her white summit for beauty. This lissom shape would seem to make the mystic letter 'Om' a better indicator of layout. The sanctuary curtain is enclosed from Lata round to Nanda Ghunti by the outer sweep and Nanda Kot included in the extended tail. For the upper moon cradling the mystical bindu there is the climax of Mount Kailash clasped in the blue expanse of Mansarover. The grand sweep of the mountain's skirts demanded more than casual geophysical description. The awesome scale and curving majesty of the black smooth basement of Nanda's walls made the trek up the South Nanda glacier a geological poem. You walk from the sharp confluence of rivers below the sanctuary portals and follow closely under the overhang of prodigious drapes of rock to measure the marvellous curve of mountain as it flows round to Longstaff Col. When complemented with the matching fullness of the northern side, the complete circle is one of the geomorphic wonders of the Himalayas.

The twin peaks of the Goddess and the sharp sublime connecting ridge form an abbreviated range of their own, parallel to the run of the Great Himalaya, unique as the briefest in length to possess such great height, and the most dramatic in the sheerness of their drop. I would follow next day the wondrous symmetry of encirclement describing a steady sweeping arc from the south base camp to the north at Rishi Tal. From the lake vantage point you could see the perfect rounding of the North Nanda glacier as it homed in to the glacier of the North Rishi. This stunning black circumambulation of Nanda Devi was undoubtedly the most exciting discovery of my visit.

A 200 ft scramble up the dirt wall of the South Nanda glacier brought us to the mess tent where Govind Singh (one of the few smiling hillmen I have met) greeted us. Inside sat the Indian liaison officer whom we had already met on the sticky descent to Dibrugheta. On that occasion he had been rushing out of the sanctuary to signal for a helicopter—in an unusual accident a falling stone had injured climbers sleeping at base. On our way to Deodhi while crashing through the jungle I had tried to photograph Nanda Devi's peak from the dense birch. When I pulled myself up on to a ledge I spotted heaps of what looked like sheep droppings—more green than black. In fact, it was the site of a musk deer latrine for these cautious animals return to the same safe spot.

I was disturbed from my findings by the roar of the helicopter drumming its way up the gorge. The Ladakhi liaison officer had got to Joshimath just in time. He was a friendly person and kept himself busy by studying general knowledge for an army exam that awaited his return. He gave me a letter for his wife to post from Joshimath assuming I would be clear of the sanctuary before the Australians finished their climb. As it happened I met him again at the IMF headquarters in Delhi some months later. The Goddess had not smiled on the Australians and they had vented their frustration on the LO for their unfulfilled plans. It was rare for any foreign party to reconcile themselves to the need of an LO.

In their book, *The Shining Mountain*, Pete Boardman and Joe Tasker who had accomplished the historic ascent of the south-west face of Changabang that announced the arrival of alpine tactics in the Great Himalaya, had effectively pilloried the institution of the LO. In what must be one of the most pathetic passages in mountaineering literature, they describe how, instead of staying to witness the ultimate ascent from Changabang's most beautiful angle, their LO turns tail and retreats.

Even the best of Indian trained climbers were years behind in technical proficiency and the habit of staging joint expeditions in the hope of improving Indian standards were just well-meaning gestures. The tragic death of Harsh Bahuguna on the fractious international Everest expedition had been caused by this lacunae in standard. After the recriminations settled few could dispute the central irony that the Indian climber's idealism and enthusiasm were the only things that would have got his more technically accomplished but egotistical team-mates to the top. The spelling out by the IMF of the kind of gear to be donated to the LO indicated the great rift in thinking. What was the point in unloading the latest equipment on a man who according to the rules was restricted to base camp duties? Was not the insistence on new gear a crude instance of Third World greed in grasping at resaleable goodies? Often enough the LO did rise to the occasion and perform heroically but for the majority of foreign climbers he was an official albatross they had to bear.

From the Indian point of view an LO was not only necessary to advise on local custom and prevent his high altitude tourists from being ripped off but also, since the Himalayas were a defence subject and a sensitive border area, to check that their concerns were entirely of the sporting sort. Thus the theory of attaching an LO to a foreign group made sense to the babus in Delhi. What their unfamiliarity with mountaineering reality did not take into account was that the official sense of duty expected of a military officer seconded to base camp as LO could never come anywhere near the passion a climber brought with him to embrace his chosen love.

What made the LO like other IMF impositions a subject of high amusement outside Indian climbing circles was the fact that many of the foreign expeditions who were booked to climb a specific peak by a declared route continued to stray from their licensed objective. How could an LO forced to remain at base camp know what was happening up the mountain? Dozens of peaks have been scaled privately to save on peak fees and the record book after the demise of the current generation of top climbers might alter dramatically when the truth tumbles out of their non-official diaries.

After the bean lunch prepared by Govind we began the easier trek back to the meadows. Kundan had been silenced by the surprise of not finding bharal. When we started up the glacier in the morning he confidently predicted we would see a teeming host. But in the three years he had been absent the sheep-dog factor—the fallout of Ummed Singh's efforts to get his flocks across the Devistan divide from the outer to the inner sanctuary—had altered the balance of nature. In places the descent was so steep that when you began to run you couldn't stop. As I whizzed down a loose slope of grey moraine a fist-sized stone spat out from the black smoothness of the mountain ramparts. Unable to stop and hardly able to swivel my head I just caught a glimpse of a retreating animal burrowing frantically up a rock gully.

Digging in the ice axe, I slewed to a halt. Kundan identified the animal as a ghooral, smaller than the bharal and presumably above 15,000 ft, very near its ceiling. Fresh bharal prints now covered the earlier ones and as we trotted down the soft moraine to within sight of the snow bridge we caught up with a whole herd of fawn-coloured wild sheep. It was a surprise to see how their colour, a Luftwaffe blue-grey in the rains had adapted itself in autumn to match exactly the changing hue of the shrivelled meadows. In fact I hadn't spotted how big the herd was and only had Kundan's word for it. Then as I stopped to focus I could make out the white backsides of the young who jostled to give away the position of their more cautious elders.

Like the musk deer these high altitude dwellers were of interest to science in suggesting habits borrowed from both the sheep and the goat. George Schaller, the explorer-zoologist, in a fine study of the problem examines the evidence from the Karakoram to Nepal. His book *Stones of Silence* is a splendidly authentic recreation of the mood at Himalayan heights. Accompanying him on the last leg to Dolpo was the writer Peter Mathiessen whose account of the expedition, *The Snow Leopard* went on to become a bestseller. Perhaps because Schaller had already won awards for his books his study of wild sheep and goats went unnoticed though in my opinion it is altogether superior to Mathiessen's bestseller with its pseudo-spiritual enquiries. Matthiessen compensates for not seeing a snow leopard by waxing lyrical on the mystical presence of absence whereas Schaller more realistically curses his bad luck.

The aura of near-invisibility that surrounds the snow leopard may have less to do with the elusive colouring of the predator than the exhausted state of its pursuer. Sightings are achieved where long residence is involved and most of the sanctuary shepherds were familiar with the depredations of this wide-ranging cat. In Ladakh many villagers report how their flocks are harried by this beautiful animal with the magnificent curling tail. An English traveller I once met recounted how he had witnessed a crowd of angry villagers clubbing to death a marauding snow leopard in Ladakh. Since then the Bedi brothers have filmed the feline more feelingly, sacrificing two years of their lives to acclimatise themselves to the punishing terrain it inhabits. The future of the snow leopard depends on its prey species and any fluctuation in the fortunes of the bharal around Nanda Devi would directly affect the survival of the snow leopard. The action of one villager who introduced domestic flocks into the exclusive grazing grounds of the wild blue sheep had thus triggered off serious ecological implications for several species. It was not just the bharal ewes that the Lata mastiffs worried. In causing them miscarriages the sheep dogs were effectively reducing the chances of the snow leopard to survive.

The bobbing herd between us and the South Rishi river was moving westwards. There must have been some seventy animals butting and trotting away from us. Experience had taught them not to trust the human intrusion. What a sad change from the day Shipton first alighted on their tame indifference to outsiders. On the way in I had picked up a spent cartridge to prove that hunting of the bharal continued. A big animal could fetch a lot of money for its meat. With the notification of national park status guns were now strictly forbidden but since the game wardens were unequipped to monitor what went on in the sanctuary such rules were treated by the villagers with derision.

The herd was extra careful not to allow us to come too near and I could not get the desired photograph. My simple camera matched my photographic talents. For these three trips I had used only the cheapest Indian cameras. Expedition expenses could double by too enthusiastic an investment in photography and I had the monsoon to thank on two occasions to help scale down my ambition. I preferred to sketch and paint the sanctuary scene in the belief that subjective appraisal would get nearer the rare essence of the beauty than any cold capture by film. With the restraint of equipment when I came to photograph Nanda Devi from her base I had to take two separate shots to get the whole mountain in and then join them up for the picture.

Back at camp, Nathu told us he had investigated what seemed to be a snow leopard kill in the direction of Devistan. Wheeling birds drew his attention to a possible source of meat but as with most destinations in the sanctuary the deceptively clear light had doubled the distance to what had seemed a strikable target. He turned back when the kill never seemed to get any nearer. This sense of frustration accompanied most marches in the brilliant air of the meadows. Everything around you and afar seemed pristine and touchable. There was no haze and the extraordinary luminosity of the air made for soft rainbow hues as if the surroundings were under a spell. But the enchantment was broken when you tried to reach your objective and found in the pure light it remained always out of reach.

In the morning we set off to have a look at the north inner sanctuary reckoning we would have enough supplies to see that as well as repeat later the abortive trek to Changabang. As always one's plans were ludicrously inflated. No matter how many seasons one spends in the Himalayas this failure to adjust to the tremendous scale of their challenge is perennial and must be the cause of more accidents than any other factor. The ease with which Shipton and Tilman set out on their sanctuary explorations speaks more of the English art of understatement than of the realities met with on the trail. To be able to read these mountains right one had to have the local experience of the shepherds plus the expertise of an alpinist. Above all the candidate needed genuine respect for the Devi and this extended to showing proper regard for the conventions that surround her. Singing and shouting would earn disfavour and the breaking of any village taboos—such as sexual provocations—might invite the fate of Ms Unsoeld.

Picking flowers was believed to trigger off rain and the playing of the flute (a feature instinctive to herders in the lower hills) calculated to annoy the Goddess. Most of these restrictions derived from the folklore that went with the Rup Kund tragedy, where a medieval king had gone to perform a pilgrimage but offended Nanda Devi by the behaviour of his court. In reprisal the Goddess had his whole party hurled into the tarn at Rup Kund and the grisly spectacle of human corpses frozen in its clasp continues to warn pilgrims to this day of the terrible fits of anger the mountain deity is prone to. A good working knowledge of local superstitions is also useful in overcoming porter reluctance. By appealing to the needs of Nanda Devi a porter may be shamed into carrying further than his own selfish instincts dictate. In every respect the personage of Nanda Bhagawati resembles a queen. She is the final source of inspiration and no one could question her ruling. She is the great mother of village destinies and overawes by her majesty the frail concerns of potential litigants. For this reason in the effective realm of the Goddess neither policemen nor lawyers are much in demand. In the Nandak revenue district adjacent to Rup Kund (where the motor road remains a stranger) the word of the Devi remains law.

Our march down to the junction of the sanctuary streams was murderously direct. As though programmed for the inconvenience of not circumventing hazards Nathu led straight along the South Rishi so that the carved-out bed of every stream debouching from the meadows had to be clambered down into and then after tricky fording climbed painfully out of. This embracing of the affliction to prefer the flight of the arrow to the lean of the contour thoroughly spoiled my morning. Unfortunately I had fallen so far back trying to photograph butterflies that I had no means of confirming my worst fears that all our switchback sufferings could have been avoided by resort to the level track via the sanctuary portals and thence steeply down to the Goofa camp site.

Cursing Nathu's mulishness and my own dilettantism that had allowed him to get so far ahead I eventually caught up as the porters sat and smoked above the narrowest point of the river just above the confluence. They were assessing the safety of the aluminium step ladder that had been clamped face down over the filling torrent to act as a bridge. An earlier wire stretched over the gap made for a reassuring grab rail should the ladder prove unsettling.

This crossing was the obvious point of entry into the north sanctuary but its promise was deceptive. The southern bank being higher it would have been easy to run and leap across the tumbling glen had not the landing stage across the torrent been confined to a two-foot ledge in front of a towering black rock. And for all the ease of access, how would one get out from a standing start back on to the higher bank? Shipton and party had been forced to ford the river and it falls so severely that even the narrowest of crossings invited the severest of risks.

The Goofa camp site as the name indicates was a cave of particularly claustrophobic proportions. To get in you had to duck under a drape of rock that went within two feet of its stony floor. There was something unappetising about the place and it was significant that Nathu had led us to it. It was only two in the afternoon and Kundan agreed that we would have no difficulty in locating a better camp further along the course of the North

Rishi. For the first time Nathu dug his heels in and refused to accept the decision of a senior. I could only put this down to some plans he had of rummaging in the vicinity of the cave. Outvoted, Nathu had to comply and storing away some items against our return we set out along the catwalk that outwitted the swing of the North Rishi.

We were now back on the flank of the mountain and circling the outer base of the main peak. The narrow passage involved some scrapes past overhanging rocks until eventually the cliffs squeezed out any possible further negotiation. We had to cross the river to hit the North Rishi glacier and some time was spent in assessing the depth of the pool that lay before us. Nathu as usual stood in as guinea pig and when the water did not come up beyond his knees we waded in and followed his line.

The snout of the glacier heaved up in a turmoil of mud, stone and badly fractured ice. At the end of the season the snow bridges were at their most dangerous and jagged-edged crevasses littered the way ahead. We managed to get down from the torment of the glacier roof to some terraces across the river. But we were still too near the huge black roots of the main peak to see anything of it, above a third of its height. Where the Changabang glacier joined the North Rishi we saw the great white rock marker I had spotted on my first expedition. Rivulets flowed in from all directions and the going was now decidedly slow as the once-freezing streams were at their maximum flow of the day and rushed musically to touch the feet of their mistress.

Nathu pointed out the remains of a shelter built by the 'Swiss' mystery trekker Thomas Gross. This giant of a man established a record by wintering for six months inside the sanctuary alone—the first man to do so—in the previous winter. The porters loved him for his strength and geniality but wherever he went strange events followed. (Inevitably Yashu was able to supply his photograph) How could he have hoped to survive in the sanctuary without the sack of flour or the metal stove so conveniently bestowed on him by a passing expedition? Was it Gross's winning personality that called forth such largesse or was he up to something in league with foreign climbers? The experience of most of us in the Himalayas when you accidentally meet another expedition is to exchange cautious pleasantries, ferret out information on the route ahead and share a polite meal. Never do these meetings end in one of the parties walking away the richer by a six months' supply of flour and a cooking range. Was it a coincidence that Gross had defected to Switzerland from Czechoslovakia and that the expedition that loaded him with the means to survive his long ordeal in the sanctuary also Czech? When all East European expeditions were sponsored by their governments why should the Czechs be so keen to heap their supplies on a defector? Almost all the details known about Gross seemed like his build—larger than life. Normally asylum seekers from East Europe had to linger long before being conferred with refugee status but Thomas was given Swiss papers in record time. He had no known means of support yet travelled around India when he wasn't lazing on Goa's beaches having a ball. What did he live on and who was paying for his lifestyle?

I wrote down the dates of his stay inscribed on a stone and was particularly intrigued to see his nickname scratched on the same rock. Was it a coincidence that it echoed the name given by the CIA to its covert operation to place a nuclear spying device on Nanda Devi fifteen years earlier? Things had gone wrong on the first attempt and the nuclear pack was cached high on the mountain side to be placed on the top the following year. But when the Indian and American climbers returned to complete their secret mission the nuclear device was missing. Had the Goddess drawn her veil of magic over its finding? And was Thomas Gross an innocent bystander, part of the *chayamaya* (illusion) created by the Devi?

To prove that generosity was possible at base camp, when we emerged from the tricky cross of streams to gain the shores of the lovely small Rishi lake we were welcomed by some expedition members from Calcutta. The porters went off to share space for the night with some colleagues from Lata while after a few introductions to the Bengalis it was discovered I had been the teacher of one of them more than twenty years earlier. That earned me a small tent of my own for the night.

After tea we headed round the lake to contact the Bavarian party whom I had met in Deoprayag. They were leaving for Kalanka in the morning and I hoped to catch the expedition doctor for treatment of my septic ankle. It continued to fester but might respond to more sophisticated treatment than my daily tin-can of boiled water and salt. As we strolled by the lake in the cool evening air a line of bharal suddenly appeared in front of us and filed past less than fifty yard away. Their healthy coats shone a glossy fawn and their faces had back markings. In the soft evening light their graceful motion seemed to turn them into golden hinds. They had left the edge of the lake after drinking and would climb to the rocky plateau above the camp to spend the night.

I could not have wished for a better close-up but then experienced the chagrin of every amateur cameraman. I had already exposed the last of the film.

ELEVEN

In Dulce Jubilo

The only dubious advantage conferred by a tent is the early morning urge to be free of its confinement. In the hushed amplitude of dawn I struggled up the hillside towards Changabang hoping to circle round and come across last night's herd of bharal. I carried neither food nor water so there was a limit to my exertions. The veto of the climbing sun would decide how far I could ascend.

It was almost as if a bridle path had swung from the lake to fringe the course of the angled Changabang-Kalanka glacier. Soon I was faced with the contrasting profiles of both mountains but preferred to sketch the wild outlines of their neighbour the Fang. Changabang from this angle is an ordinary spectacle when compared to the view from the other side.

From the east Changabang might almost qualify for the pejorative *kalank* for she is indeed a blot when compared to the peerless soar of her opposite view. The names of these twin peaks had evidently been applied by Mumm's porters. From the Bagini and Rhamani side Kalanka does appear a less enthralling neighbour than the glistening pillar of Changabang, whose sheen of grey granite easily earned her the status of 'shining mountain.' In fact Kalanka is not so much a blot on the landscape as an aesthetic anticlimax, and to level the score, that is how Changabang appears from the north inner sanctuary.

I pulled up from the breathless exercise feeling acutely the absence of any breakfast ballast. Whatever else my day depends on the inner satisfaction created by a pleasantly stretched stomach is essential, for as I have long discovered, no fight can emerge from a vacant plexus. The sight of clumps of blue poppy diverted my attention and morality being weakened by self-pity and hunger, I rearranged their spiky flowers to get a background view of Changabang and achieve a more picturesque photograph. My poor opinion of the camera's ability to get anywhere near the wonder of the total mountain experience guaranteed no guilt over these rehearsed spontaneities. Besides what greater effrontery could exceed the claim that the camera never lies? In Himalayan terms the camera seems to do little else. It cannot comprehend the scale of the subject and rarely indicates the softness of the atmospheric tones. Even less than words the gloss of photographs fails to convey the raw magic of the heights for the price of visual replication is to sever all notions of sound and smell. The sufferings of the Bedi brothers in Ladakh indicate the price real photographers must be willing to pay if they are to capture the soul of the subject.

The sharp clack of disturbed stones made me glance to the north. There browsing on the sparse khaki slopes were three bharal ewes. When I began to toil up towards them for the much-wanted photograph they seemed to assess my threat quite accurately. For all my panting I could get no nearer. The 200 yards of no man's land they had set between us they maintained without any obvious mark of retreat. Grazing nonchalantly they continued to keep the same strict divide. We were around the 16,000 ft mark and with the sun due to escape the black wall presented by the main peak of Nanda Devi I knew I had very little time left. But whenever I stopped to aim the camera the ewes backed away further, puzzled by the break in my motion.

My stomach was now not only empty but groaning at the effort to keep up and my throat painfully dry. As the first rays flooded our layer of mountain to turn the sheep a shade of fawn that blended into the colour of the hillside, we were back near the rocky plateau that overlooked the lake. The ewes leapt up the last few feet to a black buttress and looked back down at me as if to indicate the end of the chase. With difficulty I managed to draw myself up to gain a clear view of their farewell. They were trotting down to join the main herd which basked well out of range.

I gave up and lay down in the sun to get my breath back. Only then, free of the obsession to get close to the wild sheep did the magical arrangement of my movements that morning sink in. I had unwittingly won for myself one of the great grandstand views of Nanda Devi. Like the prow of a titanic iceberg the ridge leading up from the North Rishi glacier rose perpendicularly and seemed to rocket into the snows of the summit. If the main peak's contours were breathtaking in their slant, the rise of the east peak from this angle was even more grandiloquent. Here was the innermost sanctum of the Goddess, hidden to all but the most intrepid of admirers. Its rear of vertical granite was draped by the most voluptuous cling of snow imaginable. The brilliant white delicately fluted ridge that ran to link the two peaks fell into an incredible cleavage of astonishing sensuous impact.

This raw ability of nature to arouse erotic fantasy made this corner of the sanctuary seem like the boudoir of the Goddess. To have fought one's way nearer to the base of that tremendous swathe of frozen ice, its curtain falling sheer for 10,000 ft, could not have intensified the feeling of profound blessing that swept over my vision and remained with me for many hours that day.

Any attempt to get nearer the awesome inner chamber of the Goddess might have invited hostility. Already as the sun grew in strength the first artillery of the day began. The unloosened rocks free of the melting ice began to crash and crumble reverberating their hidden threat to whoever chose to listen. This was the high spot of my intimacy with the mountain yet when the chance came for a final physical embrace of passion I held back. Was it from fear or wisdom that I refused to go nearer and enter the chamber?

Whatever the motivation I had been fortunate to get this far and did not want to stretch my luck. The ultimate glory of the Devi lay in this locked up bridal chamber that yielded a mood of superlative chaste exaltation. The other unexplored parts of the inner sanctuary suddenly ceased to intrigue— having seen the centre-piece the prospect of viewing the secondary attractions lost all appeal. Too often in life over-activity can deliver us beyond the goal we wish to reach. So little is the reflective habit inculcated that many of us resemble mountaineers driven forever to look on successive peaks for a mood that, unique to the first, can only be repeated within.

It was with no regret that I turned down from that prominence to return to the camp at its base. I was halted near an overhanging rock by the sight of a bharal carcass. It was evidently a ewe to judge by the short horns at the end of the ribcage. The question was, had it been a victim of expedition poachers or prey to the snow leopard? The first of these options seemed unlikely in view of the confident tread last night of bharal so near to the human encampment. If this line was their chosen route to drink water then it was quite likely that a snow leopard could have lain in wait to cut off their retreat. The discovery of a whole flurry of wool torn out under the rock convinced me that a snow leopard had attacked the ewe in a fury of hunger. Their range was considerable and though it was unlikely this kill would have been the work of the leopard whose pugs we had seen on the South Nanda glacier, it was not impossible. Now that the shepherds had introduced domestic livestock into the inner sanctuary no doubt the snow leopards had begun to stalk them as well. They would certainly make easier targets than the cautious bharal.

Back at the tent my old student from Calcutta kindly served tea and biscuits and asked about our programme. I told him that after consulting the German doctor about my ankle (he had given me some medicine and wanted to see how it worked) we planned to set off after lunch and aimed to get out of the inner sanctuary by the new high pass of the shepherds. When I asked if he had heard about the pass he informed me that his expedition had used this entry point, hoping to get fine shots of Nanda Devi in the morning. But with the sun rising right behind the bulk of the mountain their wait had been frustrated. The only way to get a flattering shot of the mountain without glare was in the evening, but by then the sun had fallen below the level of the sanctuary curtain and invariably any afternoon shot caught the haze built up by the trapped heat.

My protege then surprised me by offering to guide us to the pass. He wasn't feeling well, he said, and wondered if he could accompany us back to Lata. Having accepted the hospitality of his expedition it would have been hard to refuse his request but I told him I would have to ask the porters first. Kundan and Nathu who had also enjoyed a pleasant stay at the Rishi Tal camp agreed to accept another member (whom we soon nicknamed 'RM' after the famous mountaineer Reinhold Messner). We were not short of supplies and reckoned that a guide would be an asset for the unknown terrain ahead. In view of RM's health the porters also agreed to carry some of his load.

If it was strange to find this sudden dereliction of base camp duties by an expedition member it seemed no stranger than the curious air of mystery that surrounded this Calcutta party. Normally objectives and routes are a source of pride and discussion at base camp but at Rishi Tal our hosts kept glancing guardedly at one another as if to signal that some secret was being kept. The cryptic exchanges in the mess tent could only suggest that they were not keen to own up to their team's real intentions but it was not till later that we learnt why. So closely guarded was the goal of the Calcutta team that not even their porters knew of it. Delusions of grandeur can be the only reason why this modestly funded expedition that could have achieved with credit the summit of the peak it had booked chose instead to go for the much more serious objective, Rishi Pahar on the rim of the north curtain. They would have come in for a lot of official criticism even if their plans had not gone awry as they did for the IMF viewed observance of its red tape as a kind of patriotic duty. Foreigners who broke the rules could be banned from the Indian Himalayas but an Indian who earned their displeasure could be effectively disbarred from climbing.

As so often happens in the romantic thirst for mountaineering glory the lead climbers veered from a heroic ascent of the mountain to a farcical descent that resulted in the death of a climber and serious frost-bite injuries to his companions. They had bitten off more than they could chew and to show how easily this could be done I now embarked on the same course. My student led the way wearing a Reinhold Messner felt hat but we had gone no further than the crossing of the river at the snout of the North Rishi glacier before he tripped near a crevasse and sent his felt trilby most of the way down it. Nathu had to climb inside to rescue this piece of mountaineering symbolism that we soon came to learn could not have been more inappropriate for its wearer.

Whatever cheerful credentials our guide possessed as a companion none of them related to that most crucial of mountain basics, the ability to put one foot in front of the other. We were appalled to realise that we had landed ourselves with a lame duck whom we would have to shepherd every inch of the trying trail back to Lata.

We did not clear the river into the south meadows till 5 p.m. My aim had been to get up the mountain towards the level of Patalkhan before we camped for the night. This would avoid the long and steep haul from the valley in the heat of the morning. But Reinhold either would not or could not move quickly. He had to be assisted, cajoled and dragged over every minor obstacle and in sheer frustration Kundan decided to camp at the level of the sanctuary portals. It was depressing to halt so low in the gorge when more than an hour's light remained.

But Kundan's instincts for the best camp site proved reliable again. We were in a soft and wind-free alcove protected by a surround of rocks. It looked out over the pink spectacular play of clouds that characterised Nanda Devi's evening performance. During the day the clouds would collect over her brows, a cold day marked by the hissing stream of cirrus that seemed to issue from the main peak.

Sometimes these resembled the triple caste marks on the forehead of Shiva and I had been fascinated to find a photograph of this phenomenon kept in the Lata temple. Had this been given by the Unsoelds or the Tasker-Boardman expedition? According to Rattan Singh the pujari it had been taken by Doug Scott who had been with Chris Bonington on the maiden ascent of Changabang.

It was the streamer effect viewed from the southern aspect that gave Kumaonis their conviction that the main peak harboured the kitchen of the gods. In the evening the cloud layers would lift and give an unobstructed view of the Goddess. In the monsoon the clouds would linger longer and sometimes not yield to the normal pattern of dispersal. Even then dawn would bring a resplendent part-clearing and the glowing mass of the mountain in a pink or orange plume would resemble a woman uncoiling on to her shoulders the luxuriance of her coiffeur.

That night Kundan made for me the best of all camp beds I had known on the mountain. This was an open-ended tent contrived from sheets of plastic stretched over a rope that was tensed at one end near my feet by the ice axe and at my head over a large rock on which a boulder was balanced to anchor the rope. Simple, comfortable and effective it was a typical touch of genius that differentiated Kundan from all the other porters. Strictly speaking as a carpenter he worked at a profession despised as beneath the status of a Rajput, but it was precisely the talent of craftsmanship that gave him an edge over his proud but unemployed caste fellows.

Kundan was also a believer in the direct method of getting a fire going. Instead of employing Nathu's system of kneeling down and putting his lips to the nascent ember to give a series of huge lung-expanding puffs, he preferred to toss in a cupful of kerosene. This caused a spectacular beginning to our meals and when Kundan was in charge of the cooking this flambé overture was invariably followed by an imaginative dish. On later expeditions I availed of the services of Govind the young cook who had fed us at Nanda Devi base. While technically a much better cook than Kundan his performance was only mediocre because being junior in years the other porters neither encouraged him to extend his repertoire not appreciated his efforts when he stuck to the staple.

Reinhold had his own tent and on this clear night the porters slept in the open. We woke to find an animal (possibly a wild canine of some kind) had raided the kitchen and removed some left-over vegetables kept in a cup from last night's meal. The theft deprived us of a much-needed cup. Most of my equipment was of the makeshift variety that would last for one trip and then be thrown away in view of the rough journeying that it had to endure strapped to a porter's back. The cups were of tin or plastic and whereas the first were apt to get too battered to serve from, the second either got kicked accidentally into the fire or were thrown away when the grease and dirt of high altitude camps made them too disgusting to drink from. Spoons were another major casualty, forever falling in the splintered landscape between irretrievable cracks or spirited away by the rats and mice that flourished in all the lower camps.

As feared our climb on that following hot morning went badly. Nathu blazed his usual diagonal irrespective of any obstacle more sensitive people might wish to avoid. We had given ourselves the optimistic estimate of reaching the pass by 11 a.m. We toiled up endlessly as each ridge that seemed to be the last translated into another and yet another. Higher and higher we panted and when snow began to appear we concluded we must be nearing the top. But the same ceaseless routine followed as ridge succeeded ridge.

I had a splitting headache and the cold wind off the snow whipped our sweating party. The one great consolation was the unexpected view of Changabang's spire. The mountain resembled a silver sabre tooth gloriously glowing amidst an array of dark jagged ridges across the Rishi gorge. Our plan had been to cross the pass before midday at the latest and get down to Trisul base camp for tea. The succession of false final ridges now had us in despair and when the last severe tug to get up yet another snow slope had been accomplished we were too far gone to celebrate our actual arrival at the crest. It was well after 2 p.m. and without a glance of farewell to Nanda Devi or a parting photograph we rushed to the less windy side of the rocky spine and collapsed in anger and disgust. Somewhat unfairly, Reinhold came in for a tongue-lashing for having slowed us down by his floundering progress up the slope. His help as a guide had been real but the altitude brought out the worst of our ingratitude.

The red tents of the Trisul camp could be spotted straight below our feet. But the vertical descent did not look too appetising. Worse, we would not be able to get to the treacherous glacier crossing until it was dark. There was only one way we could reach our objective before the light failed and that was to run. The misery of the morning's futile slog would also be shed by the exhilaration of a whoop down the steep scree. We were in line with the knife-edge ridge that led to Devistan, the snow mantle less than a thousand feet above us. To get away from its freezing winds was another pressing objective. Kundan followed my jogging descent while Nathu, caught between the instinct to join us and the need to bring up the rear was confused by Reinhold's unchanged deliberate pace. The same agonising tread he had used to climb up the slope was the pace at which he descended. It was obvious the whole party's arrival at camp would be jeopardised by this lagging member. If Reinhold hadn't looked so impressive a mountaineering figure—he was tall and handsome and dressed much more professionally than any of us—one would have felt more sympathy for his plight. But the exaggerated gap between the thoughts of Messner which he quoted while seated at camp and his own dismal inability to walk let alone climb made us intolerant to reason. Shouting back to Nathu to keep an eye on him I said Kundan and I would go ahead to let the Trisul camp know visitors were on the way. The important thing was to make sure the whole party was not benighted high on the Devistan ridge.

Kundan accepted the challenge of getting down to the glacier as fast as possible and proved to be a shrewd route finder. Many of the Lata porters have this instinct to read any likely obstacle well in advance and lacking this talent myself I was relieved to find Kundan added it to his list of virtues. Whatever decision I had taken the outcome would have been dangerous. Expedition ethics make it incumbent on a leader to go at the pace of the slowest and treat the weak member as a sacred charge. I failed to measure up to the standards of this code preferring the riskier efficacy of throwing people in the deep end and allowing shock to administer the required adrenalin. So spontaneous was our flight off the pass that it was only now I realised I had no warm gear nor sleeping bag with me. These items had been packed with Nathu's load and were getting further away each moment. But committed to the gamble of arriving at Tridang camp before nightfall every minute counted and we were oblivious even to the stunning and unusual views that would normally have qualified as the high point of the sanctuary trail.

Kundan was now far ahead zig-zagging down the scree. With an hour of daylight to go he raced off the skirts of the mountain and began the long detour round the deep and sweeping glacier off Trisul. Everything from this height and angle seemed spectacular and worthy of a photograph but our sole aim was to gain the camp. Resigned to a vast outflanking movement it came as a surprise to see Kundan dart into an opening above the dirt wall of the glacier and begin a long glissade to the crevassed floor. Now he began a brilliant glacier traverse dodging the dangers expertly and forcing a passage through the reluctant toss of ice. Just as the dark closed in he indicated the chosen point of exit. We scrambled up a shorter earth wall and found ourselves precisely outside neat rows of red tents, a brilliant piece of navigation. It was the base for the French skiing expedition and luckily for us most of the members were on Trisul. Kundan was welcomed by a group of Lata porters while I was shown to a tent by the liaison officer, Dr Acharya of the ITBP who loaned me a jacket and sleeping bag for the night.

We kept looking out of the tent hoping to see Nathu or Reinhold but neither turned up. Kundan borrowed a lantern and went with some friends to try and locate them but Nathu only arrived in time for breakfast next morning. There was still no sign of Reinhold's hat on the horizon. We organized a search party but the doctor advised me in view of my septic foot not to join it. (Perhaps he sensed my urge to put it behind our laggard guide!) I spent the morning in the luxurious mess tent forced to listen to an old French skiier who had been invalided down from his attempt on Trisul. He shook his fist at the mountain and cursed the peak for depriving him of an altitude record with which to impress his friends back in the Alps. By contrast when to everyone's relief Reinhold did show up at midday (following the same deliberate tread) he was not in the least negative about the way we had abandoned him. Instead he was full of the magnificent dawn he had experienced while still on the slopes of Devistan. Whatever his rate of progress there was no denying his genuine love of the mountains. And to prove his mountaineering judgement was better than mine he had negotiated the tricky glacier with aplomb.

TWELVE

Snow on Dharansi

I had hoped the base camp doctor's kindness would extend to putting up Reinhold for the night. Compared to the inner sanctuary the trail was now comparatively straightforward and as our plan was to try for the photo close-up of Changabang we thought we could reach Deodhi the same evening if we were not burdened by our shuffling companion. But the doctor pronounced him fit and recommended he get to Lata without delay.

It was a relief to get back to the tree line after the exposed upper slopes. As we entered the jungle beyond Bethartoli base camp we saw what looked like leopard's scat. With all the sheep pulling out of the sanctuary the predators were also beginning to move down for winter. We were surprised by a change of weather before we got to Deodhi and began to revise our plans when it got worse. Next morning the clouds billowed low with the promise of bad weather and Nathu and I decided there was no way we were going to repeat another cold night in the wet charnel house at Upper Deodhi. If the Goddess signalled her displeasure at the idea of repeating the Changabang attempt we would accept her verdict. She had given me all I had hoped for and it seemed churlish to demand more. The only irritant was that we had buried supplies across the bridge for the expected climb to the Rhamani glacier. Normally my expeditions were restricted by food rather than weather. But now at the first sign of rain I was ready to sacrifice the supplies in order to avoid getting wet. Nathu dug up certain perishables and left the rest for his next tour of duty.

As the rain clouds loomed lower we turned away from the lure of Changabang and began the long diagonal to Penikhola Dhar. The skid over to Dibrugheta past the exposed trunks of ancient birch and fir revealed the devastation caused by the rushing expedition trains. The top soil had been wiped clean leaving a bald slick down which one's boots could glissade in a muddy skid.

The drizzle had forced us to take refuge in the cave. Later the weather worsened and turned to sleet. We woke to a few inches of snow and more was falling with a steady build up. If we remained in the cave, and the snow didn't stop we could be sealed in for a few days. While rations were not short there was little to remedy the call of an emergency. Also there was the creeping gait of Reinhold to consider. He had moved satisfactorily through the jungle but would no doubt seize up when faced with the stiff ascent to Malathuni. We decided to sit and wait for the first break in the snow and then try to get beyond Dharansi before nightfall. This was an ambitious trek even in light snow but it was the prospect of having to chivvy Reinhold through deep snow that made us pack and be ready for the first sign of lightened skies.

At ten the heavy snow abated and by eleven we were ready to risk our chances with the vaguest hint of a watery sun as aid. We did well to attain Malathuni without trouble. The three inches of snow had helped firm the footholds on the otherwise abominably slippery slope. The long slog over the bleak rocks to Dharansi was performed like any Arctic journey with recriminations when we lost the line in the white mantle of snow that smothered familiar landmarks. The porter's insistence at making a move began to make sense. In deep snow Dharansi could be a death trap. The approach to the long ragged ridge is dangerously narrow at the best of times and to flounder through snow would be to take alarming risks on its knife-edge passage.

We had not cleared the worst till 4 p.m. and by then our nerves were frazzled at the helplessness of our backsliding guest. He could not negotiate the descent and had to be pushed, dragged and bodily bundled like an awkward load. There had to be a hard lesson in this pathetic withdrawal after all the beautiful moments inside the sanctuary. Why had the most inspiring moment atop the Rishi Tal camp been immediately followed by this painful reminder of human frailty? Whatever Reinhold's problems and fantasies it was the effect on our behaviour that yielded the lesson. Irritation is often the precursor of enlightenment as the Road to Damascus shows. Was I bemoaning the presence of this footless mountaineer because his predicament was uncomfortably akin to my own? We were both possessed by the fantasy of appearing as hardened explorers though in fact we took good care not to stray from the known paths. Reinhold after all was only a souped-up Shipton in a yuppie hat. My need to judge our guide harshly (when he was a decent enough person with whom I continue to correspond) could only stem from the embarrassment of a performance that caricatured my own. It was a revealing touch of the Devi that at the precise climaxing of my feelings for her beauty she should present for close examination someone who exactly captured my own shortcomings.

We struggled down to Lata Kharak where amidst a sprinkling of snow several tents announced other expeditions poised to enter the sanctuary. We hadn't had tea or water since morning and could hardly speak from the day's efforts and haranguings. I asked a group of foreigners if tea was available but they all looked blank as though they had never heard of it. Then the sun appeared for the first time but was so low in the sky that its redness seemed an omen. Not wishing to spend the night in the cold air when the comforts of Bal Singh's veranda beckoned only three hours away I shouted to Nathu (who was again carrying most of my luggage) that I intended to make a run for Lata. Kundan was well behind assisting Reinhold off the last of the rocks. Frazzled from the trying experience of helping him extract our ornamental guide off Dharansi, Nathu shouted one word to indicate his opinion of my proposed descent—*'bekhar'*. But though other porters joined in to warn that it was useless to try to penetrate the forest at night, I was convinced it was just as *'bekhar'* to spend a cold sleepless night and then have the prospect of another agonising descent in the morning. In what was clearly a rash decision from an overheated brain I rushed into the jungle as the last light of day surrendered to gathering dark clouds.

Only next morning did I learn that salvation had in fact awaited me at the threshold to the forest. As I careered down, a lone tent, well protected from the wind on the ridge, emitted a welcoming voice but having made up my mind I looked neither to the left nor right. Sadly it was the gentle Kalyan Singh poised for his last night in the sanctuary. This was his farewell to the

Goddess for the season and I had refused the hospitality of one of the Devi's closest devotees. Meanwhile, Nathu and the others spent a restful night with him and got down to Lata next morning in good time for breakfast. My panic reflected the exasperation caused by Reinhold and yielded further lessons in how stupid reactions can bring one to the brink of self-inflicted disaster.

The silent darkness of the forest was spooky and to compound the problem I realised Nathu was carrying my torch. Luckily I had my duvet jacket. Another item that turned up in my rucksack to help pass the night was a tin of condensed milk (without tin-opener). I knew the forest path turned south about a third of the way to Bhelta but in the deep gloom that engulfed the descent I hadn't a clue when to start bearing left. Eventually I descended so far that I felt I must climb back. That was hard work so I decided to keep descending until I came across a path that crossed the slope, leading (hopefully) to Lata. I was breathing heavily not so much from the stumbling progress but from the real fear of meeting a bear. According to the doctor at Tridang their expedition had spotted a bear at Lata Kharak.

My luck was in and the jungle eventually gave way to a bridle path. I groped my way along this successfully but when it snaked down into a ravine the surface turned too dangerous to traverse I was forced to make camp for the night. The sky was overcast and rumbling and the one thing I feared more than anything else was for the heavens to open. Luckily the clouds did no more than send gusts of pattering rain over the hillside. I adjudged us to be very near and on the same level as Bhelta. The dicey descent had forced me to test my navigational instincts, which I sensed had served me well. It seemed the Goddess had kept her hand on my head for when the long awaited dawn did reluctantly yield a damp grey day I only had to cross the intervening ravine to find myself exactly where my calculations had aimed. Had I stumbled another hundred yards last night I would have been at Bhelta on the straight path to Lata. But convinced I was lost I took shelter under what seemed a hedge enclosure (possibly for young buffaloes) and then began to behave like a young buffalo myself. Far up the inky forested slopes I could make out the blaze of a shepherd's fire. I could hear their dogs bark and was relieved not to be alone. I yelled and hollered using porters' names to let them know I was a friendly spirit but as expected no one rushed to my rescue. Hillmen assume all voices at night belong to discarnate spirits and hence you answered at your peril. There was nothing to do but hunker down, head on knees, and will the night away.

Sitting on the rucksack helped keep out the cold while the hedge prevented the wind from growing too restless. To alter the pattern I pierced a hole in the top of the condensed milk tin and made sucking noises to confirm to any wild animal that this was indeed a stockade for buffalo calves. Instead of feeling sorry for myself I was immensely relieved at not having been mauled by a bear and rejoiced that the threatening rain had held off. The bleak daybreak cheered me up immediately and I found myself sitting within a stone's throw of the Bhelta camp site. The stupidity of last night's hasty decision had been mitigated by the wisdom of one's uncanny homing instinct.

It now remained to cover the easy trip to Lata. Imagine my astonishment when I swung past Pratap Singh's house to find a large party of foreigners breakfasting on bacon and eggs using his courtyard wall as a table. Serving them and beckoning me to take a seat alongside was the ever-cheerful Yashu. Here was the perfect climax to my irrational descent. It seems Yashu had been forgiven his sins as comprehensively as I had. His ham and eggs tasted marvellous and as a bonus I was invited into Pratap's house for a dram of daru.

The climbers represented the Italian skiing party who would replace the French at Trisul base. The enthusiasm of the Latins for the Himalayas was something to see. Two of them had gone up to Lata Kharak and back the day before just to express their eagerness. Here were more candidates to join Reinhold and I in the sanctuary's collection of fantasy merchants.

My young teacher came marching in bravely and suddenly all the abnormal behaviour occasioned by high altitude subsided and he, Kundan and I were able to joke about our aggression towards each other yesterday. Later I called at Kundan's house which was much poorer than Bal Singh's for being the owner of 300 sheep and goats made the latter a man of considerable means in the village. It was Bal Singh who distributed the left-overs of the expedition. Kundan was delighted to receive a small pressure-cooker from the spoils. In turn he presented me with a large hand-carved holder for temple worship. He had fashioned this himself from Himalayan cedar and the sweet-smelling wood made the ideal memento from this modest village craftsman who had contributed more than any other porter to my comforts along the trail.

Kundan then accompanied me to the Nanda Devi temple to make offerings for our safe return. First we had to collect Rattan Singh from his house but that meant having tea with him before he agreed to open the temple. The happy-go-lucky mood of the villagers today was partly due to the free flow of liquor occasioned by the expedition. Visitors were sometimes shocked to find these devotees of the Goddess drunk to a man and performing worship amidst the fumes of distilled barley. But as with meat the things the hillman liked were wisely accorded sacred status and the crude whisky was first offered to Nanda. While orthodox Hinduism of later days frowns strongly on inebriating juices the evidence of earlier times strongly points to the widespread custom of sacred beer being offered as libations to the gods, a tradition that continues in the tantric schools of the unorthodox, usually far from the centres of sober Brahmanical practice.

That Lata was about as far as you could get is evidenced by the fact that this lovely old temple was served by a non-Brahmanical priest. This was the marijuana harvesting season and the plants stood tall in the pujari's garden. After he rubbed the gum off the female flower the plants would dry to yield a sturdy hemp rope. The seeds would also be dried and used for flavouring. Roasted and ground they make a tasty chutney with just enough hallucinogenic effect to induce an indolent giggle in their consumer.

The presence in every village of the cannabis addict pointed to the wisdom of not making an issue of this comparatively mild drug. I remember how before I came to India I had been taught to believe marijuana was in the same league as opium abuse. To confuse these substances and bracket them together is wilful abuse of the scientific method and illustrative of how Western culture itself suffers from a third disorder of the human mind— arrogant assumption. The most the village charasiya gets up to is opting out of responsibility in a benign cloud of stupefaction. The other property of the wild plant is to help holy men ease the pangs of hunger and this in turn makes it almost a spiritual aid to the worshippers of Shiva. By abhorring this mild stimulant Western governments foolishly deprive themselves of a useful substitute for hard drugs.

The cost of my three weeks in the sanctuary worked out to some Rs 2000, of which a part went in charity since not all the supplies were used by me. In Lata I met three young Delhi trekkers who had managed to get as far as Lata Kharak. Not having the money to pay porters they had to return when they couldn't locate the water spring. Here were more candidates to the club of sanctuary romantics and I warmed to them. They had been victims of government tourist information. Instead of keeping quiet when not in command of the facts, tourist offices seem to operate on the principle that misinformation is an acceptable substitute for no information. The trekkers were told that the sanctuary was a three-day round trek and required little in the way of provisioning. So they brought along a few potatoes just in case. To bail them out, I gladly donated some of my supplies.

Bal Singh accompanied me down to the motor road where his new shop seemed to attract more card-sharpers than customers for tea. There were rumblings that the sanctuary was going to be closed to climbers and Bal Singh confided that in the short 1982 season (from June to October) half a million rupees had been earned by the porters along the Dhauli valley. Instead of combining to make a lobby the porters preferred the macho satisfaction of individual defiance. One knew that boasts and threats were not going to affect the policy makers in Delhi. Both sides took ignorant extremes as their position and what was inevitable—the closure of the sanctuary to protect its ecology—could have been realistically modified to cushion the porters from financial distress.

I knew from personal experience that the IMF only heard what it wanted to hear. If you wrote and congratulated its president on an expedition success in the sanctuary and made the suggestion that Nanda Devi should be declared (like Macchapuchare in Nepal) an inviolate peak the reply you received waxed enthusiastic about the momentary glory of the climb but studiously ignored any suggestion that would guarantee long-term conservation of the area's beauty. My argument was that if the IMF recommended the closure of the sanctuary they should also urge the government to open up new areas to mountaineers. To allow expeditions to cross the inner line at Surai Tota and approach peaks like Changabang from outside the sanctuary rim would involve no security risk. Neither would breaching the outdated line at Munsiyari in the east. That would enable climbers to attempt the east peak of Nanda Devi plus a whole selection of peaks on the eastern sanctuary curtain. As the IMF was staffed largely by defence personnel there should have been no difficulty in pressing these alternatives that would have satisfied all lobbies. The environmentalists would have the sanctuary free of expeditions, the climbers would have a new array of peaks to challenge and the porters could continue to carry.

That things were coming to a head was clear. I learnt that a foreign expedition had bribed a forest (wildlife) guard to allow pack goats into the sanctuary at the beginning of the season in defiance of departmental orders. On hearing this the villagers, who were waiting to see which way the wind blew, plucked up courage to send their animals into the sanctuary. If penalized they would report the forest official for taking a bribe. What with the frantic ferrying of loads and the ingress of pack and grazing animals there was no way the sanctuary could withstand this pressure of population. In October 1982 there were fourteen expeditions which translated into 10,000 entrants—human and animal—over Dharansi. Both shepherds and mountaineers would have to be diverted. It was only a matter of how and when.

Bal Singh flagged down a passing potato truck and got me a ride on the roof. The truck was going all the way to Rishikesh so I decided to sleep among the sacks. Unfortunately it broke down late at night in Rudraprayag so the next morning I caught a U.P. Roadways bus to Dehra Dun. Back home in Mussoorie I wrote about the situation in the sanctuary and advocated its closure—though I would be one of the chief victims. And that is just what happened, my own recommendations preventing me from entering the sanctuary again.

At the time it seemed the right thing to do. Mountaineers had been given a great privilege and in my opinion, had recklessly abused it. Or was this more sanctimonious judgement from a romantic who resented real climbers from doing their thing? From the point of view of a devotee of the Goddess there was no doubt that the attitudes of the climbers (and many of the porters) turned on the materialistic urges of gain and fame, the latter for the climbers being the forerunner of financial success. The takeover of modern mountaineering by equipment manufacturers made success more important than enjoyment. Previously one waved a club or national flag over a summit, now the age of advertising required brand labels to the fore. Peter Boardman has described how on reaching the summit of Everest in 1975 he had quipped into his tape recorder (hardly essential equipment before the era of hard-sell) that he could not see a branch of his sponsor's bank. What he didn't say was that this seemingly casual line could well have been rehearsed before the team left England. Modern expedition members signed away their right of individual comment, ostensibly to protect the principle of collective responsibility but this could also be turned conveniently into a conspiracy to silence public doubts about claims. When one views the fluctuating status of the modern mountaineer, first a political mercenary then an advertising stooge, perhaps we should be grateful that there are still a few inept romantics left.

THIRTEEN

Mystery Lake of the Goddess

*W*ith the sanctuary officially declared closed in February 1983 the rainy season found me heading towards another intriguing area sacred to the Goddess. This lay outside the sanctuary curtain between Trisul and Nanda Ghunti (the trident of Shiva and the veil of his bride Nanda). The submarine-shaped latter peak appears on old maps as Nandakna perhaps to indicate it as a source of the Nandakini river, in my opinion the loveliest of the Alakananda's tributaries. Nanda Ghunti is also important for giving a boost to Indian mountaineering outside the aegis of the Delhi bureaucrats. The mountain was first climbed by the outstanding Swiss mountaineer Andre Roche in 1948. When Bengali climbers repeated the ascent in 1960 the whole of West Bengal was fired with enthusiasm. The healthy outcome was the growth of local clubs encouraged but not controlled by the government.

Between Trisul and Nanda Ghunti lies the Ronti Saddle at 17,500 ft, the lowest point on the south sanctuary cirque. Entry into the sanctuary is not easy however as Ruttledge and Longstaff discovered in 1927. Shipton and Ang Tharkay found getting out a bit easier when they crossed over from their 1936 mapping expedition of the sanctuary. While they leisurely enjoyed the horizontal beauty of the meadows Tilman was furiously employed in the vertical assault of Nanda Devi. He had injured his foot and was later knocked off the Rhamani slabs but overcame all the odds to climb the main peak, an exploit followed by a remarkable exit to Milam. It seemed the Goddess smiled on Tilman in spite of his stiff upper lip demeanour that prevented him from openly declaring his love for her. Ang Tharkay incidentally was the first person to take domestic livestock into the inner sanctuary when he took a sheep along for meat on the hoof.

In 1979 the *Alpine Journal* announced that a British climber had crossed from the Ronti Saddle and managed after much effort to exit down the Rishi via the Bethartoli base camp. The difficulty of crossing the Ronti Saddle should be kept in mind when the conflicting claims about the mystery of Rup Kund are considered. The small shallow glacial tarn lies high to the east and concealed under a ridge that runs before the southern face of Trisul. For most of the year the lake lies frozen and forgotten at 16,000 ft, some 4,000 ft above Bedni, considered by many to be the most beautiful of Garhwal's buggial (grazing alps).

Near Bedni Kund where shepherds have built a minor dam is a small Nanda Devi temple and alongside lies the diminutive companion shrine of Latu, a local devta recognized as the herald of the Goddess. In the juxta-position of these temples may be read the persuasive big brotherly approach of Hindu orthodoxy in the assimilation of Pahari beliefs. Increasingly Nanda Devi has been interpreted as Durga Mata in hill dress, despite the fact that her cult contains within it clear evidence of aboriginal mother-goddess symbolism as well as myth derived from hill caste practice. These several layers of devotion add to the fascination of the Goddess especially when the visitor can see the old crude customs being tidied up and sanitised to fit mainstream notions of spiritual respectability. The fact that Latu, representative of the indigenous shamanistic tradition, in his home village of Wan was known to confront the Devi on her pilgrimage to Bedni (to demand his timashi, a copper coin) and could only be appeased by his appointment as herald of the Goddess (which in effect gave him precedence) at the head of her procession, points to this process of assimilation of primitive cults by the greater vehicle of sanathan dharma.

Possible confirmation of the taking over process can be detected in the German explorer Schlagintweit's map of 1857 which depicts the east peak of Nanda Devi as 'Latu'. Today the name Latu Dhura is given to a peak behind Nanda Devi East on the east curtain above Milam, one in an extraordinary line of six-thousand footers that includes Mangram, Deo Damla, Bamchu and

Sakram (nowhere else in the Himalayas do you find so many high peaks strung out along a north-south axis). It is possible that Latu has something to do with the village name of Lata (there are others in Garhwal) although the villagers prefer the more convenient derivative of 'lat' (leg) to tie up with the mainstream myth of Hanuman carrying back the entire peak of the nearby Dunagiri mountain so that the heroes of the *Ramayana* could pick the healing herb Sanjivini. (In present day Uttarakhand one way of getting round the ban on alcohol is to sell bottles of Ayurvedic tonic whose formulae based on scripture puts their use beyond any social censure. The precious herbal input from the holy Himalayas is carefully preserved in an eighty per cent solution of alcohol and sold under the pious label of 'Sanjivani Sura')

The folklore that surrounds Nanda Devi in her Garhwal incarnation (since the cult has regional variations) climaxes at the hidden lake of the Goddess. Each rainy season the Devi is honoured in the hills by a festival that coincides with the Nandashtami phase of the moon. Annually a pilgrimage winds along the Pindar valley bearing Nanda Bhagwati in a doli, its numbers swelled by villagers who join along the way carrying their local deities with them to add to the dignity of the Devi's outing. As the pilgrims climb to Bedni the usual accompaniment of drums and trumpets is found to be missing. The higher the devotees ascend the more silent their behaviour becomes until barefoot and shivering before Rup Kund (on a special pilgrimage scheduled only once in twelve years) they are brought face to face with the cause of the Devi's grim restrictions—some 300 corpses preserved in the frozen tarn.

By a curious coincidence the Nandashtami season is the only time of the year the lake melts and for the brief space of a fortnight yields its dark secrets. Below the shallow waters the unknown victims of the harsh Himalayan elements are gruesomely preserved. The bones have been dated to around the fourteenth century AD but the explanation of how the bodies came to be in the lake has still not satisfied those who prefer wilder alternatives.

In 1942 a forest guard who visited Rup Kund wrote about his findings and the national dailies picked up his story as a sensational scoop. Thereafter for several years many researchers visited Rup Kund (which is neither easy to reach nor pleasant to stay at in view of the bleak windy site) and fuelled various theories that laid claim to solving the mystery. British observers preferred a military explanation. Bodies in such large numbers could only refer to an expeditionary force therefore it had to be the remnants of an army. British opinion then concluded that the bones must belong to the retreating army of the Dogra general Zorawar Singh who had captured Ladakh in 1834 and then went on to his nemesis in Tibet. Like Napoleon's retreat from Moscow his army was decimated by the weather and the retreat turned into a rout. But even assuming some of his men escaped over the passes into Garhwal the lake at Rup Kund is nowhere near the route to any of them. Only in superstitious village lore does Tibet lie over the next snowy range.

Another theory popular with hillmen stumbles on this same fact of stark inaccessibility. It turned on the finding by the forest guard of a very large size of leather shoe once favoured by Tibetan traders. This allowed scope for much embroidery and encouraged the belief that Rup Kund in olden times (when men were giants and took an extra large size in shoes) was on a trade route (now lost) to Tibet. The lake was their camp site and the bodies in it were of traders who had perished in a storm. Upholders of this theory embellish their narrative with traditional appeal to the vagaries of the gods. Perhaps the traders possessed magical powers that could unlock a secret underground passage to Tibet. Surely the possession of such a large size of shoe indicated special spiritual powers of some sort? If the Buddha boasted long ears as a sign of wisdom and the avatars of Hinduism are portrayed with long arms to symbolise their all-embracing power, the sign of big feet had to refer to magical journeys performed in double quick time!

The most persistent researcher of the mystery was Swami Pranavananda who went to Rup Kund for ten consecutive years. This remarkable explorer applied scientific technique to his gifts of intuition but his theory sounds the most bizarre of them all. He was of the opinion that formerly the villagers would dump their dead in the lake after an epidemic (this would account for the religious paraphernalia found in the lake). In another variant of this morbid act of disposal, a modern American anthropologist has come up with the possibility of ritual suicide, which was certainly practised in Garhwal—albeit at an individual level—up to British times. But so many bodies could only suggest a medieval equivalent of the Reverend Jim Jones sect.

The most likely scenario for the Rup Kund tragedy is the obvious one of the Nanda Devi pilgrimage that was scheduled to pass the lake (weather permitting) every twelve years (or more according to the pundits). Led by a four-horned ram the long line of pilgrims bearing banners and parasols trudged up to the tarn to cross the ridge under which it lies in perpendicular expectation. Weary and barefoot, they would hardly be in a condition to practice snow-craft on the sheer 300 ft ascent from the lake to the ridge. Their goal on the other side was the enclosed valley leading to Hom Kund, a minor tarn at the base of Trisul whence the four-horned ram is set loose as messenger to bear the procession's gifts in its saddle-bags to the feet of the Goddess.

The smaller pilgrimage annually culminates at the Bedni Kund temples. Villages around Nauti (situated above the confluence of the Pindar with the Alakananda at Karnaprayag) send their patron deities to accompany the pilgrimage undertaken by Nanda Bhagwati. The significance of Nauti is that its inhabitants the Nautiyals (amongst the best known and most advanced of Garhwali clans) were the gurus of the rulers. Their village is situated not far from the original capital of Garhwal at Chandpur (now the village of Kansua) and traditionally the descendants of the Chandpur Raja patronise the Bari Nanda Jat (or Raj Jat) as well as announce the propitious birth of the four-horned ram which indicates the approval of Nanda Devi to proceed with this big twelve-yearly pilgrimage.

There is no written evidence of the Raj Jat before the nineteenth century but a lot of oral tradition that makes its continuity from medieval times seem more than likely. If it is remembered that the greatest pilgrimage of them all—and the hardest—to Kailash-Mansarover in Tibet was well-established by the time of Kalidasa in the fourth century AD and that the Puranas give a detailed breakdown of pilgrim places in Kumaon and Garhwal in the centuries that followed, there should be no insurmountable difficulty in accepting that by the fourteenth century the journey to the outlying flanks of Nanda Devi had become a routine pilgrimage.

The evidence from the lake thus inclines more towards the pilgrim theory than to any other. Religious articles have been recovered, amongst them the most characteristic feature of modern processions, the ceremonial umbrella of woven bamboo carried on a long pole to shade the Goddess in her palanquin. The discovery of female slippers and bangles is taken as a sign by the orthodox that the party could not have been on the Raj Jat pilgrimage since no one is allowed to wear shoes and women are forbidden to take part. This is to stultify enquiry by arguing backwards. Granted that in present-day hill society no woman would dare disobey the custom of an all-male Raj Jat but 600 years ago the rules may have been different.

There is every reason to assume that it was only after this accident that the penitential mood hardened and women were no longer allowed to take part. There is much to suggest that after the calamity the Brahmins accustomed to use the female sex as scapegoats—perhaps as a sign of racial guilt at having married into local aboriginal stock or at least of having satisfied their carnal lusts at their expense (for example the custom of devdasis maintained until independence at many Uttarakhand shrines) fixed blame on the presence of women (and low castes) and thereafter established the tradition as we know it today where neither of these low-born species is welcome on the Devi's spiritual circuit.

The Nanda Devi folklore emphasises Brahmanical disgust at the inherent uncleanliness of women and attributes the Rup Kund disaster to the impurest condition of all occasioned by the toils of child-birth. If it seems weird and contradictory for male worshippers of a female deity to consider the profoundest of her lunar mysteries to be a defiling factor for their ritual this is the plain fact of life in Uttarakhand. The paradox of worshipping woman as a goddess yet treating her daily as a beast of burden is central to the religious and social code of the U.P. Hills. Until this neurotic dichotomy is squarely faced, the petulant spite of males will continue to breed disharmony and increase the frustration of men habituated to blame all their woes on the actions of those they deem less worthy by the accident of birth. (The curse of defilement extends from the Rup Ganga to render the course of the Nandakini unfit for ritual worship)

The most favoured version of the lore surrounding the Raj Jat's progress to Rup Kund makes the king of medieval Kanauj a kinsman of Nanda. The king wished to celebrate the expected birth of an heir by undertaking a pilgrimage to 'Kailash'. (To a hillman every holy mountain is referred to as Kailash just as every stream is referred to as Ganga) King Jasidhwal arrogantly observed none of the rules of the pilgrimage and insisted on including in his entourage a group of dancing girls. As if this was not enough to anger Nanda, the wife of Lord Shiva, the foolish king committed sacrilege by allowing his pregnant queen Balpa to accompany his party. When Nanda Devi heard that her sister (from the house of Chandpur) had given birth to a child on the mountain—thus polluting holy Kailash—she called on her demon herald, Latu to destroy the king and annihilate his party in a hail of heavenly bullets and throw them into the lake. To prove that this story was invented by a Brahmin, Latu was commanded to go easy on the

Brahmanical contingent who thus lived to record for others the perils that awaited those who did not toe the line of the Devi or her high caste interpreters.

It is a mystery why the British when putting forward the Zorawar Singh remnant theory failed to mention the possibility of the Raj Jat pilgrimage. Could it be that they were reluctant to accord their humble hill subjects the status of mountaineers and were loathe to admit that native Garhwalis could attain great heights without the aid of boots? From the beginning the British accorded prestige to their highest possessions. There was a matching of Alpine achievement with the enjoyment of empire and the ultimate one-upmanship developed in the scramble to be first on Everest. This need for physical confirmation of European superiority extended to the intellectual arena and there was a colonial compulsion to belittle native talent. For example Radhanath Sircar, the Bengali computer of the height of Mount Everest (as it became), lived to see his contribution deliberately downplayed. Racial relations worsened after the 1857 mutiny and Sircar whom George Everest had considered his right-hand man found his fortunes fading in the new order. By the end of the nineteenth century his authorship of a Survey manual had been suppressed and in the twentieth Professor Kenneth Mason pretended that this mathematical genius had been a mere clerk.

That the British were aware of the Raj Jat is vouched for by mention of its details in Atkinson's *Gazetteer*. 'A procession is formed at Nauti which accompanied by the Goddess in her palanquin proceeds to the Baiduni Kund at the foot of the Trisul peak. A great festival also takes place every twelfth year when accompanied by her attendant Latu, the Goddess is carried into the snows as far as the people can go beyond the Baiduni Kund and there worshipped in the form of two great stones glittering with mica and strongly reflecting the rays of the sun.'

Note however the curious omission of any references to the lake at Rup Kund. This only goes to show how random were the sources of Atkinson's information. On the whole however his general presentation of the Nanda Devi lore is remarkably accurate and his own research limitations are frankly admitted: 'There is a local *Upapurana* devoted to the worship of Nanda and description of the places sacred to her in the Kumaon Himalaya which I regret that I have been unable to procure.'

There ought to have been sufficient clues for the British to have guessed at local pilgrim involvement in the Rup Kund tragedy. Nothing of a military nature has been found in the lake and even a retreating band of men would have possessed some weapons between them. But most damaging to the military theory is the absence of any geographical logic. Not even a shepherd would seek out Rup Kund since it leads to a dead end. Why should a retreating party seek to compound their woes by climbing into such an inhospitable cul de sac? Geography emphatically demolishes the argument for any military involvement.

As for large-footed traders, why should anyone want to cross two dangerous passes above 16,000 ft when they could follow a river route to Tibet in a fraction of the time? Science suggests the rivers flowed before the rise of the Himalayas on either side of them so that even if the configuration of the ranges had changed it was still always more profitable to keep to the easiest route along the river. The dating of the bones to medieval times ought effectively to settle the matter in favour of the pilgrims but so perverse is the human urge to prefer fantasy to reality that people unacquainted with the terrain continue to maintain both highly improbable theories against the overwhelming weight of common sense and scientific data.

The Indian mountaineering historian Shambhu Nath Das has examined the Rup Kund evidence and made a detailed study of the surrounding folklore. He concludes that there is no alternative to the pilgrim disaster. He had the advantage of scrutinising the terrain and in a reconstruction of the calamity has recreated with considerable authenticity the most likely scenario. From Bedni the pilgrims do not wear shoes. (Note however that this does not preclude them from carrying footwear to put on when they re-emerge from holy heights). The long straggling party of pilgrims follows a steep grassy slope to the outstanding image of Ganesh near the miserably windy camp site of Bhagubasa. Along the way as is often the case with pilgrimages for simple peasants, landmarks have been identified with reference to the folklore. A stand of pillared rocks symbolises the wrath of Nanda Devi and is known as Patar Nachauni. The rocks are said to represent the dancing girls who came with the king of Kanauj and were turned to stone as a warning to those who dare sing or dance on the holy mountain.

Beyond the beautiful jade Ganesh is Balpa ki Sulera, the polluted spot where the sister of Nanda gave birth. A more miserable site would be hard to discover and the grey flinty platform of rock offers no protection to campers as I was to find out. The last few kilometres up to the lake (invisible under a ridge) is unsurpassingly bleak. Rearing up behind the sunken tarn is a 300 ft steep snow slope now known as Jyuri Galli indicating 'death alley' (some say it refers to a local spirit, others see it as a corruption of 'Zorawar'). This steep slope may have been the cause of the bodies in the lake and in Shambhu Nath's reconstruction everything seems to point to this dangerous feature as the solution to the lake's mystery.

Tired and dispirited the long straggle of pilgrims would reach the lakeside in the evening when Himalayan weather is always at its worst. The clear mornings cloud up and by afternoon it starts to rain. The rain turns to snow and storms rage briefly before the weather again clears to yield a peaceful evening. As they filed up the steep and slippery snow slope perhaps a sudden storm hit the lead climbers and caused them to slip down on top of those following behind to create an avalanche of human dominoes on a Cresta run that shoots down straight into the Kund.

The bare bones of the disaster were embroidered by Brahmanical lore to attribute the accident to Nanda Devi and Latu. Instead of wind and sleet blasting the party iron shrapnel was hurled by the gods. Anyone who has stood on the Jyuri ridge directly above the lake knows exactly how poetic this reconstruction is for the hail actually hits you like bullets and the wind like a shrieking demon seeks to hurl you down the snow chute into the waiting jaws of the lake.

'Rup' means the form or image of the Devi and it is difficult to understand why such an inauspicious little lake should be accredited with such an impressive title. This was a minor mystery I set out to solve and I wrote to Lata to ask Nathu to accompany me. We met in late July at Kausani where I had gone to visit some friends. The signs at the outset were ominous. While loading our kit bags on to the roof of the bus Nathu lost his balance and dropped a load. Fortunately no one was injured. Then the bus up to Gwaldam became so overcrowded it could hardly groan up the hill. We spent the night at the tourist bungalow but mist obscured Gwaldam's main feature—the huge frontal view of the trident peak of Shiva. Next morning aided by a Dhotial porter we scuttled down the mountainside to the old suspension bridge over the Pindar at Nanda Kesari, a temple that announced we were now on the pilgrim trail of the Goddess. Yesterday before leaving Kumaon we had passed another famous Devi temple at Kot, a place— according to the missionaries—of evil reputation. Rumours of tantric rites abounded at many of the interior temples and certainly if one went by the mood occasioned by these spooky old buildings invariably overhung by a clump of gaunt cedar trees you could easily imagine the blood of innocents being sprinkled as libations to unsavoury presiding spirits.

On the other hand the mist-scarfed mountains in the monsoons unfairly added to the effect of sinister goings-on which the onset of a sunnier season would immediately dispel. But it was an undeniable truth that the further you penetrated the mountain's defences the more unsophisticated the worship of the Devi became. The impact of the motor roads had been to directly facilitate the mainstream of Pahari culture. One of the least admitted aspects of the caste system is that those it demeans most seem to harbour amidst their antagonism a secret hope of inclusion. This conflict of interests must be one reason why caste has been able to flourish for 2,500 years. To prove this argument is the increased tendency in Hindu society since independence to include the lower castes in its age-old system rather than support the secular demand for the abolition of all caste.

The most obvious sign of mainstream infiltration into hill life is the increased use of Hindi and other plains fashions. Women now adopt the sari and also have begun to use Hindi. In matters of religion minor deities are in the process of being matched with figures in the main Hindu pantheon and in towns like Naini Tal and Almora it is easy to see Nanda Devi as Durga or Santoshi Ma. The most interesting feature of this process of Sanskritisation is that it involves no missionary effort. Apart from the government sponsoring of Hindi the urge to return to supposed Aryan roots has caught the hillman's imagination. Curiously this cultural longing for the traditional pattern of plains Hinduism is held along with an increasing political desire to be free of plains economic domination.

The agitation for a separate hill state grows while the difference in attitudes between plainsmen and hillmen is narrowing. A motor road that links Kumaon with Garhwal runs down from Gwaldam to join the course of the Pindar flowing to Karnaprayag. From Tharali it turns inland to enter the realm of the Devi, continuing along the route to Mandoli near the Loha Jung pass. As a sad comment on how hill affairs are run by plainsmen we had read in the newspaper of a government-sponsored tour to Rup Kund a few weeks earlier.The tourist officials were under the impression that you could do Rup Kund in three days from the roadhead at Mandoli when in fact five days would be required for an acclimatised trekker and more for those who had come from Delhi by bus. However the road to Mandoli had been built ten years earlier and had collapsed while waiting for some crucial bridges to be built along its course. Nathu and I availed of short lifts by jeep between the broken sections and ended up for the final pull to the Loha Jung by exchanging our Nepali porter for a horse.

Rajuli was going home riderless to Wan and her owner Narayan Singh offered to take our baggage all the way to Bhogabasa the last stage below the actual lake. Narayan Singh was a droll companion but his horse went like the clappers. She wore a garland of nine brass bells round her neck to scare off leopards.Unlike most horses which preferred to jingle along in packs Rajuli forever forged ahead. It was only later when we came to unload her near our destination that we discovered what may have been the cause of her getting the journey over quickly—running sores under the saddle.

That night was spent in a new tourist bungalow where to our astonishment the main suite turned out to have a luxury double bed with the sort of laminated inlay that went with the nuptial scenes of a Hindi film. Narayan Singh slept in the chowkidar's quarters while Nathu prepared to sleep on the floor of the suite. I insisted he put his sleeping bag on the other half of the commodious bed. Rajuli meanwhile weathered a cold and stormy night outside. After ringing the bell dangling from a deodar branch to announce our arrival at the pass we walked along the valley of the Neel Ganga, a delightful corridor of conifer that looked on to the glowing green buggials which rose above the dark layers of dense oak and bamboo jungle. On the trail to Wan we were passed by a party of agitated villagers all wearing the traditional garb of brown blanket pinned across the chest. A thief posing as a herb contractor had dug out a villager's savings from a hiding place in the house where he had stayed for the night. Had we seen any suspicious characters on the trail? We hadn't and it seemed unlikely that the thief would have chosen to travel by the main bridle path. There was a short-cut to Bedni Buggial from the Loha Jung pass but we preferred to take the longer route via Wan in order to see Latu's ancient temple.

I was not disappointed. The forest bungalow where we stayed is a mile above the village and situated right next to the huge lone cedar under which Latu has his eerie ramshackle shrine. This deodar is said to have been the tallest tree in the whole of the Kumaon division until its top was snapped off by lightning early in the twentieth century. Even now Latu's tree is enormous, each bough branching out over the temple equivalent to a full-grown tree and the trunk measuring some thirty feet when I surreptitiously ran a nylon climbing rope around it.

The bungalow chowkidar effectively supervised the welfare of the unpredictable godling and in Par Singh I found the very last of the old breed of faithful retainers. The bungalow was dilapidated but not without charm. Alongside a new government tourist bungalow had been built in a style that entirely lacked the serene lines of the older building. The siting of the British bungalows as well as the quality of workmanship that went into their building make these a bonus to the trekker who values aesthetic architecture. The village of Wan was a collection-centre for forest produce and medicinal herbs were being dried on the roofs along with mushrooms for commercial use. In the evening we attended a jagran ceremony to call up the spirits for oracular purposes where all the men seemed to be far gone on daru and staggered around unable to get their drumming act together.

The climax of the relaxed evening was a loud-mouthed villager who appeared doing the goosestep. Next he performed an exaggerated '*Heil Hitler*' and then broke into pidgin German. He had been made a major in the Indian National Army after his capture by the Germans in Europe, preferring promotion to prisoner-of-war status. With such enterprising military adventurers on its doorstep, Rup Kund hardly had need of irregular troops from outside.

FOURTEEN

Mirror of the Huntress

Our information was that so far this season no visitor had been able to get to Rup Kund because of the snow. According to the chowkidar, of a dozen visitors who went to Bedni only one made it to the lake. This accorded well with the twelve-yearly cycle of the Bari Nanda Jat though like any other Himalayan expedition its successful outcome depended on the weather.

Sometimes the procession could not get beyond Patar Nachauni because of the hostile conditions. Presumably this journey in honour of Nanda Devi qualifies as the most arduous pilgrimage in the history of religion especially when the participants are not expected to wear shoes on the higher sections. For some three days they toil over harsh slopes of scree, across a steep snow field, and then a glacier confused by a sea of boulders; all this performed between 12,000 and 16,000 ft.

As there was little chance of our crossing Jyuri Gali and exiting down the Nandakini valley we had to leave our supplies in Wan and return by the same route. I had in my possession a bank draft for Rs 10,000 which belonged to another expedition and was in two minds about where to leave it. It seemed pointless to take it to Rup Kund so I left it with the other luggage in the safekeeping of Par Singh.

The next day we heard Rajuli's bells toiling up to the bungalow where

Par Singh had very kindly dug up some fresh potatoes for us from his field. Narayan Singh had loaded a bundle of firewood on top of the luggage and we set off round the hill where the barley fields were still green at 8,000 ft. in July. The path dropped steeply through the glossy foliage of kharchu (the high altitude oak whose leaf resembles holly) to cross the clear stream of the Pila (Yellow) Ganga. Then we strove to get up the muddy trail to Bedni as quickly as possible to avoid the jhonks (leeches) which lay in wait during the rainy season. They only operate in the conifer band and once we hit the bamboo and birch level we were safe from their depredations. But the lower jungle was lush and leafy and the bridle-path extremely muddy from the passage of buffaloes. We squelched a way through by leaping nimbly from side to side, never daring to halt lest the blood-curdling leeches got a chance to attach themselves to our boots. At last the fronds of ringal (hill bamboo) bent gracefully over our path and we passed from the last of the trees to emerge on to the green and glorious meadows.

It is impossible to describe the happiness that enfolds from the roll of Bedni's pastures. Part of it is due to the thrill of beholding great herds of horses running wild with their manes flying and their hooves thundering as they career before the spectacular nearness of Trisul and Nanda Ghunti, whose peaks provide a vast panoramic close-up of mountain delight. The contrast from dark green where the trees end to the sudden rapturous onset of emerald grassy slopes adds to the sense of delirious well-being.

It is here the bliss-giving Nanda arrives in her palanquin and all along the route of her royal progression we had passed her resting places (it would never do for the hem of royalty to touch the ground). From the villages along the way the local devtas are hoisted on to the backs of their devotees, each palanquin joining the ranks according to strict protocol in theory, but in practice only after a lot of heated argument. It is a feature of hierarchic Hinduism that though it seems to be immutably fossilised in its usage, thanks to an inherent flexibility the pecking order is forever changing. The terrible tragedy caused by stampedes at those other twelve-yearly gatherings the Kumbh melas, are invariably the result of fights over precedence in the bathing ritual between different akharas of sadhus. Similarly the Nanda Devi yatra is marked by civilized proceedings when it sets out from Nauti to cover the Pindar tracts accustomed to the manners brought in by the motor road. Once past Nanda Kesri however the rough and tumble of crude interior politics begins. Quarrels break out over precedence and abuse flies freely but to illustrate how accommodating Hinduism can be in reconciling these violent differences over the naked ambition to be seen first, the royal cavalcade manages to continue.

To add to the leaping sense of joy triggered by the exhilarating spread of Bedni is the convenience of two log huts built for visitors by the forest department to overlook the snow peaks. In the evening the horses galloped past whinnying to their fold while their herders converged on the huts to hear the latest news. Soon the log fire leaped into flame and the pressure cooker was balanced on the first of its coals. Nathu haggled about the price of milk and mutton then shared cigarettes to prove he was a man of means. (Most shepherds could only afford to smoke bidis). Our equipment was next fingered by the shepherds and suitable wonder expressed at the invincible claims of our sleeping bags which alas did not live up to their rating.

Narayan Singh moved to the other hut to sleep and left Nathu and I to the welcome embers over which some of our wet clothes were strung to dry. During the night a love-sick buffalo kept moaning softly outside the hut and when the morning came it stuck its head round the door to look forlornly in at what (when visitors were absent) was clearly its favoured resting place. Narayan Singh had begun the day by unceremoniously kicking the door open. Instead of shouting disapprobation I leapt out of bed to confirm the astounding vision of Trisul I had glimpsed, framed huge in the doorway. To add to the pleasure a couple of shaggy sheepdogs frisked up and gambolled in front of the hut. After we had made offerings at the tiny Nanda Devi shrine Rajuli led the way from Bedni across the most marvellous expanse of greenery. Nothing comes near to Bedni in the rains for the mood of pastoral plenitude. The sanctuary meadows inspire because they represent the prize after a difficult approach. Surrounding Nanda Devi they share her mystique and the presence of wild blue sheep adds to the uniqueness of the memory. Bedni is a more democratic experience, easier of access (if one can outrun the jhonks). The magnificence of its carpet of flowers in the monsoon has to be seen and smelt to be believed. It is an orgiastic occasion beyond the normal reckoning of any pen. The Goddess' definitive grace lies in the riffle of breeze over these vibrating pastures and the goodness and mercy of the Psalmist follows one's gaze over these voluptuous alps that lift up the heart.

Jim Corbett seems to be talking about Bedni in his big-game hunting story describing the strange behaviour of his porter Bala Singh. The porters had sung around their camp fire cheered by the beauty of their surroundings but by morning had turned gloomy and uncommunicative. Bala Singh was ill having swallowed, as Corbett puts it, the demon of Trisul. As outsiders his porters would not be aware of the Devi's restrictions. Had they known the Goddess frowned on singing they would never have dared open their mouths unless, drunk with the arrogance of being attached to scoffing sahibs, they had deliberately flouted local beliefs. But Naini Tal is too far from Wan for its residents to have heard of the vengefulness of Latu. Otherwise Corbett could have narrowed down the identity of the spirit Bala Singh had swallowed. It was more likely the porter had been possessed by Latu for this was just the kind of trick this impish spirit was always up to. Instead of removing the possessed porter to Wan for a local cure to be effected (by the sacrifice of an animal), Corbett took Bala Singh all the way back to Naini Tal. There his depression grew worse and the affected porter had to be discharged from service. Bala Singh thereafter returned to his village and died. According to Corbett this was the only way the demon could get out of his stomach and return to inhabit Mount Trisul. Had he been more alive to local remedies, Bala Singh might have been saved by a little ritual that involved an apology to the Devi for breaking her rules and some blood shed in the name of her more primitive herald. Magic, not medicine, was the cure for the strange happenings at Bedni.

As we passed the Dancing Rocks the spell of the Goddess seemed quite real in changing the destiny of expeditions. *Chaya maya* is how the hillman describes the curious magic effected by the gods and this combination of the spooky and illusory is the expression an American anthropologist William Sax used for the title of his doctorate thesis on Nanda Devi's pilgrimage. As he lived in Mussoorie while doing his research I was able to meet Sax. Beneath the academic surface one sensed something rather unusual in an American scholar, a sympathetic understanding of hill religion. This made him stand out in a place like Mussoorie which remains a prominent name on the map of evangelistic fervour. It contains the Landour language school which taught foreign missionaries the languages required for converting the North Indian from the polytheism of his Hindu heritage to the multiplicity of Christian sects that clamoured for his custom.

You can just see the main peak of Nanda Devi from Mussoorie but you have to stand outside the Scots cemetery in Landour to fix the angle, and it has to be in winter to reduce the haze. Two temples in line with the peak are dedicated to local goddesses. The first is at Sarkhanda Devi along the high ridge towards Tehri, a peak that is probably the highest in the whole Mussoorie range (which runs all the way to the border of Nepal as the first great rise of the Himalayas after the low chain of the Shivaliks). Above Tehri and commanding both the Alakananda and Bhagirathi rivers as they conjoin to become the Ganga at Deoprayag is the lofty temple of Chandrabhadni. Both these temples have tantric associations and like those of the Nanda Devi cult involve the use of the Sriyantra as an object of worship.

The Sriyantra is an abstract design involving interpenetrating triangles that is often worshipped in lieu of an image in a temple dedicated to the Mother Goddess. According to tantric beliefs the raw energy inherent in the power of the maternal shakti should not be worshipped indoors for its explosive strength would surely shatter the roof of any structure. For this reason the Sriyantra is often buried to diminish its destructive potential and at the climax of the Bari Nanda Jat is said to be one such Sriyantra buried at Hom Kund far below the Ronti Saddle, a spot marked by the flicker of mica from the huge black stone mentioned by Atkinson.

The path got steeper as we continued and the glory of marching through swathes of wild flowers dimmed when the sun was overtaken by blustery clouds. We passed horses chomping on the long grass and looked down to the sweep of Bedni now dotted by molecular herds of white and black sheep. Ahead Rajuli's bells began to slow and then they stopped. The path was blocked by a snowdrift. After a lot of tugging the horse managed to clamber through but round the next bend there was deep snow blocking the way and Narayan Singh had to admit defeat. We were within striking distance of Kailu Binayak and Nathu insisted that since the pony-man claimed the full amount, he should lug up the firewood to where the Ganesh image guarded the threshold of the mystery lake.

As Rajuli's bells faded away into the mist we offered wild flowers to the lovely image of Binayak and began the level plod to the barren camp site of Balpa ki Sulera. The cave at Bhogabasa had been constructed by Swami Pranavananda and must rate as the most chilling dormitory I have ever clapped eyes on in the Himalayas. At least in the tent we would be protected from the gusting rain. Nathu got the tent up and we shuttled between the two sites, arranging our kitchen back in the cave. That evening it took Nathu more than an hour to get a fire going. Bhogabasa seemed to be oxygenless to add to its other miseries.

The morning saw more relentless rain but by ten there was a break and we could glimpse Nanda Ghunti through the strands of cloud that sped away in the warming draughts of wind. Quickly we lined the goat pens with our wet clothes and prepared to strike camp for the last march up to the lake. We couldn't see Rup Kund, only the black jagged ridge whose lowest point we guessed was Jyuri Gali.

The ridge ran down to Chanoniaghat where we had been told the pilgrims returning from Hom Kund entered the narrow rapids of the Nandakini. But all this was guesswork and even speculation went blank when after fifteen minutes the clouds blotted out the way ahead. From warm sun we switched to cold driving rain. Luckily we hadn't taken down the tent and could hastily stuff our clothes back inside. Now as the weather grew nastier the plan was to ferry a load up to the lake (as far as we could go in the mist) so that tomorrow we could move up quickly and find a camp site without the burden of supplies on our back.

We set off over the snow slopes diagonally and slogged away towards what we assumed was the goal. Light snow sleeted down and we slipped over the polished scree finding the wind colder all the time. Below us the valley of the Rup Ganga dropped away from a sudden shelf that made one gulp at its abruptness, especially when Nathu after the incorrigible manner of all Lata porters insisted on beelining up narrow gullies which swept down to open in awesome chutes to the very edge of this abyss.

By one o' clock we were in the middle of a whiteout and had to cache the load in a prominent place marked by a cairn. Then we slithered back down to our sopping tent and spent a miserable afternoon trying to blow up the wet firewood in the cave kitchen. The night was even more miserable and without a flysheet the tent was beginning to ship water. The wind made it billow and several times Nathu had to go out and check the anchored ropes. Owing to the rocky terrain there was no question of hammering in pegs. Oppressed by the never-ending night I had to stick my head out of the tent porthole to suck in some oxygen. Then I remembered the medicine a friend had given me for such mental agitation. The homeopathic remedy Kali Phos did the trick and I found I could sleep without fear of suffocation.

In the morning the rain still slanted down and the prospects never seemed gloomier. It was impossible to see the way in the mist and now we were stranded with lean supplies at camp while all the goodies lay out of reach up the hill. I sped along to the cave in my bare feet, skidding on the ice, as it was too much effort to fit on our soggy socks and boots. Nathu was again heroically engaged in blowing up a fire from two soaked branches and after an hour of dedicated puffing managed to provide a breakfast of lukewarm, lumpy porridge. The day dragged on as we stamped around trying to keep warm, yawning from the boredom and too disgusted to go back to the tent where the water now had begun to form pools. The wind whistled through every crevice in the cave to add to Nathu's difficulties as he hunched over the chula. I vowed I would never camp again at Bhogabhasa and made up my mind that tomorrow we would retrieve our load and retreat to Bedni. Clearly we were not welcome.

That night our sleeping bags had to be fitted inside plastic covers to keep out the water slurping at the bottom of the tent. While making tea on the stove Nathu had knocked over the hot water and this gave rise to the day's only laugh. Nothing had changed in the morning and all we knew was that tonight come what may we would be back in Bedni. But first we had to retrieve the load. We set out through the misty sleet and followed yesterday's angle. By ten we had located the kit bag and visibility had improved up to 200 yards. Nathu thought we could explore a little ahead and if the mist clamped down we would return. The slope steepened and rocky outcrops now had to be negotiated. Still there was no landmark to fix our aim and we continued towards what we had assumed was Jyuri Gali.

A whoop from Nathu signalled eureka. He had found the lake. There was no sign of him as I struggled up a band of wet rock. Then I looked down into a magical bowl of white snow surrounded by red cliffs. The impact of Rup Kund was stunning in spite of the poor visibility. It was as though we were wearing subtle glasses and were privileged to see an angle on the lake hidden from most. The jade purity of the ice covering the small tarn made it seem like a precious stone set in the clasp of the surrounding snow and capped by an impressive ring of red rock. No one had led me to expect the beauty of this perpendicular wall of rock as it encircled the end of the lake in a dramatic setting. It was as though the virgin snow slopes were in the embrace of a red granite chastity belt. The mystique of the pre-sexual aspect of the Goddess put one in mind of the worship of the virgin Kumari in Kathmandu. Her juvenile innocence with the potential of a bloodthirsty Kali seems to have some crossed lines with the Nanda Devi cult. Uttarakhand has had close cultural ties with Nepal and Kedarnath in theological terms can be viewed as a subsidiary of the Pashupatinath temple.

The wallowing in the sacrificial blood of animals suggests that the attainment of womanhood by the Kumari is a subject more for the student of female psychology than the theologian.

Now Nathu clambered down to the unsure edge of the immaculate pool but snow concealed the overlapping of rock and ice and it would have been dangerous (and sacrilegious) to have tested the surface. Nathu yodelled to test the impressive rebound off the cliffs and I had to remind him that the same sanctuary rules applied here. Before I could suggest it, Nathu had set off up the steep climb to the Gali towards the point we could see from our camp. He flailed a way through deep snow and then got stuck in a drift that came up to his armpits. It was now one o'clock and as the weather was still holding there was no reason to restrain Nathu's enthusiasm. I followed in his trail and looking back half-way to take a photograph allowed the cover of the camera to slip from my frozen fingers and slide away down the slope. It was a re-enactment of the Rup Kund disaster. The black cover ended up at the lake's edge and Nathu recovered it on the way down.

Now battling his way up the 'alley of death' he soon crested the slope and yelled his success. But the wind was so strong his voice was swept away. I panted up alongside and took his photograph holding a red flag with Sathya Sai Baba's logo on it. Nathu had discovered a stick on the ridge and tied the flag on as a marker for other expeditions. We were the first to reach Rup Kund that season.

In order to take a shot of the lake straight under our eyrie I had to ask Nathu to clasp my knees. The wind buffeted so hard that I felt unsafe. But the mystery of Rup Kund had been answered in the blowing of the wind. It was with satisfaction we turned to slide back down off the snow on to the black rock slopes. We were immune to the rain as we skidded and slithered back to camp, whooping with pleasure at this unexpected bonus. Our tentative beginnings groping in bad weather had turned to a timely seizing of the spoils. To Nathu went the credit for route finding and it was his opportunism that gave us the ridge.

We wore sheets of bubble plastic that doubled up as raincoats when not used for mats on hard ground. Now to speed our escape I used mine as a ski-seat, sitting on the plastic to skid over the frozen snow. The danger was to know when to stop for the snow was broken in patches by sharp rock. Nathu with the load proceeded more cautiously. Where the sweep of snow thinned and the scree slopes began I shot past him on my ski-seat having failed to judge the mixed terrain. I went hurtling from a smooth ride on the white cover to a most violent upending on the black. Nathu collapsed in helpless laughter at the undignified end to my descent but I had the malicious pleasure of watching him take five minutes to get off the same rock shelf that I had cleared in a fifth of a second.

It was still pouring around the camp site and Nathu told me to collect essentials and set off down the path to Bedni. He would pack the rest and catch up with me by a shortcut. I set off running and was hammered so hard by the rain that it felt like being coshed over the head with a wet towel.

As the green meadows hove into sight below the jade presence of Ganesh I saw from the corner of my eye Nathu descending like an express train, straight down the spine of the ridge. I preferred the zig-zag of the path as it helped me brake. The brilliant clutch of flowers at one's feet was the reassuring sign that we were beyond the misery zone and back with a chance of survival. We ran to the huts sodden and frozen to our innermost cores. A young shepherd boy waved a greeting and I bet him ten rupees he couldn't get a fire going within five minutes. Indra Singh rushed off to his camp downhill and sped back with some glowing coals. Within minutes another shepherd trotted in with an armful of rhododendron wood and my bet was gloriously lost as the flames licked out to caress our stricken bodies. We ripped off several days' wet clothes to revel in the glory of Agni, lord of the leaping fire.

FIFTEEN

Beyond the Power of Thought

After the successful outcome of the 1983 encounter with Rup Kund I decided to go back in the monsoon of 1984 with extra porters and try and cross Jyuri Gali to Hom Kund. On our earlier trip (after the life-saving bonfire of Bedni) Nathu and I had decided to return to Lata via the Kuari Pass. This voyage of several days passed through some of the most magnificent forest glades as well as lead over the crest of the Great Himalayan range. The trail ran all the way from Tapovan (near Lata) to Gwaldam and had been given the ultimate trekking accolade under the name of 'Curzon Trail'. The Viceroy, himself no mean arbiter of mountain scenery, believed this to be the most desirable walk in Garhwal. He had entered half-way along at Ghat but his party never made it to Kuari. They were attacked by wild bees and the tour was called off.

At Wan, Par Singh, the old chowkidar, returned my luggage (with the bank draft untouched) and suggested that to make the going easier, we should take along his son Gopal. Gopal turned out to be an immediately likeable young man, well informed on local matters, so when Nathu did not veto the lightening of his load, I took Gopal as guide.

The walk from Wan to Sutol is without doubt one of the most beautiful stretches of mature jungle I have ever passed through. We climbed from the lone deodar of Latu into the gaunt elegance of crowded ranks of cypress. According to Par Singh the next deodar bole you met on the trail after Latu lay some eighteen miles away. The significance lay in the fact that the Himalayan cedar is a gregarious species. It prefers to be amongst its own. Latu's solitary tree in the middle of a cypress colony was a sylvan oddity, as weird as its resident tree spirit.

There is never any perfect season for walking in high Garhwal but each one is exceptional. The most convenient is post-monsoon when the days are clear and the mountains shine in friendly companionship. But the flowers then are shrunken and their special brand of intoxicated exuberance, and the growl of virile torrents, are absent. No matter how miserable the monsoons in their passage, the magic they give rise to is undeniable. The glowing greens amidst the cold swirling greys have a special appeal known only to the minority who tread against the accepted trekking fashions. In the forest, particularly, the colours when the sun does manage to break through are unforgettable. The vast range of nature's green palette is stunning and the eye takes in two dozen shades as it covers 200 yards of slope.

On the crest of the Curzon Trail around Kanol is the loveliest of clearings at Kukhina Dhar. From Kanol you plunge steeply through the thick undergrowth to hit Sutol on the Nandakini and the brilliance of the meadows left behind with their emerald sheen now contrasts with the sombre chrome of the silent forest where gnarled trunks groan against the wind, and a thick carpet of viridian creepers and vines spills everywhere in a riotous tangle of affirmative sap. No other season comes near to the Gerard Manley Hopkins effect—'the dearest freshness deep down things.'

Sutol was deserted and lacked even a tea shop. Perhaps the somnolence of its setting or the presence of two charasiyas sitting stoned in a veranda decided Nathu and us to change our plans. Since the expedition had been successful, why spin out another three days toiling up and over Kuari to Lata when by tomorrow night we could be there by bus if we headed down the Nandakini valley from Sutol? The temptation proved too great and we paid off Gopal. But we insisted he stay the night in Sutol and return to Wan the next day as there were fresh bear and leopard tracks on the path and it was unwise for anyone to be abroad in these jungles away from daylight.

Nathu and I found a PWD bungalow at Pheri on the descent to Nanda Prayag. We had to wait while the chowkidar freed himself from a meeting of village elders. The democracy of a panchayat is a vigorous sight and amidst hurled abuses we could detect obscene signs meant to clinch forceful arguments. The chowkidar agreed to let us spend the night but in view of his odd behaviour we deemed it advisable to lock the door. In the enclosed valleys with their tight matrimonial arrangements madness is not unknown and in this example of local nuttiness the chowkidar imagined himself to be a PWD foreman forever noting things down in an imaginary notebook with an impressive flourish of a non-existent pen.

We were relieved to make a quick getaway in the morning and hurried down through the line of villages to re-enter the heat belt as the path evened to follow the rushing river. At the Chefana bridge (known as Silli Buggair— 'the shady rock') before the coming of the bus we had fresh pakoras and tea in the metal beaker so typical of hill paravs. The shopkeeper advised us to take the less-used track along the far bank of the river as it did not undulate. It turned out to be a narrow and delightful path that passed for much of the way through head-high stands of marijuana. They were so tall that one did not realise what the plant was until the sweet milk from the broken stems began to assault the senses, followed by our giggly sense of well-being.

We arrived at Ghat too late to catch the bus that would have got us to Joshimath by nightfall. While Nathu ate I climbed up to the village primary school to try and reach the village of Krur where the Devi was said to be worshipped according to traditional rites. The school-master welcomed my enquiries but advised against trying to reach Krur which lay another three miles away. Spread out below the school Ghat appeared as a very dramatic hill parav with the river curving away sharply past a tiny bazaar. The beauty of its setting was about to be destroyed as two new roads slashed their way across the valley and an ugly red girder bridge was being lugged into position to overshadow the elegant old suspension jhula.

That night we stayed in the tourist bungalow at Nanda Prayag and next morning while waiting for a bus to Joshimath we found a truck going all the way to Lata. Perched on the roof was S.S. along with a group of Lata HAPs returning from an expedition to Kashmir. I decided to go to Lata to find out the latest from Bal Singh on the closure of the sanctuary. Surprisingly the locals had accepted the situation without a fight. I climbed up to have darshan of Nanda Bhagawati and called on Rattan Singh to produce his great hooked key to open the temple doors. Inside the Devi's silver mask gave off the appearance of an Easter Island monolith. A red sari completed the royal regalia and chunky silver jewellery worn through the nose after the custom of hill women accompanied the representation of the Goddess. There was a restrained dignity in the appearance of Bhagawati, almost a Victorian figure in her plump dress of marital red. If the slit eyes in the silver mask spoke of tribal totems there could be no doubt about the queenly arrangement of the Devi by her Rajput pujari.

A year later but earlier in July I summoned Nathu to Joshimath with two other young porters to meet me in Yashu's 'Nanda Devi' hotel. One of them was Gopal, the cook I had met at Nanda Devi base, and the other a novice whose lowly status qualified him for the name of dogsbody (DB). I left it to Nathu whether they wanted to lug up loads over the Kuari Pass (a two-day undertaking from Joshimath) or catch the bus to Ghat and work our way via Kanol to Wan. As expected everyone opted for the bus.

The rooms in Yashu's hotel were cubicles partitioned by plywood and much to the delight of the junior porters but to the embarrassment of Nathu (who was supposed to keep them under control) from the room next door came groans and sighs that could only signify 'couple at it.' In the confines of the flimsy surrounding every squeak from the other side of the partition was followed by a giggle from the porters and every groan of passion with a choked guffaw. When I looked into the visitors' book next morning I noted that our neighbours in the throes of passionate love-making were a British couple from Lyme Regis. Yashu concluded they were honeymooning.

In the morning there was a panic when no kerosene was available. So serious was the shortage that not even Yashu could produce any in Joshimath. Nathu waved away this crisis certain that some would be available in Ghat. Knowing Nathu's ability for wishful thinking I was not in the least surprised to find Ghat also completely out of kerosene. Nathu now stoutly maintained that Wan would be well stocked, an absurd presumption but we were too far on our way to be bothered by niggling details like kerosene.

As we moved along the river bank opposite the marijuana plantation there was a shout from a house above the path followed by the sight of Govind in the warm embrace of a local farmer who identified him as a close relation. This led to offers of a mule to carry our supplies which we refused and a plastic jerry-can of daru which we accepted. Our plan had been to push on to Sitol but the constant sampling of our liquid acquisition got us only as far as the bridge at Silli Buggair. The porters decided to sleep off the effects of our windfall inside the shop on the stone slabs that acted during the day as benches. I chose to put up the tent in a terraced field near the Nandakini and allowed her swollen roar to lull me asleep—not difficult in view of the empty jerry-can.

The morning was crisp and clear as we crossed the Nandakini to follow its white tumbling course to Sitol, a village tucked below the great sweep of mountain that rises to Bedni. Nandakini signifies the daughter of Nanda and the point where she meets the Alakananda at Nanda Prayag is said to be the site of Kalidas's great Sanskrit drama *Sakuntala*. Here in romantic circumstances a king out hunting was smitten by the beauty of a hermit's daughter. The river undoubtedly is one of the most lovely affluents of the Ganga, seeming to laugh throughout her course and resembling a youthful goddess figure forever tumbling in innocent delight with none of the sinister threat that belongs to her close neighbours the Patal and Birehi Gangas. It is true that at Nanda Prayag the angry emerging torrent has washed away the ancient temple of Nand erected in honour of Lord Krishna's father. Also it was the lurid inflow of the Nandakini that assured Sir Edmund Hillary's jetboat expedition up the Ganga would proceed no further, stalled by a raging waterfall across the Alakananda. We would now not cross the Nandakini again till we reached her source near Hom Kund.

Sitol was further than we had bargained for and in the sticky heat of the hot valley we were tempted to stay the night when we arrived early in the afternoon. The bungalow was one of the most beautifully sited I had seen in Garhwal, surrounded by thickly wooded mountains ablaze with a dozen different varieties of conifer. The river bored a way out of a steep grassy gorge and swept round in a magnificent tumult of glacial grey. Nearby the seasonal bridge linking Sutol had been swept away and until the level of the river dropped no further logs would be lashed to make a temporary crossing.

We decided to move on and get the steep ascent to Kanol behind us. The climb was sheer and sticky, made worse by the drenching rain that now swept in to accompany us. On the way we had to ford the Mane Ganga, a small swirling stream of brilliantly clear water. All around the jungle exploded in an abandon of growth and the slanting rain only added to the celebration of berserk greenery. Velvet moss dripping with moisture underfoot and parched lichen dangling from branches above were passed on the plodding grind uphill and in between were elegant flowering trees that seemed to cascade in the exuberance of the season.

So loud was the sylvan chorus of these enchanted slopes that it completely erased the misery of our muddy slog to the ridge. The narrow path zig-zagged mercilessly up as the rain beat down but as we neared the bungalow overlooking the four corners of the Nandakini basin the clouds cleared and a benevolent sun arrived to begin to dry out our soaking gear.

The porters met a village school teacher who had once taught them in Lata and that helped break the ice with the bungalow chowkidar. Though they were always eager to make a little money on the side by opening their bungalows to non-departmental arrivals, by the very nature of their calling in far-out places most chowkidars conscious of their official status felt they were persons of consequence invested with the testing responsibility of maintaining the dignity of government. When they stooped to the corrupt sidelining of procedures and allowed us to stay in official accommodation without the prescribed permit, it brought out a compensatory display of disdain. While they would open a room to infringe on major laws they would refuse to carry water lest this minor act be interpreted as conniving at our illegal entry. It was very important to maintain the dignity of a sahib on these occasions and let the porters do all the talking. If there was one thing any self-respecting chowkidar could not abide it was egalitarian behaviour. A dishonest sahib was preferable any day to an honourable upstart.

The onward stage to Wan over Kukhina Dhar was done in a relaxed manner and we all lay down to rest on the magic meadows when the sun chose to light up their face. Then down we passed softly through the mighty stand of cypress to Latu's great branching deodar. Along with Gopal we met his brother who when he first saw us dodged behind the bungalow. We learned he had been the wildlife guard on duty at Renni who had allowed the foreign mountaineering expeditions to take in pack goats to the sanctuary despite the ban on their entry. The young man had been disciplined by his superiors and during his summons had heard of my writing on the subject. Now he concluded that I had come to harass him since those amenable to accepting bribes assume they are the proper prey of blackmailers. He emerged only when Nathu (who had met him in Renni) assured him that my interest in the sanctuary was purely devotional.

As Gopal would prove useful as a local guide to our party I decided to take him along to help with route finding. He knew all the landmarks and would be able to identify pilgrim associations. This was borne out when we arrived at Kailu Binayak and offered flowers to Ganesh. Clutching the image to his chest, Gopal staggered round in three circuits of the cairn. This, I was told was the local way of honouring the god who removes obstacles.

Before leaving Wan, we had sent Gopal to Mandoli to fetch some kerosene. He had only been able to get half of the kerosene we had asked for but it would see us through. No one warmed to the subject of kerosene and of all porter loads it was the most detested. No matter how well it was packed it would leak. A common scourge in hill eating places is to find your food taste of paraffin, the flavour having seeped through in transit from the plains.

We had left Wan late and ambled along the ridge to drop down to the Pila Ganga. We strode smartly up the incline to beat the jhonks and then slowed again in the muddy bamboo thicknesses above. By four o'clock we pushed aside the last of the sombre spruce and stepped out on to the idyllic greensward. I saw Govind's face crease with delight at his first encounter with the much talked-about Bedni pastures. The men from Lata had all heard about Bedni, for shepherds meeting in their camps automatically swap stories of where the grass grows greenest. Govind was not disappointed. The horses were there while the foals cavorted in the afternoon swirl of mist, their tails flying, and the carpet of flowers was incredibly bewitching in a bold pink swathe of bistort spiked by clumps of brilliant yellow and blood-red potentilla.

As we passed the small Bhagawati temple—the porters doing their namaskar to the Devi—we saw carved on the door of the log hut in large new letters the words: 'Love is energy beyond the power of thought.' Delighted and intrigued by this banner of welcome whose insight seemed exactly to capture the mood of these deliriously dancing meadows we were soon enlightened by our friend of a year ago, Indra Singh, faithful stoker of our survival fires. It was hard to recognize him. In the space of a year he had grown from an awkward adolescent into a confident man. When he described how the lines had come to be written and gave details of the young English couple who had devoted two or three days to their carving, they matched exactly the pair who had been so much in love in the room next door to us in Yashu's hotel. To clinch the honeymooning aspect of their labour the couple had astonished the shepherds by spending all their time indoors passionately entwined, emerging only to carve into the planks the findings of their impassioned research. Love in a hut—what better mantra could hint at the secret to be found in the mystical fulfilment of maddening desire?

That night Trisul glowed by moonlight through the small triangular window of the hut and we kept our fingers crossed for a clear morning. At 5 a.m. Govind got up and described the weather as *'mamuli'* which was the excuse we all needed to turn over and go back to sleep. When I awoke later, prodded by Govind to accept his sweet tea, I felt cold and ill. Yesterday's climb had been another encounter with miserable relentless rain and its gloom seemed to have penetrated my bones. Nathu agreed I should stay in bed until the shivers passed. In the meantime we decided the porters would go back to the forest and collect fallen wood for the next camp at Bhogabasa.

I woke again at noon feeling much better, to find the porters sitting round the fire playing cards. They hadn't collected any firewood but proposed to do so in the evening. After a meal of rice and dal I felt better so I strolled over to the Devi temple for a walk. The image here though small is exquisitely carved and shows the Goddess in her Durga form slaying the demonic buffalo. As I put my face down towards the niche where the Goddess was installed I was aware of a pair of bright eyes level with mine. Appearing alongside the image was an adventurous nid, the tailless rat (known as the mouse-hare). There it sat nibbling, and looking straight at me and even posed while I took a photograph.

This fearless state of a realm unvisited by human feet reminded one of just how much divine concerns have been trampled underfoot in the grasp for material comforts. Up here was true freedom. The worldly search ended in the dissatisfaction of stored-up funds the body could not enjoy. The result of a lifetime's toil was only to make your bank manager happy. Here on these transcendentally lovely fields of the Goddess one was aware of the limitations of the intellect to embrace the truth of the moment. Only love could penetrate the essential spontaneity of the witnessing self. And one agreed with Willi Unsoeld's assessment that death is not too high a price for a life lived fully.

Exposed as we were to the physical constraints of altitude and the crude attempt at comfort the hut provided we ought by the logic of modern life to have been miserably served by our situation. But quite the opposite mood prevailed. We exulted in the exposure to the elements and rejoiced in the inconvenience of a smoking fire that made one weep and cough. To extract the magic virtue from sizzling logs, and respond to the deep glow of ember, it was in the gazing that one realised it is more important to ask questions of the soul than wrest answers from the mind.

Alongside the tiny structure dedicated to Latu a young holy man had erected a temporary shelter to spend his summer on the buggial. Unlike most sadhus who lapse into the conventional borrowed wisdom of their calling, reciting the parrot-like formulae of Sanskritic truths their dull existence could never hope to comprehend, this young man had a healthy physical respect for his sadhana. He did not pretend to be beyond the pleasures of the Himalayas and discussed enthusiastically the various high points he had visited. He had been over the top beyond Rup Kund and strongly advised us against camping at Bhogabasa. If we cooked enough rotis and stuffed them with dal before we left Bedni they would see us up and over Jyuri Gali and we could then camp on the meadows above the Silli Samuder glacier at a lower altitude the same day. This man obviously knew the terrain and had learned the hard way. When he confirmed that Bhogabasa was the worst place to camp because the firewood did not burn, I accepted his presence as a sign from the Goddess. I returned to the hut where the porters had stacked up the firewood for tomorrow's haul and told them to burn it now in making a big pile of rotis for the new plan. Govind got down to the job with a will but it took him till bedtime before the last of the great stack of stuffed rotis was made.

The sadhu's plan worked splendidly and putting the meadows behind us we passed the Dancing Rocks by eight next morning. Cheered by the absence of rain we made it to Bhogabasa by eleven. We got the stove going in the familiar rocky camp site of Balpa ki Sulera and soon heated the rotis to be followed by some hot Maggi cube soup. The porters were a bit chary of foreign-sounding food lest the contents included beef with the resultant threat to caste. But the cubes were vegetarian and their salty flavour was exactly what the body cried out for.

As we cleared the last of the scarred scree slopes to pass the frozen Kund the weather turned blustery and it was a major disappointment to find that the magical hollow that a year before had seemed so dramatic in its contrasts of jade, ermine and rust red now seemed just a bland merging of muddy tones. The snow had drifted over most of the lake leaving a damp green patch in the middle while the background rocks rose undistinguished amidst the murky swirl of a brewing storm. There was no cause to linger for puja as we had hoped. Govind in these matters was much more sensitive than Nathu while Gopal quietly bringing up the rear also impressed with his readiness to show devotion.

Nathu made short shrift of the Jyuri Gali slope and urged everyone to cross before the gusts of flurrying snow worsened. I was the last to get up to the ridge and wanted to take a parting photograph of the lake but Govind appeared out of the mist and confirmed that the porters had all descended the other side. This turned out not to be true for I found them sitting snugly under some rocks having a smoke while they waited for me. Nathu was grinning. He had cleverly sent someone else to interrupt my photographic session knowing that I wouldn't have listened to him.

Reunited, the party then began the steep rocky descent towards the final goal of Hom Kund. The valley was clouded over but the lower we stumbled the more the visibility improved. Then in a brilliant patch of sunlight the view opened up as though we were in an aeroplane piercing the veil of clouds on a descent to the airfield. Ahead through an extraordinary triangular gap our gaze was led to focus on a big black rock that marked the union of two tumbling streams of white water. The source of the Nandakini with the great black 'bindu' at its centre was the true Sriyantra at Hom Kund, buried to the outer eye but revealed in a startling moment of awareness.

Sixteen

Silly Season

*T*o find the tantric symbolism so glowing and real made one overlook the agonies of pilgrimage faced by ordinary walkers. During our treks along the lower trails we had met a few veterans of the Bari Nanda Jat and it was interesting to compare their expectations with our own. The villager sees a pilgrimage as a practical opportunity for spiritual investment. Its troubles confer on him the right to ask the gods for a boon. Invariably the spin-off from the difficult yatras of Uttarakhand is thankfulness at having been able to offer a prayer at the doorstep of the gods, where it will be difficult for them to ignore your petition.

Perhaps the bulk of prayers are for family welfare and success in marriage and career. Ascetics are assumed to ask for realization but they too are usually thankful for the lesser bounty of guaranteed meals during their stay at a holy tirtha where merit is gained by feeding them. It is one of the most remarkable features of Garhwali character that despite the subsistence level of the peasantry, never in the twenty centuries of known custom has a holy man ever been denied a meal. For a hungry society to continually share its food means that a force greater than the acquisition of non-edible merit is at work. It is in this simple humanity of the unsophisticated hill villager that the profoundest teachings of true religion are revealed. And as a corollary it is the neglect of institutional religion to share its wealth that has divided modern civilization and made acceptable the bizarre notion that the haves and have-nots exist in a divinely intended conflict.

One of the most beautiful pilgrim moments I have experienced occurred in the most debased of institutional situations. This was in the church of the Holy Sepulchre in Jerusalem, erected on the site of Jesus' crucifixion. So commercialised and sectarian-ridden are the concerns of the conflicting churches that the key of this prime site of Christendom had to be entrusted to a neutral Muslim. As I stood before the altar at Calvary two groups of pilgrims entered simultaneously, one a party of nuns led by a Franciscan friar, and the other of lay composition led by a Greek Orthodox divine.

The two priests jostled and elbowed each other vigorously to try and make sure their own party would get the best vantage point. Disgusted but by now familiar with the brazen antics of churchmen touting pilgrims around the Holy Land, I was surprised to see, as both parties hurried off after the obligatory genuflections, a young nun detach herself from the rear and spontaneously kneel in a true expression of devoutness to her calling. The sheer flowing grace of her submission said everything of her feelings for Christ. Such impulsive behaviour and breach of group discipline might have to be confessed but the nun's surrender to her divine desire restored my faith in the ramshackle credentials of institutional faith. I concluded that if such souls spent their lives in prayer the world could not but be a better place.

I was not over-familiar with organized pilgrimages having been put off by the only one I joined which went around the border abbeys of Scotland. It was led by some English Franciscans and the man in charge was a former army officer who even in the garb of a humble friar continued to bark out his unsolicited staff-college wisdom. While visiting the Uttarakhand shrines, which I did regularly, one was forced to join the queue of eager peasant pilgrims from all over India. At Badrinath the jostle was so severe that old ladies desperate for a glimpse of their god would not hesitate to fight their way past less ardent candidates for darshan. It was an animal urge to prostrate before the divine, the crude physical shoving being overwhelmed by the immediate sense of grace that flowed into the supplicant spreadeagled at the foot of her chosen deity.

At Badrinath I once had the good fortune to be present in front of Lord

Badrinathji when a party of pilgrims arrived from a Marcha village. These tribals on the border around Mana are the winter custodians of the shrine when the deity moves down to Joshimath for the winter. The party I witnessed bore amongst them an oracle possessed by Nanda Devi. Shivering and vacant-eyed he held a dagger between his clenched teeth and uttered yelps as other pilgrims sprinkled him with libations of very holy but exceedingly cold water.

In his Ph.D. thesis on the Bari Nanda Jat published under the title *Mountain Goddess* (1991) William Sax describes the hurly-burly of the Hom Kund yatra which he joined in 1987. As a student he had been fascinated by the Rup Kund mystery and felt blessed that the pilgrimage took place so conveniently for the furtherance of his research. However the reader wonders what Sax really made of his boisterous village companions. The men of Nauti were acceptable with their respect for the niceties of ritual but once the group was swelled by other village deities joining in and the yatra entered the interior areas away from civilizing influences the attitude of the locals became crude and lumpen and their behaviour distinctly loutish.

Friction over precedence soon turned into hostile confrontation and instead of a pilgrim atmosphere Sax records perpetual petty political feuding between the reformers and the 'junglis'. The unpleasantness extended to include the rival oracles of the warring groups and one village medium possessed by the Devi shrieks his opprobrium at a lesser (representing Latu) who dares doubt the wisdom of the Goddess. Fortunately the basic trappings of the tradition were strong enough to withstand the stresses of local pride (and greed) and the dignified presence of symbolic royalty in the figure of a descendant of the Raja of Chandpur (who activated the circuit of the holy mountain only when convinced all the omens were propitious for its start) was sufficient to quell the ugly aggression of the interior party. The problem arose over the modernisation of devotional practice. The climax at Hom Kund had been to let the sacred four-horned ram run into the snows bearing gifts for the Goddess in its saddle bags. It would return with its head miraculously cut off—an emphatic euphemism for having received the sacrificial chop. When I talked to Sax in Nauti (before his participation) he described how in the interior buffalo sacrifice was still practised and involved horrendously gory scenes with rampaging villagers giving hot chase to the stricken beast, baying for its blood in religious frenzy. This is not quite the picture of rural India modern politicians want to project and since the U.P. government had been asked for a grant to subsidise the pilgrimage to Hom Kund it not unnaturally insisted that the cruder aspects of former pilgrimages should be removed. Instead of animal sacrifice a vegetarian substitute would have to be used, and the restriction on the female and low-caste participation lifted.

These Gandhian reforms were welcomed by the enlightened Nautiyals but violently resisted by the high-caste villagers who lived in valleys remote from the changing fashions of the world. India's image abroad (whatever that meant) was not as important to these conservatives as following the time-honoured customs of the Devi. The reformers accused the orthodox of using their defence of ancient ways to guarantee there would be Brahmanical pickings from animal sacrifice. In return the men of Nauti had to face the reckless charge that they only sought government aid in order to embezzle the funds intended for the Goddess.

At the centre of the storm was the one man able to withstand it, the remarkable Dev Ram Nautiyal, a notable devotee of the Devi and indefatigable Secretary of the Raj Jat Organizing Committee. I had first met Dev Ram in his shop in the upper bazaar of Karnaprayag in the monsoon of 1981. This was on my return from Joshimath after the disastrous attempt to reach Changabang base. Everyone interested in the worship of Nanda Devi knew about Dev Ram and his enthusiasm extended far beyond the hills of Uttarakhand. At every opportunity he sang the glories of the Goddess and would deliberately stimulate discussion of the Rup Kund mystery in the press to gain more mileage for his lifelong mission—organizing the Devi's Bari Nanda Jat.

He had been partly successful in 1968 and made a start in overcoming the inertia of tradition. Money and a film crew had been supplied by the U.P. government on condition that no animal sacrifice would be performed. Apparently at every halting place Dev Ram had to plead with the locals to resist their blood-letting urge in honour of Nanda Bhagawati. But at Hom Kund the incensed opinion of the traditionalists finally overcame official objections. The four-horned ram was slaughtered according to local rites after the main pilgrim party had turned back from Hom Kund—and only after the film crew was out of sight.

I had ended up in Karnaprayag by luck because the motor road was broken. The night had been spent in the tourist bungalow which was jammed full of visitors held up by the road block. Luckily I met the two young trekkers who had been at the Helang landslide on the way up. Then they had taken the only available porter and had felt guilty at leaving me to sleep on the roof of the bus. Now in reparation they invited me to share their room. The night passed pleasantly for one of them, Tomar, a young doctor from Bikaner had a ready fund of jokes. Each yarn was followed by his booming laugh and we laughed so much that complaints were made to the chowkidar about not letting other people sleep.

Dev Ram suggested I should have darshan of Nanda Devi in her natal village so changing my programme I enquired about the bus to Nauti. It would not leave till midday. One could have walked to the village but it was a very steep uphill slog that would have claimed the whole day. I went back to the upper bazaar to meet Dev Ram's son Bimal who had inherited his father's love of Nanda Devi and is today his natural successor in the struggle to keep the Bari Nanda Jat going .

Part of the ongoing friction between the reformers and the traditionalists lay in the familial nature of Uttarakhand society. Nauti represents the native village of the Goddess, the place to which she is most attached. The lore of the Devi follows local custom closely and this meant there would always be sadness and resentment in having to move to the in-laws home in another valley on marriage. The intense conflict the outsider sees in the faction-ridden quarrels along the yatra trail would be viewed more philosophically by local villagers for they had undergone a similar experience in losing their daughter to distant and untried neighbours. It was part of life in the hills and like the unfairness of the soil's low yield, there was nothing to be done about it. Most hill songs reflect the poignancy of the daughter of the house leaving her maternal abode to dwell amongst strangers. They would have chosen her for an ability to work hard on the land and expect her immediately to get down to an unrelenting round of chores her mother-in-law was waiting to provide. It might be noted that this unromantic economic status of a newly married hill woman (acquired quite literally as a work-horse) was no different for a hill princess—as Nanda Devi is widely held to be. It is only in the towns of Almora and Naini Tal that the romantic fairy tale princess strand is emphasised.

The Goddess in the Kumaon heartland is viewed as the daughter of the Chand Rajas, the dynasty that once ruled from their capital in Champawat. For the annual Nanda Devi mela in Almora it is imperative for the Raja of Almora to be present as the lineal descendant of the Devi. At present the line flows through the former royal house of Kashipur and if any better evidence was needed to illustrate the finer side of the Nanda Devi cult there is the remarkable figure of Princess Sita, the Raja's sister, who now lives in Mussoorie. This real-life princess is a stunning replica of the Nanda Devi ideal. Beautiful to look at, elegant of manner and socially concerned she spends her whole morning in puja to the family Goddess. Her afternoon is devoted to the courtly graces of entertaining (or playing cards after the custom of Mussoorie's blue-blooded). Another strand in her family attachment to the Goddess was the emergence for a short spell in national politics of her son Arun Singh who held the portfolio of Defence under Rajiv Gandhi. Many people were impressed by the superior values he brought to bear on his stewardship and were not surprised when they resulted in his prompt resignation after a scandal involving commission on armaments surfaced.

While the top end of Kumaon society maintains the full dignity of its noble lineage, at the level of conventional religious practice the standards plummeted after independence. Having lived for twelve years in Kumaon I was aware of the huge increase in the theft of religious works of art from temples. It was well-known that what started innocently when the wife of the Deputy Commissioner picked up broken images littered around ancient temple sites like Dwarahat and Jageshwar, to display them more reverently on her lawn, soon turned into a lucrative business when art experts identified local masterpieces and arranged through Delhi's diplomatic bag to have them whisked out to a New York auctioneer. Too much indignation has been spent on the American millionaire buyers and too little on the Uttarakhand priests who cynically sold their ancestral deities. So deviously was this trade practised that an image of the Chand Rajas from Jageshwar was sought to be smuggled into Delhi by the expedient of carrying it aloft in a palanquin in simulated pilgrimage to try and outwit the police.

The scurrilous reputation of temple security staff led to the image of Nanda Devi herself being stolen from her main temple in Almora, something that could not be done without priestly connivance. Nauti was saved these embarrassments only by cleaving to the yoni symbol and investing in the buried Sriyantra.

The bus was jam-packed when I boarded it at 11.30 a.m. and the conductor continued to ram people into its bulging interior for another two hours. We groaned our way up to the village over bumpy roads washed out by the rains, the misery of the journey being amplified by curses at the squeeze of passengers and imprecations on the bus company who allowed it.

This was not the most conducive atmosphere for building up a religious profile of Nauti and when we were free of the claustrophobic bus neither did the surroundings help. An already treeless plateau stood above the dark plunge of the Pindar valley as motor roads in all directions incised their surgical gash.

The inhospitableness was diminished when the gathering at the tea shop understood my interest in the Devi. Plans to spend the night on a bare wooden bench were vetoed and I was shown to more comfortable quarters in the house of an old soldier. He explained the pecking order of local castes and informed me that the priests of the Nanda Devi temple in Nauti were not Nautiyals but Maithanis. (The Nautiyals were gurus to the Raja and the Maithanis were priests to the Nautiyals) In the morning I climbed down to the small, modern temple and was surprised by its undistinguished appearance. It had been renovated after his Rup Kund researches by Swami Pranavananda. On questioning the villagers about details of the Raj Jat and in particular the exact whereabouts of the matching Sriyantra said to be buried at Hom Kund, their faltering and contradictory replies made me conclude that the lore like the temple was of recent manufacture. The miserable weather prevented me from furthering my own researches into the geographical significance (if any) of the place of Nauti on the physical map of Nanda Devi. The hill that rose above the village was dedicated to the Goddess Ufrey, apparently an early indigenous form of the Mother Goddess and still worshipped by an annual fair which preceded the setting out of the Raj Jat. (For those who favour the Assyrian origin of U.P. hillmen the name Ufrey conveniently refers to the great river of Nineveh, the Euphrates)

Was Ufrey the aboriginal form of the Devi on whom these high caste settlers from the plains had grafted their formal notions of Durga Mata? Could the devotee from the summit of Ufrey Tak view the peak of Nanda Devi towards which the pilgrim party set out ? Was it just a coincidence that Hom Kund lay in a line, drawn from Nauti to the main peak of Nanda Devi? It was unlikely that the villagers could distinguish between one peak and another. Easily identifiable shapes like Trisul and Bankatiya (the axe-like Nanda Kot) would be referred to by name but Nanda Devi (except from the east) was not easy to pick out behind the other peaks.

What then made the men of Nauti undertake the long and arduous month-long Raj Jat? Was it from the satisfaction of working out on the physical level the tantric exercise of raising the serpent power through ascending bodily centres until it flooded the being with the light of certainty? Sax's description of the Raj Jat hardly suggested the bliss of oneness in a cosmic moment of union with the Goddess.

But as I viewed the goal on our descent to the Silli Samuder meadow camp that physical thrill was hard to deny. One was moving in a higher gear and to prove it as we ran down the rocky slope in drunken exultation I stumbled and performed an amazing somersault that put my head within a half-centimetre of total annihilation from a jutting rock. Like an unconcerned witness my body righted itself from the incredible loop and after a wobbly reaffirmation of new-found knees I discovered myself continuing the downhill charge, death or at least unconsciousness cheated by a fraction. Again the Goddess had chastened with hard lessons and taught that immortality was hers to give, teaching simultaneously the dangers of the way and the grace that lay at the end.

From Nauti with its copper-capped modern Sriyantra (presented by the missionary Shankaracharya of Sringeri) I walked down to the old fort at Chandpur past the villages that still offered their feudal tribute to Nanda Bhagawati's Raj Jat. One would provide the auspicious bamboo umbrellas (found in the lake) another the articles of regalia offered by tradition to the Devi's palanquin. The fort was an impressive little ruin with some fine stonework. Not far away was the lovely collection of temples at Adi Badri. Now off the beaten track of pilgrimage this small cluster boasts of the best architecture to be seen anywhere on the round of the Panch Badri temples. It was the coming of the bus that took away the spiritual significance of Adi Badri (and other shrines en route to the main temple). Hinduism, ever practical in adjusting to the swing in pilgrim economics, accepted the inevitable and concentrated on swelling arrivals to the main Vishal Badri shrine even if this meant stimulating tourists whose primary concern was to picnic rather than have darshan.

In the same way the Raj Jat committee based in Karnaprayag accepted the need to bend to modern demands. The frayed tempers that accompanied the palanquin of Nanda Devi as soon as she entered the jurisdiction of her in-laws village of Devrara in 1987 came to a head at Bedni with the interior faction insisting that evil omens would befall the Raj Jat if the Nautiyals insisted on diluting the ancient rite of animal sacrifice. What saved the pilgrimage from turning into a battle was the presence of uniformed policemen normally unknown in these backward villages where crime remained under restraint from the feudal fear of brute reprisal. When it became evident that the main procession led by the reformers and backed by the clout of government would not heed the advice (or threats) to toe the line of tradition, the interior party was forced for the sake of their self-esteem to withdraw from the pilgrimage under protest but not before issuing dire warnings that the outraged Goddess would visit terrible retribution on the reformers.

The Raj Jat continued on its way from Bedni without any of the predicted disasters befalling it. Women and low caste participants did make a token appearance though significantly local women were persuaded not to go beyond Bedni. This sop to the traditionalists at the expense of women's liberation shows how hard it is to change the female lot in the hills. But no animal sacrifice was reported from Hom Kund so that reform in one crucial area had been achieved. The sacrifice of a coconut signified further inroads into hill religion by Gandhian values.

In his account Sax is more concerned to relate the tensions than describe the physical hardships. His position was invidious since he was known to both factions and liked by them all. As an initiated devotee of Nanda Devi (a fact he appears shy to acknowledge in his book) performance of the Raj Jat meant a lot to him. But strangely little of the beauty of the march or the joy of the experience comes through. His journey is a catalogue of the abusive interfacing of the factions, a travesty of what the Goddess is believed to stand for. As a *mleccha* (foreigner) some of the traditionalist party feared his presence might anger the Devi and pollute her mountain but Sax sidestepped this embarrassment by his knowledge of local custom. He announced that he was willing to have his application for joining the Raj Jat put up to Latu through his oracle but when they drew near the place where the oracle resided, Sax cleverly bypassed the village and the question of his acceptability was never put to the test.

No such energy-sapping brawls occurred on our circuit to Hom Kund which passed over Jyuri Gali two years before Sax went with the main procession. It was a tribute to Dev Ram's tenacity that the pilgrimage got underway at all in view of the government's reluctance to fund any overtly religious occasion. Only faith in Nanda Devi could have overcome all the hazards that Sax describes. Which brings us back to the individual impact of this tough pilgrimage. In spite of the crudity of her village followers and the animal passions they indulge in they sincerely believed they were acting in the Devi's interest. Their loyalty to Nanda Bhagawati could not be questioned. In their own way they saw the royal circuit as a magical act that without the prescribed ritual would not work. If my private vision of a tantric exercise enlarged and re-enacted in the mountain arena seems fanciful when compared to the grim disharmony that characterised the main march, it was real enough to convince me of the underlying truth of the symbols. The glory I had found around the Hom Kund parting of the clouds was fixed forever as an exalted memory.

In that breath-taking moment the unlikely coming together of dreamlike elements convinced me that I had been shown one of the Devi's choicest secrets. In the glimpse of the bindu at the heart of the yoni the sense of perfect wonder had been aroused. Beside that any physical goal would have seemed ersatz.

We camped under the terrible fall of Trisul's flanks but the mist revealed only her black skirts that rose in huge ragged formations. We camped in the lee of a rock in the middle of the meadow afraid of stones falling during the night. The enclosed valley was entirely different from the Rup Kund side of the divide. Protected from the wind it seemed to boast a different carpet of flora. Here the beautiful purple spread of gentian claimed primacy. In the morning when we moved down to the glacier we passed whole colonies of the blue poppy which many consider to be the supreme beauty of Garhwal's buggials. In the rains however the wet petals lose their irresistible blueness and one is more aware of the rarer yellow poppy standing head-high on what seemed to be an enchanted slope with extra hormones at work. I have never seen more lush growth in the Himalayas.

While I admired the monsoon display of riotous colour the porters were busy scrabbling at the roots of a pink hyacinth. It was a medicinal plant with a white-fingered root and fetched good money from the herb contractors in Wan.

Rhubarb also grew to a lavish spread and as we drew nearer the Silli Samuder glacier—the ocean of boulders—we wondered what more spells this remarkable hollow hidden at the roots of Trisul would reveal. Leaping up to balance our way over the rocking blocks of granite I was confronted with a sudden conflagration. The whole glacier was ablaze with the magenta hue of witch-herb, the extraordinary signature of our unpredictable fiery hostess as we approached the turning-back point of her pilgrimage.

SEVENTEEN

The Dancing Daughter

*K*eeping under the overhang of Trisul we skirted the outflow of the glacier which was joined by the tumbling torrent off Ronti Saddle to herald the start of the gorge section of the Nandakini. The day's vivid colour helped overcome our soured mood brought on by the continual downpour. We now struggled up the slope towards Hom Kund and discovered that Gopal, the local man, was not really sure of our target. Like most things on the pilgrimage the effect of the Devi's *chaya maya* was to confuse and confound the landmarks. (Devotion was more important than the honouring of outer signs)

Gopal indicated we had a choice of two places to turn back from. Not far above the Chanoniyaghat gorge was a lone black square-shaped rock which he seemed to recall was the turning point of the ordinary pilgrim. Higher up lay the great black rock with its reputed reflecting inlay of mica. Because of the weather (or the *chaya maya*) we never saw the sun glint on the rock which lay up the steep slope leading to the distant Saddle. It was frustrating to be in a bowl of such dramatic mountain beauty and not be able to see an inch of the mighty ramparts of Trisul on one side or of Nanda Ghunti's impressive bulk on the other. The clouds whirled angrily as the wind funnelled down from the saddle between the two peaks. Since it was important to do a little puja to the Goddess at her sacred crater we decided to halt for the night under some cliffs near Trisul base camp.

Normally Trisul was approached from inside the sanctuary along the Rishi Ganga offering a comparatively straightforward snow plod to the summit in Longstaff's footsteps. Longstaff had shared Lord Curzon's opinion that few areas could match the mix of scenery found in Garhwal. To offset his cosmic sense of clinging on to the edge of the curving planet as he viewed the plains from Shiva's trident, General Bruce's Gurkha orderly Karbir (who had made it to the top with the Swiss guides) declared afterwards that he had seen the next best thing to Vishnu's golden pavilion. Echoing another old soldier's thoughts on Everest in 1953 (when news of the first ascent was suppressed till Coronation Day) Karbir loyally declared he could see Buckingham Palace in the distance.

When the sanctuary was closed the summit ceased to be a plod and turned into a real challenge. The new approach followed the Nandakini to its source and serious climbing skills were thereafter required. After the British climber's crossing of Ronti Saddle to Bethartoli base, a German climber waxed more ambitious in 1979 by attempting a similar traverse of Trisul. He climbed right over the mountain to exit from the sanctuary in an extraordinary solo crossing of the trident peak.

The most awaited traverse of Trisul's three prongs was accomplished by a mixed Yugoslav team in 1987. Sentimental value attached to their climb when Vlasta, the daughter of Ales Kunaver who had climbed Trisul I and II twenty-seven years earlier, completed the hat-trick in her father's memory. The lady then went on to paraglide from the main peak to base camp. (*Nae bother at'aw*)

We had a cold night and gave up any idea of exploring further than the crater when the weather grew more moody. It was a day's march to the Saddle (now called Hom Kund Khal) and there seemed little point in struggling so high when we wouldn't be able to see anything. The sense of power these hidden mountains possessed seemed to grow in the drape of mist. Possibly their menace was increased by the veil of cloud that teased their roots and sifted their awesome battlements. The price of travelling in the rains was to be deprived of the larger grandeur of the peaks for the more intense pleasure we had experienced on the flaming Garibaldi glacier. Instead of the soaring white snows witnessed by most expeditions we had been treated to a taste of lesser-known intimacies that would last long in our list of Nanda Devi's rare and unheralded beauties.

The thunder rolled as we toiled up the sharp ridge to complete the formalities of pilgrimage. The 'crater' at Hom Kund turned out to be a very small depression which was filled with a foot of water at this season. The big rock had no dramatic distinguishing marks and the modest size of the Kund made me wonder if we had arrived at the right place. But there was no mistaking the centre of the triangle I had seen. The twin streams of the infant Nandakini tumbled to a spectacular confluence below our offerings. A few stunted yellow potentilla managed to take their final bow and we offered them along with incense before fleeing from the worsening weather.

The morning was miserably wet and polished the rock along the descending bed of the Nandakini to a glistening black sheen as we skidded down its course. Several times we had to wade through side-streams and the worry was that we might not be able to ford the river at Chanoniyaghat and have to make a detour round the Silli Samuder glacier again.

Some good route-finding by Nathu brought us to the crucial fording point and there in place were two logs, recently cut to allow our escape. This was a boon from the Devi since our party did not carry an axe. But the bridge was flimsy and while the porters walked across nonchalantly I was filled with the same indecision the sanctuary streams inspired and had to sit on the ·tree trunks to hump myself across with great effort, my boots shipping a lot of water. The roar of the river filled the gorge and a last glance back to the culmination of the Nanda pilgrimage showed the oppressive tumble of boulders that had given the glacier its name.

Nathu led the way into dense forest as the rain beat down. What followed was the hardest afternoon I have ever spent in the mountains. Also because of the labour involved it was the most invigorating. The mix of birch, rhododendron and bamboo in the tangle of virgin impenetrability made for impossibly hard going. Our clothes and equipment caught on the bamboo and tore, while our feet skidded off the slippery curving rhododendron branches underfoot and catapulted us into the back of the person ahead. This forward rush would be met by the vicious swish of an elastic bent bamboo returning to its upright position after the drag of a rucksack. The jungle tore and maimed us and the plastic sheets—supposed to keep out the rain—were soon in a hilarious state of shred. Crucified by the tear of birch and battered by the backlash of bloodletting bamboo we still did not give in. Nathu continued to bulldoze a way above the swirling river and stepped at times to the brink of the mushy slope that threatened to collapse into the raging water. Sometimes we had to make detours and climb fifty feet above the loud river but always the clods at the edge crumbled dangerously as we tried to sidestep the snatch of the forest. The rain coursed down to make us so wet that we seemed to be part of the monsoon drench. By some perverse logic our misery made us laugh and as the cane lashed back to whip our bodies we began to make a joke of it. When the person in front stumbled over a treacherous rhododendron root for the next clump of bamboo to boomerang him back upright we hooted with delight. The body having passed the conventional parameters of discontent suddenly found the challenge liberating. The mind too had sailed across the barrier of normal grief and matching the body's drunken rollings now became intoxicated with its own possibilities. We knew no defeat and sang as we slashed a way through the thickets.

At last we emerged into a clearing which Gopal declared to be the camp site of Jamandhali. It was still early in the afternoon and there was no rock shelter of any sort. The rain continued relentlessly and after a smoke Nathu shouldered his load and said we should look for a more promising place to spend the night. Gopal felt peeved at having his wisdom questioned but I sided with Nathu. The more of this snagging jungle we put behind us the better. Unfortunately Nathu's route-finding instincts now deserted him as we thrashed around looking for some kind of trail. After the ordeal of being caned by bamboo we were desperate for any place that offered shelter. A skid down a slope to the river seemed promising and in my hurry to get clear of the constricting jungle, I tripped over a concealed root and went head over heels to land with my feet kicking out of a clump of cushioning azalea. The porters rushed down to make sure I was in one piece. (They also knew I was carrying the expedition brandy)

One more bruise after a day of pummelling hardly mattered and now on the river bank Nathu signalled he had found a rock shelf under which we could camp to keep out the worst of the rain whose volume caused some anxiety. If it continued to rain heavily the river might rise in the middle of the night and necessitate evacuation. As the only alternative was to climb back into trackless jungle we decided to risk the danger. Within minutes the porters had erected my tent and fashioned another for themselves from sheets of plastic. Soon the stove was humming as they sorted out the supplies for the evening meal. I stripped off the wettest of my clothes and changed into a warm sweater. Best of all was to find a dry pair of socks to change into. Once the extremities were back in circulation one could settle down for the further pleasure of Marmite on cream crackers.

The rain weakened to a friendly patter and when I glanced through the tent flap I could see the porters happily playing cards. The day's agonies were forgotten and thanks to the punishment we were all aglow with a sense of achievement. No other camp would possess the same magic.

Further thrashings in the morning at last yielded the makings of a path to betoken a fall in altitude and the thinning of the bamboo stands. The more open jungle of birch allowed us to stumble faster and near the next camp site of Lata Kopri a huge fat pheasant whirred away from under our galloping progress. Now we were in tracts visited by villagers and by following the track along the river we emerged from the verdant gorge where the first village went by the unlikely name of Good Buggair. Next came the familiar cluster of fawn stone houses at Sutol but not a single villager was in sight. Apparently all the males had gone on a honey collecting expedition. This involved the extraordinary mountaineering technique of lowering a man off an overhanging cliff by a rope. While dangling in mid-air he would smoke out the bees and cut away the combs to be collected by his companions below. Many of the men were badly stung but this was accepted as part of the job.

As there was no question of finding a cup of tea in the house of old friends we continued our 'crash programme' and followed the valley path as it dived steeply to the temporary bridge at Sitel. Before losing height we bade farewell to Gopal who returned with his wages along the path to Wan.

As we skidded down the muddy path to cross the boiling river we passed a group of village labourers who cheered us by announcing they had just got the bridge operational after several weeks of disruption by the river in spate. We passed over the logs safely and made for the Sitel bungalow. The chowkidar was as nastily disposed as the bungalow was beautifully sited. For a handicapped person it seemed his soul was more twisted than his body. He was surly and unhelpful and when we came to pay next morning I asked for the local register explaining that I was an Indian national. A separate register was maintained for foreign guests who had to pay more (a discriminatory policy followed by the forest department that extended to the entry fee for wildlife parks). When I opened the register I saw the familiar name of William Sax who had apparently been in the area quite recently. Puzzled why an American should use the register for Indians I added my name under his. Then the chowkidar triumphantly demanded extra money, gloating that I had signed the wrong register. I paid the money but tore in half another crisp new note in his face to spoil his triumph. The porters threatened to beat him up but were restrained by Nathu (who made a point of picking up the torn halves of the note). The message was that we were back from the realm of the Goddess to the real world of commerce and the sooner we adjusted to the crooked habits of government servants the better for all of us rarified pilgrims.

The march down the lovely leaping Nandakini from the coniferous delights of Sitel to the pine slopes that rose above the bridge at Chefana was done smartly in the cool of the morning. For the first time since we had set out ten days ago there was no rain. The contrasting greens of the different species were an added delight to the lyrical tumble of the frothing river. Compared to the snarling Rishi the Nandakini really did come across as a dancing daughter of the Goddess.

After pakoras at the Silli Buggair shop we repaired to the river bank for a hearty scrub. Higher up it had been too cold to apply Lifebuoy soap. Back at Ghat my idea to climb up to investigate the temple at Krur was effectively vetoed by Nathu who had gone and piled my luggage on top of a mini-van taxi. We returned along the last section of the Nandakini to Nandaprayag where I said goodbye to the porters and caught a passing bus to Srinagar to spend the night at the tourist bungalow. The first ritual there was to enjoy an open-air shave and haircut. Only then did one feel qualified to re-enter the company of the civilized.

I made up my mind to revisit Krur at the earliest and the opportunity arose the following April when I accompanied a photographer friend to Garhwal. First we went to Tunganath to catch the rhododendron in bloom against the winter snow. Then from Chopta we drove to Tapovan to get the rare view of Nanda Devi from the motor road out of Joshimath. Next we ascended in four-wheel drive to Auli to stay a night at the ITBP mess for which Ashok Dilwali had supplied some enlargements of his mountain photographs. As a not very bright beginner in photography it was fascinating to see how a professional was devoted to detail and how much sweat went into recording what seemed a casual shot. That night as we walked back to our room in the chatteringly cold air we were inspired by the luminous spread of Nanda Devi's face as the light of the full moon climbed upon it. I asked Ashok if it was possible to get a clear picture of the mountain by moonlight and he said you undoubtedly could if you used a long exposure. But the result would depend on the brightness of the moonlight. If I woke him at two in the morning when the moon was full on the mountain we could try the shot. Before going to bed he set up his cameras and mine in the glazed veranda facing Nanda Devi. The alarm went off at 2 a.m. and we both struggled out of bed to shiver in the cold. The mountain looked magnificent in the reflected beauty of the moon and both cameras were clicked. Ashok then spotted that the veranda windows were reflecting our images and decided to move the tripods outside into the clear but grippingly cold night air. The shots turned out to be the best I have ever seen of Nanda Devi. The glare during the day prevents a clear portrayal of the main peak. At Auli you get the same view as from above Tapovan but being so high on the buggials the entire massif is visible.

The following winter I revisited Auli with a party of Delhi students to ski on these slopes. The snow was a bit wet but the views of Nanda Devi and other peaks around Joshimath must make Auli the most spectacular of all bases to ski from. On that trip I walked over the snow slopes to drop down on Lata in winter. All the villagers had moved down to their second home built near the motor road. Even in the kinder altitude along the river bank life was hard and while the women wove their carpets the men smoked in the sun shaking their heads sadly at the unkind closure of the sanctuary.

Bal Singh was doing good business as a building contractor from the sale of sand found in abundance along this stretch of the Dhauli Ganga. During the summer he was a contractor for the controversial sale of deodar. The local women led by Gaura Devi of Renni had sparked off the Chipko movement by hugging the Himalayan cedar to prevent the contractor's axe from felling them. But though it is fashionable to blame the rip-off on unscrupulous plainsmen, the real enemy of the environment was the acquisitiveness of the hill male. It was easy to posit the innocent Garhwali and wronged Kumaoni at the mercy of the greedy Punjabi and cunning Marwari but this was like blaming the American millionaire for collecting sacred images that originated in hill temples. The fact was hill people were hand in glove with the outsiders and the impoverishment of hill life whether by the export of prime timber or the smuggling out of religious antiques was not done without the active connivance of influential local people.

In winter, however, the men of Lata could only drown their woes in home-made daru. Theirs was the last village before transhumance was made necessary by the altitude.

Most people in the higher villages moved down to lower grazing pastures leaving only a skeleton staff to supervise the locked-up houses of the deserted village. I climbed up to the summer Lata with Nathu and went to the temple courtyard. In winter when the grass was subdued one could see the details of the beautifully carved naula (water spring) next to the temple. The superior style of this early medieval structure suggested Lata had once been patronised by the rulers of the area. I was interested to meet Bal Singh's family pujari who hailed from Sevai, a village above the motor road between Renni and Tápovan. The small temple in Sevai is beautifully proportioned and connected Nanda Devi to the circuit of the Panch Badri shrines. We have already seen how Chandpur fort next to Adi Badri introduced a common bond. When I met the rawal (chief priest) of the main Badrinath shrine I noted that on the wall of his room was painted a large Sriyantra. Although Nanda Devi is the wife of Lord Shiva and not immediately recognizable as Lakshmi the consort of Vishnu, Hindu viewpoints are too fluid to allow for suppositions to remain unmodified for long. Based on a realistic understanding of the confused randomness of the human psyche Hindu theology differs from the monotheistic insistence on a choice between black and white and offers the subtle options of the rainbow. Not to closely identify Nanda Devi with Vishnu's spouse does not mean all affinity is denied. It will be remembered that on the peak of the mountain exists the golden palace set in the midst of a lake whose centre-piece is Lakshmi enthroned on her mystical lotus. Thus the bindu reappears in another form.

On the way to Badrinath are the temples of Pandukeshwar, amongst the oldest and best preserved in the whole of the Himalayas. It is from a tenth century copper plate here that we find one of the earliest written references to Nanda Devi: *'Nanda Bhagawati charan kamal kamalas nath mirthah'* — (Resembling in his complexion the lotus feet of the Goddess Nanda and the lotus seated Brahma) In the *Devi Purana* popular in Bengal the Goddess Nanda is mentioned by name and equated spiritually with her husband Lord Shiva. Shiva in turn is stated to be the true destination of all pilgrimages. The physical characteristics of the Goddess are entirely feminine and bliss-provoking even when attired as a yogini covered in ashes with her top-knot coiled: 'She wears a royal tiara on her broad forehead above bright eyes. Her body is as beautiful as the full moon, her breasts so full it is an effort to carry them. Her whole body is studded with precious stones and smells of sandalwood. She is soft-spoken with four hands bedecked with flowers, one hand raised in blessing. She wears a blood-red sari and is waited upon by Jayadevi her maid.'

After the moonlight photo of Nanda Devi we climbed to the village of Sevai to solve the puzzle of Bhavishya ('the future') Badri, fifth and forthcoming of the shrines. According to legend the image of Nar Singh in the old temple of the same name in Joshimath (where Lord Badrinath is brought down with ceremony to spend his winter) has an arm that is withering. When the limb breaks there will be a great landslide blocking the canyon road to the main Badri shrine. Bhavishya Badri will become the next in line for worship.

Here is a myth of highly profitable potential and we wanted to check out the latest development. According to varying lists of the Panch Badri temples there is no agreement on what constitutes the actual five of the circuit. Their importance has changed according to the needs of pilgrims at different times. Availing of this fluid situation it seems some pundits recently contrived to rediscover Bhavishya Badri high on the mountain above Sevai. Sevai lies near the hot springs of Tapovan and it is certain that the convenience of hot water to bathe tired bones made this the original temple of Bhavishya Badri.

Ashok and I climbed past the temple waved on by villagers who told us the new site was ahead. We got higher and higher following the same advice until the original one-mile climb extended to five. Just when we began to doubt the existence of any temple we arrived amidst the dense canopy of spruce that clothes the towering slopes leading to Ronti. A shepherd pointed out a tiny stone box above which had been erected a hastily painted tin notice. We had been conned. This absurd anti-climax that claimed to be Bhavishya Badri was a ludicrous end to our search.

The shepherd was offended by our laughter and pointed out a spring that he said had miraculously appeared to justify the embryonic temple—a crude Brahmanical trick to elicit offerings from simple pilgrims that is quite likely to catch on since the public wants to believe in miracles. Once this humble structure is made more presentable traffic, to the hill top will swell.

Certainly the green gloom of the forest made for a beautiful backdrop to this future investment on the outer curtain of Nanda Devi's sanctuary. The exercise had been valuable in demonstrating how cult practice grows to meet market demands. The increased number of pilgrims to Badrinath brought by the daily convoy of buses had stimulated public interest in the ancient myths and now the local Brahmins were catering to this new audience who were not averse to adventuring uphill for merit.

Such ploys have been the mark of all institutional priesthoods and Hinduism's takeover of the small local cults is matched by examples in every continent. To show the universality of the strategy I picked up in the Joshimath tourist bungalow a junked plastic bottle of Buxton mineral water from a British expedition. The label declared it had been filled at St Ann's spring, then went on to describe the pre-Christian beginnings of Buxton's tonic waters which to the Romans had been known as 'The waters of the Goddess of the Grove.'

EIGHTEEN

Temple Tracking

*I*n the spring of 1985 I continued tracking the lore of the Devi and after the climb to Bhavishya Badri returned to Nanda Prayag to catch the crowded taxi to Ghat. But first I explored the tiny bazaar of Nanda Prayag which in spite of its size has had a considerable impact on Garhwal's culture. I was particularly interested to see the tiny printing press operated by the Bahuguna family which for two generations has brought out a news-sheet entitled *Dev Bhumi,* an independent weekly that constitutes a remarkable labour of love.

From information gleaned in Nanda Prayag I learned that the temple at Krur had ceased to have much significance in the Raj Jat in the hundred years since Atkinson had mentioned it. On the other hand it seemed likely that the village would jump back into prominence with the building of a new motor road from Chamoli to Ghat, an artery that seemed colossally wasteful in view of the river route already existing via Nanda Prayag. Sadly hill planners never apply their mind to the useful alternative of upgraded jeep roads for the interior with passing places regularly spaced to save on the expense of double lanes.

Wedged in the mini-van running along the lower Nandakini valley the villagers were forthcoming in indicating the current sites sacred to the

Goddess. The problem was that everyone assumed only his own village worshipped the Devi according to true tradition while the others—whatever the official list might say—were upstarts not to be trusted. But everyone seemed agreed that the Goddess' native village was Nauti in Dasohli and her sasural at Devrara in Badhan, the neighbouring revenue district (known as patti). These subdivisions had survived from ancient times and represented realistic cultural boundaries for those accustomed to travel on foot. The coming of the motor roads had made most of them redundant but those interior pattis sacred to the Goddess, Painkhanda (which included the Rishi valley) and Nandak (which followed the flow of the Nandakini) were still real entities in the eyes of the devotees, and local loyalties were strongly invoked. (Dr Sax writes of Pratyeka along the Pindar river)

The jealousies that surfaced on the Raj Jat reflected this sense of attachment to one's valley. It was naturally assumed that the patti beyond one's horizon into which the daughter of the house would marry was peopled by men of less superior parts. This led smaller villages to borrow from the Nanda Devi legend and boost the status of their village when far enough away from the main road not to be caught out. According to a villager I sat next to, the taxi ran past the foot of a hill on which two temples sacred to the Devi stood and in his own village of Kot Kandhara he claimed there was an image of the Goddess.

As I had never been able to locate an actual full-length representation of Nanda Devi the news sounded too auspicious to ignore. I decided to continue to Krur later and get off there and then to begin a long climb up to the village of Kot. It was a hot morning and the path went up through slippery pine jungle but at least it was too early for the mental racket that came with the cicada chorus of summer. By midday I had struggled up to the ridge and was directed to a tiny temple capping the last field on the climb. It didn't seem much of a temple but when I ducked under the low entrance I was struck by the handsome and authentic feel of the image. Done on an eighteen-inch slab over which a wash of *bajri lep* (black gravel) had been baked, here at last was the Goddess as the villagers visualised her. She had the thick lips of aboriginal extraction plus the strapping beauty of hill thakur women. She displayed big breasts and exuded the luscious come-hitherish quality of a male fantasy figure.

In contrast to the full bosom, the waist was narrow and the bottom half of the image undeveloped. As I had no flash to my camera and did not want to risk the anger of the Goddess (or her devotees) by carrying the image outside I had to be content with a sketch. The sketch shows the huge bosom matched by enormous earrings (which appear to fulfill the Gorakhnath sect requirement of passing through the cartilege). The figure holds a trisul-shaped lotus upraised in her (first) right hand from which hangs a mala presumably of the sacred Rudraksha bead. In the left upper arm is held a lotus-shaped mace and in the lower a kamandalu, the sadhu's water pot shaped out of a dried gourd. A large mala also garlands her neck and nestles between the enlarged breasts.

Instead of a classical crown the Goddess wears a cap bearing the lotus motif. The effect of a voluptuous free-standing figure is enhanced by a pair of supporting maidens in miniature waving flywhisks. These attendants stand in different postures, the one on the left before a crouching lion, the *jhamp singha* that in tantric symbolism marked a place where the cult of ritual suicide was practised. The alluring woman and her attendants wear knee-length dhotis with the centre-fold firmly draped to make the lower part of the body of no consequence. A stone mala girdles the two attendants across the puny stylised legs and the feet stand on a half-lotus motif. The whole is balanced by the two lower hands of the Devi resting near the heads of her sportive attendants who also wear the heavy earrings derived apparently from the aphrodisiac rhino horn.

Looking at this crude yet beautifully crafted and powerfully erotic image my thoughts immediately went to the Roman goddess of hunting, and the succeeding apostolic refrain 'Great is Diana of the Ephesians'. Derived from Artemis, daughter of Zeus we have in her both the Goddess of nature and of the moon, a combination that yields the essence of all feminine mysteries. When we learn that the image with its many paps in Ephesus was worshipped in August—the same time as Nandashtami is observed in the hills—we can detect common elements in the universal urge to worship the great Mother Goddess.

Many of the details of the legends of Attic Greece and ancient Rome overlap the Nanda Devi lore. Amidst the sylvan innocence of Nemi lay buried blood-stained weapons and as at Lata the meat of the hunted animal was offered at the temple. In the sacred grove the Goddess at Nemi likewise held aloft a torch in her right hand very like the lotus-shaped trisul seen here at Kot Kandhara. Also Diana shared her sanctuary with two lesser deities. Her chief blessing lay in granting couples offspring and in staying the birth pangs of expectant mothers. In Garhwal the Devi is prayed to for the gift of fertility. Brahmanical prejudices may account for the modification to view the act of childbirth as inauspicious, local lore being twisted to suit high-caste hang-ups. Nanda was said to be jealous of her sister and had caused the holocaust at Rup Kund out of spite because she had no child of her own.

The psychology of high-caste sexual attitudes makes for a fascinating study. Not only are hill Brahmins obsessed with the ritual horror of menstrual impurity but some hill thakurs observe the custom of never kissing their wives' breasts lest it lead to the unmanly association of being reduced to an infant in suck. Many of these restrictions may derive from the unspoken fear found throughout Hindu society (with its emphasis on the joint family), of the unspeakable subject of incest, the universality of whose overhang is reflected daily in the most common expletives of the sub-continent. According to Dr Sax this subject loomed large in his findings but was not likely to get aired owing to its explosive potential.

Two other villages merited some interest. Hindoli near Kot was reputed to supply some of the Goddess' regalia for the Raj Jat. However when I went to enquire no one of any responsibility was available to show off the relics. During the day the only people who remained at home were the very young or the elderly. Able-bodied women would be out working on the hillside while the men would be busy gossiping in the teashop. Across another ridge was an old established temple to Latu at Nauli, but that could be best approached from Karnaprayag whence a new motor road had just been opened. Now there was just time to check out Kalimath a popular *bali dan* temple hidden in a defile. I got the vegetarian's distinct sensation of unsavouriness that often accompanies temples where animal sacrifice is actively pursued and was glad to get clear of its morbid associations. When the actor Victor Banerji set out to film the Rup Kund mystery I recommended he visit these temples. Bowled over by the vibrancy of their icons he confirmed that they were in honour of the Goddess Kali; and these rare glimpses of the Shakti of Lord Shiva appear in his documentary *Splendours of Garhwal.*

On passing through Kot to get back down to the road I was apprehended by another species to be found in the deserted village. This was a young man aggressively drunk who decided I was a threat who needed to be chased away. For the whole of the five kilometres back down to the motor road I was forced to trot to try and shake off my unsteady but persistent pursuer.

Another shared taxi brought me to Ghat with its small, hot and fly-blown bazaar. Primitive shops selling basic items and tumble-down eating places (that only ravaging hunger would make one enter) were passed for the climb up to the primary school poised half way to Krur. The school teacher whom I had met on the earlier visit was still in residence and made me welcome. Of course I could spend the night on his school veranda. As a sign of the Goddess' favour there was a teacher from Krur now on the staff. As his name, Bhagawati Prasad, suggested he was a devotee of the Devi. He was also modern and clothes-conscious and to be photographed was his ultimate ecstasy.

From a neighbouring house he brought up three tiny schoolgirls to sing for me the Krur rendering of the Nanda Devi hymn of praise:

> *Jai Nanda, Jay ho Jadamba Bhavani, Jay ho Mahadevi Chatra Dharini, Daksha Prajapati Raja Rishiyon ki ben, safal hoya devton ki dhyah, Nauti Almora Dasholi Badhan, Maithur yo reo tero Kururan gram cha Sauryas yo tero Devraran cha, Doli Ma bithe ke teri jat lijan cha, Che maine Kurur che maine Badhan.*

This stanza succinctly captures the popular theology of Nanda: Long live Nanda Devi in her awesome majesty, greatest of Goddesses from whom all blessings flow. Daughter of kings, sister of rishis, She alone makes plain the way of the gods, honoured in the eyes of both Nauti and Almora, worshipped in all the villages of Dasholi and Badhan. Mother, thy home is in Krur and thy husband's dwelling in Devrara. Seated in thy palanquin shall we not bear thee aloft in procession? Thou residest six months in Krur and six months in Badhan.

These rustic notions of divinity's seasonal cycle following the marital pattern of a village girl were sung by Babita, Usha and Jyoti who also wrote the words down for me. (They also sent a letter for their reward: 'Plege you sent me Photo hurry up. Good night') Soon they too, despite their opportunity for education, would be forced to marry into a distant village and renew the cycle of separation. By making the Goddess accept the lot of all hill women the pundits who composed these hymns cleverly strengthened the male cause while outwardly honouring the status of women. If married daughters suffered the unfair wrench of exile from their native surroundings it was due to the divine dispensation of the Great Mother and had nothing to do with the manipulative minds of her male devotees. Such craftiness would continue as long as hill women subscribed to the low opinion their menfolk had of them. Too many had grown to cherish their abject state.

Bhagawati Prasad took me to Krur in the morning and climbing the badly eroded terraces we gained the new motor road that had devastated an already bare landscape. The village was poor and the temple a small stone structure that overlooked more stricken slopes. The sullen reality of the lives of the Devi's village devotees was brought home in the harsh and unappetising landfall around Krur. Some village boys accompanied me to the temple and provided the only cheer by swinging on the jhula of the Goddess, which comprised of a hefty chain dangling from a gnarled tree. They took me back to the village house in which the Devi was currently residing, for the custom was for each family to entertain Nanda Bhagawati for a specified period. The backwardness was depressing and the crudeness of the rites did nothing to lift the heart in temporary respite. The image worshipped was a small silver conventional Durga seated on her lion and the mood was of affected enthusiasm adopted for my benefit.

The climb to Krur had been an unrewarding experience except for the cheerfulness of the children. The new road seemed to blight the prospects of the village rather than improve things. It leached away what little virtue remained in the land. To be fair to the villagers their situation only reflected the general level of indifference I had found throughout Uttarakhand. The Goddess was an object of annual fuss when the festival season drew near. Only then did the temple committees spark into life publishing brochures that suggested local culture was thriving when in fact the publication had been paid for from a government grant. The greatest irony of all was that the Bari Nanda Jat could not take off without official funding and could not have completed its circuit without a police escort. On the other hand the determined exuberance of young people like Bhagawati Prasad to combine the best of the old ways with the latest trendy hair style of Bruce Lee suggested the worship of Nanda Devi would continue but in a modernised form.

Architecturally the cult temples of Nanda Devi do not amount to much. The tantric requirement of burying the Sriyantra made any structure superfluous and the earthquake-prone belt of the middle Himalayas anyway guaranteed that few ancient buildings could withstand the constant trembles. Those that had survived like the temples at Gopeshwar and Karnaprayag (the latter in honour of Uma Devi) were distinctly broad in the beam, having been given a low centre of gravity deliberately to try and outwit the earth tremors. The main temple to Nanda Devi in Almora is too inelegant to be anything but modern though the small shrine to the Goddess in the civil courts' enclosure is a superlative example of the art of the Chand Rajas. Naini Tal's lakeside temple to Naina Deva, sought nowadays to be related to the Nanda lore was right in the path of the terrible landslide of 1880. East of Naini Tal is Devi Dhura where the curious bloody rites in honour of the Devi are channelled into a stone-throwing contest between parties. The Bhotiya area of Milam claims to boast an important Devi temple but apparently it is no more than a conventional enclosure of modest dimensions and unambitious design. Another stands at Saudhara marking the source of the Sarju river that flows through Bageshwar.

On the way to the Pindari glacier I was disappointed to find ahead of the last bungalow at Phurkiya a modern lean-to structure built by a publicity-thirsting sadhu who autographed with a paint brush all the rocks he passed along the way. At least by the imposition of a Durga image placed there in 1980 (and no doubt claimed to have lain there undiscovered since the creation of the universe) he has indicated how easy it is for one individual to hijack the original animistic shrines and replace the hill devtas by mainstream members of the Hindu pantheon.

Back in Ghat I hoped to walk to Devrara, the contentious marital village of Nanda Devi which lay two days' march away. But on hearing that 'Badri Prasad Nautiyal' (alias William Sax) was in residence in Nauti I decided instead to go and see him. It was a sensible decision because I learned more about the Nanda Devi cult in one night from this American scholar than I had from local devotees in thirty years of questioning. It was valuable because Sax viewed the subject as a devotee. Unlike most Westerners he tried to understand rather than judge the often crude excesses of the Devi's followers. Sax also had the advantage of studying the local languages whereas my acquaintance with hill dialects was limited. As a Fulbright scholar he was happy to share private thoughts that his Indian director of studies might have deemed too sensitive to find their way into print. By appointing its own cultural academic watchdogs the Indian government felt reassured that any feudal skeletons in the cupboard of religious practice would only be rattled and not allowed to fall out into public view. For their part American anthropologists were so excited by India's vast choice for original field work that they promised to keep their more lurid findings to the footnotes of their Ph.D. theses.

After a rich evening's haul of information I was forced to conclude Nanda Devi had displayed her trump card in enabling me to find so many answers to my questions from the first—and only—foreigner qualified to speak on the subject.

Another scholar Sax referred me to was Dr Shivprasad Dabral, a Garhwali historian who lived at Dogudda between Pauri and Kotdwara. I decided to maintain the tempo of my enquiries and visit him on the way back to the plains. Dogudda was hot and sticky after the cooler environs of Nauti and I had to walk a mile into the valley to approach the retired historian's home. To my disappointment I found instead of a traditional village house a large rambling construction in cement, the sort of cheap and quick solution many hillmen now resort to in a time of dwindling skills and resources. But when I was welcomed inside by the old but extremely active owner I found to my utmost delight that the big barn actually protected the original hill house which was now revealed beautifully preserved inside.

Dr Dabral laughed at my bewilderment. His imaginative solution to a teasing problem summed him up. Here was a scholar-extraordinary, possessed of original ideas and fearless opinions. Since orthodox academic channels were not eager to publish anything but received wisdom he had set up his own Hindi press on which to crank out his books. He has published (in ten volumes) the only serious alternative history of Uttarakhand to Atkinson's *Gazetteer*. Most refreshing of all was to find a scholar who checked out the facts on the ground. In the trying terrain of Garhwal only a local could hope to do this. Dr Dabral was an enthusiastic trekker who had covered most of the pilgrim routes and his love for the mountains remained evergreen. His concern to preserve the best in local culture was what had caused him to build a protective shell around his original family house. Now he showed the carvings on the veranda and explained the traditional designs, referring to books on iconography to extract more symbolism.

On Nanda Devi's religious evolution he had no opinions but agreed that in the absence of local characteristics (the silver masks were signs of minor hill deities that extended also to Himachal Pradesh) it could be assumed that her status had been inflated to satisfy the needs of mainstream religion. I quoted the startling example of Vaishno Devi in Jammu who in recent years has shot into prominence as one of the most sought-after deities in North India. Her modest cave-dwelling could hardly cope with the crowds after it was known that the Goddess was a great favourite of Bombay film stars. Eventually this minor deity was turned by popular demand into the chief manifestation of Durga for our age. So profitable were the offerings that the government stepped in to take over the administration from the Maharaja of Kashmir.

Significantly access to Vaishno Devi was largely by motor road and the final climb involved but a few kilometers of graded footpaths that evened out at the modest height of 5,000 ft. Presumably Nanda Devi could be considered an Uttarakhand understudy of Vaishno Devi waiting in the wings for public exposure. In view of the traditional appeal of Badri and Kedar it seems unlikely that Nauti or Lata, Almora or Srinagar will suddenly aspire to draw crowds of plains pilgrims. On the other hand it only needs one miracle (in theory) to set in motion the popularity of any shrine. But fiscal students of religion will point out that the world's richest shrine at Tirupati is remarkable for combining two basic requirements of popular pilgrimage. First, it is perched on a modest hill to give the pilgrim a sense of some token effort having been made to reach his god. Secondly, it is well served by road, rail and air. In short, it provides what mankind feels bashful to acknowledge in seeking to make easy our contact with the divine—the best of both worlds.

NINETEEN

The Curzon Trail

*T*he year 1985 worked to a natural climax in one's travels around Uttarakhand. It began in January with a circuit of Kumaon which brought me close to Nanda Devi in the view from Chaukori. A more dramatic scene was captured from Chandak above Pithoragarh where both peaks present an unforgettable mountain portrait in the gold of the retiring day.

After the midnight shots of Nanda Devi from Auli I was invited by Ashok Dilwali to accompany him in August to Sahastra Tal to discover 'seven sacred lakes'. This was accomplished at the steamy height of the monsoon and yielded Garhwal's western buggials at their most resplendent. We were too near the Gangotri end of the Himalayan chain to be able to see Nanda Devi but hard up against the face of Jaonli we discovered this traverse of the Halmot Dhar to be one of the most delightful in Garhwal's unending repertoire of high magnificence. It is rare to be able to walk along buggials with a completely unobstructed view of the great peaks close at hand. Looking south we could see the limestone gashes that marked Mussoorie.

In October I decided to splurge on four porters for an exploratory expedition east of the Kuari Pass down to the source of the Birehi Ganga. This would complete my chain of investigation from Lata to Phurkia, a semicircle of peregrinations around the south outer curtain of the sanctuary. From the outset the expedition was doomed. I made the fatal mistake of allowing Nathu to bring along an older man with Govind and DB. He was immediately christened LS (lead-swinger). Lazy and a cunning opportunist, LS was everyone's idea of a British shop-floor steward. We had only climbed up from Tapovan half way to Kuari on the first morning before this insidious layabout began to look for a camp site. His demoralising behaviour served to put into perspective my rather uncritical boosting of Lata porters. Most expedition leaders complained they were rude, aggressive and light-fingered. Now I had to witness daily the depressing example of a professional cadger wheedling for extra rations but determined to do as little as possible to earn them.

The climb from Tapovan couldn't have been steeper. But it passed through some friendly villages where the children swarmed out to greet us. Karchong was the poorest—so our lunch was guaranteed. Throughout India the pilgrim finds that the poorer the village the more likely its hospitality will be pressed on the stranger. Harvested clusters of millet (mudwa) were drying on the stone flags and some tiny tots were learning the Hindi alphabet from their wood-bordered slates. With our meal we had some deliciously sweet freshly dug potatoes and I made Nathu pack some for boiling up in the pressure cooker along the trail. Just then Pratap Singh arrived from Lata. He seemed embarrassed to meet us. He had cut his leg while chopping wood and had been unable to accompany Bal Singh's sheep to the pastures around Niti where the sanctuary sheep now grazed. So he had become an itinerant salesman of home-spun woollens travelling from village to village for custom, a calling far less noble than that of shepherd. Then I realised why LS was such a poor specimen of Lata manhood. He too was a pedlar of high altitude produce but spent his winters in the plains hawking rare Himalayan herbs, spices and minerals. It was his contact with the plains that had turned him from a sturdy shepherd into a shifty salesman.

But it was too glorious a day to be perturbed by human failings as we toiled up past a spectacular waterfall. October is the best trekking season when the golden days yield the full fragrance of harvested sap. The sky is a celestial blue and the air perfectly attuned to vigorous marches. Sun-dappled trees and the roar of rushing water coursing off the mountainside stimulate the taste of salt on one's lips while the sifting wind soothes any regret at the sweat. It is good to be alive in high Garhwal in October as the crickets fill the clear air with a deafening drone of plenitude. The intensity of the sky with a few puffed clouds abroad by early afternoon contrasts with the map-like spread of fields below. Crops of ripening red buckwheat shock the eye as do the yellow stalks of scarlet coxcomb. The multihued greens of the jungle begin to enclose one's progress and range from the deep chrome of oak and dark viridian of spruce to the fresh gloss of chestnut and maple.

We marched on to break the back of the climb, emerging steeply to camp on a north-eastern shoulder of Kuari. Misty weather now clamped itself over the ridge as we sheltered under some rocks. The autumnal green-brown patches of bracken ran down to the lower ridges where a plume of blue smoke indicated that the last shepherds of the season were ready to start down before the cold of winter. In the evening I set off to explore, climbing eastwards to break through the mist and gain Delisera buggial that ran gloriously for miles towards the beckoning (but hidden) snow peaks.

After an hour of slogging uphill against the grain of rocky rivulets I had to turn back just before I reached the great void down which I hoped Nathu would be able to find a route to the source of the Birehi. The porters had made a huge bonfire of fallen birch when I got back and Govind had prepared an excellent cabbage stew to go with the rotis. It was a viciously cold night but I was up at six to pack two chapattis laced with Marmite for my breakfast. Govind gave me a glass of tea and I set off with my camera to catch what lay across the void. The porters would pack and join me on the great dividing ridge later.

Looking back I could see the first rays of the sun on Chaukhamba. Nearer but still shaded because of their shorter stature were the giant outlines of Hathi and Ghori Parvat, the elephant and horse-headed peaks. It is only from Kuari that the aptness of these descriptions is made clear. The fluted contours of their summits perfectly match those of a horse and elephant. As an example of how the current urge to Sanskritise can overcome objective mountaineering sense it is common to find in Indian climbing literature 'Ghori' (the horse) replaced by 'Gauri' (the wife of Shiva). The sheer bulk of these two shapely peaks viewed from Delisera must make this one of the most distinguished viewpoints in Garhwal.

After spending a whole roll of film on their massive profiles I found that the camera wasn't working. This had happened so many times before that I could only laugh at my misfortune. As I drew nearer to yesterday's limit the sun arrived over the ridge to thaw my fingers (and hopefully the camera shutter). I sat next to a small sheltered seasonal lake and ate my breakfast against a clump of flattened rhododendron bushes which dazzled in the morning sun with the brilliantly reflected shine of their bark.

By now the clouds had begun to level out the castellations on Chaukhamba and erased the controversial tip of Nilkanth. Next they threatened the titanic outlines of Hathi Parvat. Could I top the ridge before the clouds rose from the Birehi basin and would there be any peaks left worth photographing? So often the effort of cresting a hard-won ridge in the Himalayas is the agonizing anti-climax of another ridge looming to test you. I decided to try a little magic to prevent that painful outcome and would not look up until my feet had touched the edge. The magic worked and I came out on the brink of the huge fall overlooking Ronti, Nanda Ghunti and Trisul. Fatally the clouds had just begun settling on the furthest of these three peaks and I had to scrabble to get off the lens cap. Luckily the camera had shaken off its morning sloth. The sun was strong and one breathed contentedly before this Great Himalayan crescendo where the green meadows turning brown fell away beneath our feet in an awesome sweep of undiscovered basin.

Nathu arrived and went straight over the lip to reconnoitre. After a lot of casting about in several directions he came back and glumly admitted that it was possible to get down but not up again with a heavy load. We would have to skirt the divide and look for a south-easterly way down. A shepherd had told us of this alternative and we began to track diagonally over tumbled rocks hoping to locate it. Then out of the blue it began to snow. We couldn't believe it. At first it was just a light patter of small hail and we thought it must be the flurry of a passing shower. It never rained seriously before noon in these mountains and in October the pattern was so predictable that you could give it in writing.

We were wrong. The hail changed to big soft flakes of snow that blotted out the way and balled up the soles of our boots. Progress became a slanging match as we were committed to an ugly traverse of tumbled rock near the edge and no one could agree on the best line. We sheltered under an overhang but had no water to make tea so as the cold intensified we decided that it was less miserable to plod on. We tended to veer away from the edge for fear of going too near in the whiteout and then had to climb back amidst curses of indecisive navigation. Frozen and bedraggled Nathu and I agreed we would never find the path in these conditions. We must retreat and get our bearings from the Kuari Pass. As soon as we pulled out from the competing elements on the ridge they relented and we were below the worst of the storm. We stumbled cold and wet to the pass in mellow sunshine. Govind brewed up tea as we debated whether to continue or retire.

The weather grey and overcast hardly indicated scope for experiment. To the north Dunagiri sailed patchily through the clouds but was soon misted over by squalls of scudding hail. This was certainly not the sort of weather in which to take loaded men down steep untested trails from the crest of the Himalayas. I voted for withdrawal south of the pass and attempting access to the source of the Birehi along its banks. LS who was always a natural supporter of negativity vociferously seconded my proposal to get off the mountain. Nathu whom I hoped would scorn such cautious counsel felt unsure about the strange turn in the weather and decided it was safer to retire and watch how it would behave.

For a long time I blamed LS for the turning back of our resolve. But in hindsight it is also possible to argue that the Goddess had attached him to our expedition expressly for his role of spoiler. Had Nathu been in charge of the younger porters he might have feared their scorn in turning back from the brink. In the event the weather did not improve and had we got down to the Birehi basin forcing a passage along its unknown and little explored basement it would have been both dangerous and miserable. LS had acted as a brake on our impetuosity. The Goddess may have been trying to point out that exploration of the outer world is not as important as learning about oneself. It was better to be one's own modest unadventurous personality than pretend to be a latter-day Shipton.

We raced along the smiling meadows where the path to the pass veers evenly and caught a parting glimpse of the huge majesty of Dunagiri. Ahead the welcome rays of the sun played on the rocky horns that guard the portals to the pass. Lord Curzon might well have learned of Kuari's glories from Mumm's book. The Swiss guides had their minds blown by the number of peaks that greet the visitor early in the day. (The problem is always to get up the steep pass before the clouds descend). To the devotee of Nanda Devi however Kuari yields no view of the mountain. Contrary to the normal pattern in Uttarakhand it is the southern side of the crest that peels away in a sheer drop and the portals of Kuari present a dramatic threshold to the forested valleys running at its feet. The northern aspect of easy plateau country makes for a gentler descent where the softness of the contours is helped by the weaker growth of trees that characterizes the arid uplands between the Himalayan chain and the Tibetan border.

Everything contrasted south of the Kuari to underline the highlander origin of the phrase 'the other side of the mountain.' The greens were greener, the trees more lush, the crops infinitely more plentiful and bird and animal species more abundant. The oak now replaced the gloomy spruce and the dense thickets of hill bamboo heralded the beginning of sub-tropical largesse. The pass was in a horrible condition with most of the zig-zagging bridle path washed away. A black pack-horse with its neck broken from a skid froze us in our advance. For a moment the fertile face of our enchanted valley turned sour until we noted a golden eagle (actually the bearded vulture) waiting to tear its carrion prey. The evening's silent descent over the mossy dripping path was broken by the screams of disturbed monal, those exultantly-hued pheasants that scurried downhill in panic making easy targets for any determined shikari. At Dakwani we passed a shepherd in the dell who directed us to a dry cave facing south. It was an ideal camp site overlooking a magic world of deep wooded clefts with booming cataracts echoing from below and misty bewhiskered forests all around. Our embowering trees were overhung with long strands of lichen that held the dew while avenues of overarching bamboo indicated the line of tomorrow's march. As a final capping to the visual bliss we had our new potatoes baked in the ashes and eaten with the rapturous combination of ghee and salt.

Govind kept up the culinary delight with pakoras for breakfast. Our ample supply of ghee had been intended as encouragement for unexplored terrain but the morning's weather decided us to lighten this difficult load. Ghee was second only to kerosene in the messiness of its transportation. We eased our way steeply down to a gloriously shaggy mist-draped glen then crossed a stream by a slippery log to fall upon a bank of blackberry bushes not quite ripe enough to enjoy but still too succulent to resist. We zig-zagged up to the meadow of Surtoli to enter a layer of wreathed rising mist and discovered we had been walking for three hours. (The stomach we decided, was a better guide to fatigue than a stop-watch) Nathu raided a shepherd's hut for firewood while Govind went to squeeze out water from a trickling stream. LS pulled some leaves of mustard growing in profusion on a pile of sheep dung while DB assisted me by chipping off splinters of wood for kindling with the spoon of the ice axe.

The bonus of leafy mustard decided us to extend the tea break to full meal status and we lazed pleasantly on a green bank while Govind prepared rice with jholi (a Garhwali dish prepared from gram flour) to which was added the tasty spinach. A lone shepherd returning from Wan to Lata suddenly turned up almost in a spooky replay of the myth of Latu the Devi's herald who was credited with flying over the Kuari pass to settle scores with a famous local bully of Lata. Then another shepherd appeared and we felt guilty when he entered the hut from which we had plundered the firewood. Luckily he hailed from Sutol, the most friendly of villages, and soon joined us for the meal. As we continued on our way the path began to lose height severely and dropped towards the first village of Pana, where a man was rubbing out the marijuana gum from his patch of cannabis. It was the most hectic time of year with potatoes to be dug and the fields to be ploughed for winter wheat. After that many of the men would follow the shepherds who were now moving down with their flocks to the lower ranges.

We dropped further through the wooded delight of the upper Birehi to come to the booming gorge at Jhenjhenipatni, the aggressive torrent spanned by a fairly new and long overdue suspension bridge. Any bridge seen against such a dramatic background would appear to take wing and here was a fit subject for a Daniells aquatint. We stopped for the night at a village hovel which exceeded my elastic standards of primitive acceptability. For once I decided the tent was a better bet.

The villagers of Irani said that it would have been difficult to make progress along the river bank to the source. But the question was rendered academic by the weather which showed no signs of clearing. We could only retreat and hope to outdistance its gloom. It was an irony that after all my monsoon forays done on a shoestring, this first expedition on which I had splurged Rs 3,000 to avail of the clear October season should have reverted to the wetness of chaumas, the four months in the hill calendar when the gods slept.

By nine the following morning we had climbed to Sem Kharak set amidst magnificent chestnut groves. On the muddy path we detected both bear and leopard imprints. Alongside some stone slabs we found a pile of monal feathers, their purple, blue and green sheen aquiver with an uncanny beauty that transcended their flimsy physical form. Puzzled I stooped to look at what seemed a small stone shrine made up of a quartet of slabs. It was a crude trap made by the villagers to catch the monal. The bird would stick its head into the chamber to eat the grain spread on the bottom stone and the inserted neck would dislodge the carefully placed upper stone which would then flatten the bird. I kept the electric blue feathers to add to my Nanda Devi scrapbook. Their improbable intensity spoke of Lord Krishna, the most comely of the gods who chose peacock feathers as the symbol of his divine sporting nature.

The mist continued to baffle and the season seemed more like winter than autumn. A young English couple appeared on the trail behind us and asked the way to Ramni. When the rain started we all adjourned to a shepherd's hut where Govind prepared more rice and jholi. It would have been too much of a coincidence for the couple to have come from Lyme Regis and their accents confirmed that they were from Preston. I was struck by their discrimination as tourists. They had latched on to the very best of India and in the space of three months had prised out the most rewarding destinations. Uttarakhand is often underestimated in modern tourist literature despite Longstaff's appraisal of Garhwal as the most scenic area in High Asia.

When the rain lessened we walked down towards Ramni and saw the mist evaporate to reveal the infinitely fresh green spread of the Nandakini valley. Ramni had dry stone walls and the disused bungalow of an early British forester. The tourist couple wanted to spend the night in the travellers bungalow while we decided to make our way to Sutol in the hope of the weather improving for tomorrow. If it did we would try and cross back in the direction of Birehi by climbing up the course of the Nandakini, then strike north to follow a line parallel to the Hom Kund valley. According to the shepherds there were seven small lakes that lay up that route. But as we neared Sutol the rain clamped down heavier and the whole valley seemed to settle in a gloom that suggested finality to our hopes. One was simply not prepared to face monsoon conditions when the expedition had been designed to enjoy the sunny delights of October.

Apparently the Goddess scorned our softness. She also rammed home the message that success does not depend on money. This was my most costly expedition and it proved to be the least fulfilling. My financial graph showed clearly that the tighter the funds, the more memorable the outcome. Nothing in Nanda's domain is won easily.

My decision to keep retreating may not have seemed at the time to be of the stuff that signified field marshall material but in hindsight it is possible that Nanda was tempting the masochistic instinct that some mountain travellers respond to. If the expedition was an expensive flop and cost me more than a month's salary then any lesson learned in the process of retreat could at least help cut future losses. Rashness to enter the valley under Kuari might have led to loss of life and insistence on breaking in to the Birehi headstream could only have resulted in a blind groping in the mist. The weather was a factor not to be toyed with. One expensive teaching of this October outing was to accept that no matter how mechanical Himalayan weather patterns had seemed in my twenty-five years' acquaintance, it was a subject I obviously had more to learn about.

There seemed to be only one course left and that was to try and salvage our morale by sidestepping the miserable conditions. We would veer westwards across the Alakananda and try the high route from Rudranath to Madhmaheshwar via Nandi Kund. The jungles there were even more pristine than those along the Curzon Trail and from Rudranath temple there was the bonus of a view of Nanda Devi. So we turned down from the viceregal bridle path to leave the upper Nandakini as though driven out of Eden by the Devi's scowling herald.

This chance turning back of our plans brought us to the village of Burha Ala for the night and we stopped over at the remarkable Panchayat Ghar, the village meeting hall cum jail. It was the most superior village building I had seen in Uttarakhand, made of beautifully carved and enormously endowed deodar timbers. To sleep on its upstairs veranda seemed like a special dispensation had not the fear of bed bugs (that inhabit all village situations where wooden beds are employed) dampened our desire to lie down. Like us, the villagers were complaining of the maverick weather pattern that had upset the drying of their crops. The Goddess was angry at the way the world was progressing and part of the blame we were told, was due to the influx of foreign expeditions that now filed up past this village on their way to Trisul base camp. The villagers faced the dilemma of joining the expedition baggage train to earn a porter's wage and then complaining of the foreigners lack of respect for the Goddess' customs. They arrived in her sacred enclosure near Hom Kund singing and drinking, unaware that according to legend a sacred Sriyantra lay buried in the nearby crater. Obviously the weather was a sign of Nanda's displeasure and any suffering our small team might be put to was no doubt well-deserved. This was surely the kind of negative teaching that LS would respond to and we left the village next morning with him agreeing wholeheartedly with everything the village elders said.

Another lesson awaited me the next day when we smartly cleared the lower Nandakini (not even stopping for pakoras at Silli Buggair) to catch a bus to Chamoli. There we fought our way on to the famous Bhukha Hartal bus which ran from Badrinath to Kedarnath over the highest road in Garhwal. At the summit the day's incessant rain turned into snow and much to everyone's surprise we saw two bedraggled pilgrims waiting at Chopta, the 10,000 ft-high bus stop under the temple of Tunganath.

To my astonishment the man who got on with snow in his beard was my friend Gurmeet Thukral from Mussoorie. Behind him was his American wife Liz and on her back their six-month-old daughter Sarah, none the worse for her exposure. Gurmeet was producing a book of photographs on Garhwal and had sat up at Tunganath for several days waiting for the weather to clear. I compared his dedication with my own promptitude to withdraw and wondered why the Goddess had arranged such an unlikely meeting on that freezing bus. The answer came when Gurmeet asked me to write some chapters on Nanda Devi for his book *Garhwal Himalaya,* which turned out to be a reasonably good trekker's guide to the pilgrim places of Uttarakhand. It encouraged undecided admirers of the mountain Goddess to take the plunge and get to know her better. It was only later I learned that Tunganath had a temple of Nanda Devi.

TWENTY

Mount Dulcitude

The affair with the ravishing Goddess had occupied a third of my life and while the physical passion nominally subsided the subtle attachment remained. What began as a headlong lust metamorphosed into an abiding love and the fire that stirred the loins of youth was transmuted into the tender warmth of affectionate regard. But the friction (so necessary to make possible any meaningful resolution of opposites) has also remained and forever one continues to face the challenge of translating understanding into action and of measuring up to the demands of that power higher than thought.

There remains the basic conflict between the inert rear of massy granite and the sensuous image of a bliss-giving female. Is the Devi a physical fact or more, and is there any real link between the physical and religious facts? Are the masks in her temples and Sriyantras buried at her sacrificial shrines related to one particular peak or are they of general application to any mountain? Is the original Goddess of Uttarakhand a daughter of aboriginal hill custom or an Aryan deity imported to the Himalayas? Did Nanda begin her career worshipped along the Euphrates or was she native to the Indus and Ganga, a modified version of the mother figure of the Hindu pantheon, both terrible and fair?

The questions are endless and my research though fascinating had proved nothing. Strangely the more I went into the various versions the problems seemed to lessen in importance even as they grew more imponderable. It was as though the Goddess was spelling out the importance in all religious questioning of getting beyond the conventions of the mind and letting the intuitions play.

This change from the masculine mental demands for black and white reasoning to the elusive understanding of slippery psychic subtleties was an essential gift of the Devi to this devotee. Whatever my bafflement in understanding her nature, moods and unpredictability I knew that if I listened long enough, her message would help. It was a kind of poor man's revelation to wait on the Goddess for her sign of approval or otherwise. I was convinced she wanted me to pen these experiences of search along her Himalayan trails and in spite of despair at never coming near an adequate rendering of what astounding beauties of nature she had revealed, I stubbornly stuck to my stultifying task of recording them.

When those first painfully set out reminiscences were rejected on the grounds of their wearisomeness—with suggestions that if trimmed of their prolixities they might be reconsidered—I returned to the task like a doomed prophet who has no choice but to obey the voice he hears. No one can set out adequately the feelings of love and it is surely a ludicrous task to try and give an inkling of the passion that I feel for this particular peak.

Mountain literature is rich in capturing the mood of the heights and often in the midst of the most dull expedition account the flavour of the Himalayas manages to seep through into the narrative—the dull beaten brass 'tonk' of a goat's bell, the acrid smoke of green oak or the exhilarating flute of a shepherd on a distant slope. Books have been written on the spiritual aspect of mountaineering and some climbers feel called to analyse the philosophical and psychological summons of high ground. The symbol of a peak is one of the few uniting theological features between monotheists (with their awful god handing out the law from Sinai) and polytheists (whose presiding spirit resides on Sumeru). Rene Daumal's *Mount Analogue* is probably the most profound study of a mountaineer's real drives (assuming the mountaineer is 'real'). Whatever the psychiatrist may say about infantile obsession with Alpine mammary glands (and the irresistible male lure towards the promise of expansive snowy white breasts above dark cleaving wooded valleys) the fact remains that even after expensive sessions on the analyst's couch many mountaineers are possessed of motives besides sexual sublimation.

The British in India moved to their hill stations in summer to preserve their sanity and improve the chances of colonial continuity by giving their families a break from the heat and dust. Most modern climbers originate from the urban competitive situation with its unhealthy and cramped artificial routine. To escape to the mountains is to give their minds space and their souls oxygen. Reasons can vary from the Californian on social security who climbs the Yosemite canyons as part of an exclusive club of daredevils (apparently out to convince polite society that bums lack neither skill nor daring) to the Bengali babu who annually catches the Doon Express to Haridwar and then boards a pilgrim bus to Kedarnath from where he will trek over the great buggials armed only with a cloth shoulder-bag and a blanket.

The greatest shortcoming of the Indian Mountaineering Foundation has been to invest in the foreign habit of large environmentally hostile expeditions rather than underpin the traditional pilgrim mode of approach rich in respect of the Himalayas. The Western sporting approach supposedly inspired by romantic and heroic contests with the Alps coincided with colonial compulsions and were fairly easily sidetracked to political ends like the conquest of Everest. The pilgrim tradition would have made a more solid base to build on for it instinctively revered the Himalayas as the home of divine powers. Its ethical influence might even have shamed the brown sahibs of Delhi's bureaucracy into not bringing such beautiful peaks as Shivling and Nilkanth into disrepute with their narcissistic and unprofessional claims and saved Nanda Devi from the polluting presence of a nuclear time bomb in her sanctuary. To those who love them the mountains are sacrosanct and a false claim from a true worshipper is unthinkable.

The climber alone with his beloved communes briefly with the mountain spirit and can at that moment distinguish between the personality of his peaks. His breathing is affected and the simple act of drawing in fresh mountain air is to clarify the nature of selfhood and accept the responsibility for one's individuality. Total trust exists between the climber and the rock he rests against. For all practical purposes he is a committed pilgrim dedicated to expressing through his hand-holds a hymn of ascent.

Often when tragedy strikes and the climber fights back to overcome terrible odds a book emerges to honour the indefatigable will in man.

Always it is implied that life is foreign to the peaks themselves: and that they signify baleful blind forces as opposed to the well-disposed climber's. There is a profound truth in the unconquerability of the human will but its proper harnessing has been prevented by a Semitic distortion. The Old Testament commandment to subdue a supposedly inert nature invites hostile reprisal which is evident today in our depraved environment striking back in global warming that threatens to submerge coastal civilisation.

The long Hindu traditions of honouring the Himalayas show the late nineteenth century flowering of the Alpine sport (and twentieth century politicking on Everest) to be but the flickering of an eye. The human regard for mountains and an affectionate feeling for peaks like Nanda Devi precede the sporting era by thousands of years. As Daumal perceives, the mountain is a visible bridge linking earth to heaven. Its obstructing loom is often the physical boundary of nations and cultures and by its barrier-like undeniability the mountain is both a symbol of security and threat. The foothills of the Himalayas were traditionally the inaccessible tracts where robber gangs would withdraw to evade pursuit, and the same role continues to this day as terrorist guns supplant the presence of armed dacoits.

To the popular Indian view unfamiliar with the discipline of the char dham yatra the Himalayan snows appear regularly as a fantasy diet in Hindi films. *Love in Simla* manages to catch exactly the perfect mongrel mix of colonial hill station snob appeal married to ancient erotic legends that began with Shiva copulating for aeons with Parvati on Kailash. The extraordinary flexibility of Hindu attitudes makes permissible on the one hand the shedding of Shiva's seed on the holy mountain and on the other rises in wrath—as in the Rup Kund lore—at the pollution attendant on the female fruition of the very same act. The laws of Manu rigorously forbid any defilement of a mountain's sanctity and lay down impossible restrictions on even the simplest of human activities (such as the need to seek out flat ground on which to relieve oneself).

It was somewhere between the literal physical actuality of the peak and its religio-symbolic mystique (that includes the sporting appeal with its octausend magic) that the answer to my quest to identify the Devi lay. The peak was only as real as my passion for it. Those profound delights of nature so hardly won by financial and bodily suffering were not exclusive to the outer sanctuary but part of the wilderness we all have inside ourselves. That noble granite thrust of marvellous mineral shooting from the deep green of the gorge into the vaulting blue ether was an arrow of enlightenment fired by the Goddess to penetrate the stoniness of my own vision. What my travels around the skirts of the mountain had amounted to was a working on the self (which Daumal hints at) and the important outcome was not the conventional sporting achievement of any impact on the mountain's vertical scale for the record books. It was in the changes wrought in my understanding—stimulated by the mountain's heady effect on my feelings. Daumal derived his inspiration from a Gurdjieffian striving for conscious being, a state that like a summit could not be arrived at without goading the body well beyond its normal limits in a super-effort.

It became clear the more I trod the Nanda Devi trail that my motion was more magical than peripatetic. If the villagers of Nauti did not avail of the opportunity to turn their twelve-yearly procession into a tantric exercise of joy to celebrate the coursing juice of intoxicating nature as it soared to ecstasy on Bedni buggial here was one pilgrim who set out determined to experience that natural bonus of the Devi whatever the effort.

A lively awareness of the mystery of the divine impermanence of flesh overcame any lasting sense of misery inflicted by the doubting mind and the grey matching weather. The mountain was a trigger to my soul, its arrival on the horizon a kind of heavenly descent that liberated my heart from the thrall of the intellect. Together animal and spiritual instincts came close to a rare union of nirvana. The danger and exposure that dogged one's tread only enlivened the raw appreciation of planetary beauty. The exclusion of the inhibiting mind and its analytical faculty worked to make one momentarily a child of the cosmos, intoxicated by the wonder of being, a small but significant part of this miraculous garment whose texture wore the wondrous erotic feel of *samsara*. Like Milarepa one could only gape: 'Void is its nature yet everything is manifest.'

Along with the insights of the alchemists went the intuitions of the poets. Wordsworth and Blake, Kalidas and Rumi were echoed in the background trumpeting of a nakedly transcendent nature, the Goddess made flesh in the intense colour of her flowers and maddeningly near in the fragrance of her sensuous overhang. One trekked from the extreme of leaden-booted misery to the wafted lilt of exaltation and always the hardest work lay in the aftermath of reconciling the veering moods of nirvana and *samsara*. The nearest one could come to formal resolution was to practice the yoga of honouring the Devi. Whatever brought one nearer that goal was the way. The male mountaineer desperately needed a female guru to encourage his undeveloped intuition. Expeditions too often like clockwork monsters in their macho lust to reach the top ignore the feminine route of discretion that alone guarantees a return match.

Savage encounters (like Joe Tasker's on Dunagiri) might be thought to have imprinted a conviction of immortality forever on the survivor's forehead but no theory fits when the human vessel insists it is too small and any overflowing is mistaken as a leak that needs constant replenishment. Like greatness sainthood is thrust on the climber who decides his mountain is worth dying for, and who can judge that such singular (seemingly suicidal) devotion in surrendering the gift of individuality (and causing unbearable grief to companions) is not a valid way for some? 'Better to die trying to wake than live in sleep.'

The conflicts sparked between the attitudes of Unsoeld and Roskelley are healthy in making us question our motives. Willi for all his swashbuckling lack of safety will outlive his critics not because he was right but because he had learned that love is more important than truth. Perhaps mountains are there to teach us that lesson. Only they are big enough to overcome our ego.

In my benign walks around the sanctuary meadows, viewing the peaks and considering some of the achievements on them, studying the religious feelings of the local people and noting the natural glories in the rare beauty of the forests and the riotous sexuality of the flowers, I followed my inmost instinct to worship. I got nearer to the Devi in the mountaineering mode than in the religious and was never further than when reading William Sax's sad account of the Bari Nanda Jat. Intellectual enquiry into the nature of the Goddess, I discovered, shrunk her stature and any investigation of her temples invited serious disappointment. Those blank African masks with their tribal lack of individuality was exactly the mood exuded by the captive Goddess in her hill shrines. The Sriyantra was a more liberating option contriving to combine an amazingly rich yet deceptively simple arrangement of angles and triangles that lead into a mystic central point then explode into infinity, a model of the universe and a representation of the mystery that we are.

But its symbolic power could never approximate to the feelings generated when close to the Goddess in her physical sanctuary, when her feminine allure got the adrenalin flowing in this male devotee's veins. Nanda

Devi could never be portrayed as the mother figure familiar to the Hindu pantheon because she was too near the ordinary flesh and blood of a desirable hill woman of unlimited passion and unpredictable desires. The buxom beauty of the Kot Kandhara image was the nearest to the real Devi I discovered and she needed no replication because she had an abundance of human lookalikes. Those tough, handsome cheerful hill women one admired for their sheer mountain craft and character (combining physical fitness with a stubborn refusal to admit defeat) were the archetypes of my Goddess, sustaining by their cruel chores the noble myths of Uttarakhand lore.

It seems fitting that these extraordinary performers on the physical level should include in their repertoire the lineaments of a superhuman entity. These remarkable women in the midst of their sweaty grind and so avidly despised by their menfolk during their lunar flux teach most vividly that human well-being can only derive from the honouring of all natural cycles. In the tender farming of the earth's limited resources the Chipko message of Gaura Devi is the real voice of the Goddess for our times, warning against a sullied environment. As it happens 'Gaura' is local scriptural usage for Nanda Devi.

As a male writer I make no apology for viewing the mountain Goddess as a village woman for that in fact is the way hill theology pictures Nanda Devi. Mountaineers married to their craft have perhaps realised that it is more pleasurable to learn the many moods of feminine unpredictability from the stern lessons of the Alps or Himalayas rather than have the same gripe voiced daily down the years from a contracted rope-mate over the breakfast table. To find the real woman of one's choice is indeed a mountaineering task since achieving the impossible is what climbing is all about.

The conviction that the outer and inner, the spirit and the flesh are no different may be the ultimate discovery of he who seeks to know the essential nature of his mountain Goddess. But equally important I discovered is the prayer that implores the beloved never to withdraw her favours. For the few who spurn the static state of oneness and prefer to place themselves between the pull of the magnet and the lodestone there can be no peace. Only the dulcitude of desire.